THAT WHICH GROWS WILD:

16 TALES OF

DARK FICTION

Also Written by Eric J. Guignard

Baggage of Eternal Night (JournalStone, 2013)

Crossbuck 'Bo (forthcoming, 2019)

Anthologies Edited by Eric J. Guignard

A World of Horror (Dark Moon Books, 2018)

After Death... (Dark Moon Books, 2013)

Dark Tales of Lost Civilizations (Dark Moon Books, 2012)

The Five Senses of Horror (Dark Moon Books, 2018)

+Horror Library+ Volume 6 (Cutting Block Books/ Farolight Publishing, 2017)

Pop the Clutch: Thrilling Tales of Rockabilly, Monsters, and Hot Rod Horror (forthcoming) (Dark Moon Books, 2018)

Exploring Dark Short Fiction (A Primer Series) Created by Eric J. Guignard

#1: A Primer to Steve Rasnic Tem (Dark Moon Books, 2017)

#2: A Primer to Kaaron Warren (Dark Moon Books, 2018)

#3: A Primer to Nisi Shawl (forthcoming) (Dark Moon Books, 2018)

#4: A Primer to Jeffrey Ford (forthcoming) (Dark Moon Books, 2018)

#5: A Primer to Han Song (forthcoming) (Dark Moon Books, 2019)

#6: A Primer to Ramsey Campbell (forthcoming) (Dark Moon Books, 2019)

THAT WHICH GROWS WILD: 16 TALES OF DARK FICTION

ERIC J. GUIGNARD

Harper Day Books
New York, NY

Cover design by Lynne Hansen
http://lynnehansen.zenfolio.com

First published by Cemetery Dance Publications,
electronic format in July, 2018
ISBN-13: 978-1-58767-692-5

First Harper Day Books paperback edition
published in July, 2018
ISBN-13: 978-1-949491-00-5

Library of Congress Control Number: 2018908106

HARPER DAY BOOKS
New York, NY

Made in the United States of America

Dedicated as always, and with love,
to my family—Jeannette, Julian, and Devin.

TABLE OF CONTENTS

A Case Study in Natural Selection and How It Applies to Love

YESTERDAY I SAW JAMIE GOODWIN BURST into flame.

He was just sitting on one of those cheap aluminum-back chairs we all have, eyes closed in the shade of Hester's old RV, trying to get some relief from the heat, same as everyone else. I was checking the stock of coolers, seeing if any held even a bit of water left to siphon out, when Jamie let out a tiny gasp like he woke from a bad dream. If it was a bad dream he had, he woke to something worse, 'cause little glints of light popped and fizzed off him like the sparklers we used to wave around on Fourth of July. Smoke or steam or something else rose up, then Jamie's eyes went cartoon-big and he turned into a fireball.

Jamie's the fourth person to spontaneously combust this month. Two women burned last Wednesday, and old Tom Puddingpaw blazed the week prior. Before that, we averaged only one or two fireballs a month, but now it's getting worse. And after Jamie burned, Ms. Crankshaw didn't even cancel lessons like she normally did, as if coming to terms that folks fireballing was the new natural order of things.

"That's another lesson in evolution. One day we're apes, then we're humans, now we're fireballs."

She didn't really say that, but she might as well have.

At least Loud John and Rudy were there when Jamie burned, and they contained his cinders so it didn't spread like when Quiet John caught flame. But I still saw the whole thing, and it still scared me, even if others pretend to somehow be getting used to it.

"I watched him die," I tell my friends. "Jamie didn't scream. I think he tried, since his mouth opened wide, but nothing came out except flames."

"Why is this happening for no reason?" Ogre asks, though that question is rhetorical because he doesn't expect an answer. His voice hitches and he overcompensates for it by yelling, "When's it going to stop?"

That's rhetorical too.

We're not supposed to be outdoors because of the heat, but we're wearing protection, and sometimes out in the desert is the only place we can talk without everyone else listening in.

"I told you we weren't safe," Liz says. "Ms. C.'s wrong or she's lying to us. Anybody can fireball."

"No one ever tells us the truth," Tommy adds. "It's stupid going to lessons if everyone shields us from what's really happening. I mean, what're we learning? Facts or make-believe?"

Me and Tommy and Liz and Ogre are shooting at sand lizards with a pair of slingshots. I oughta clarify we'd shoot at anything daring our range of rocks and marbles, but it was too hot for anything but lizards to come out under the sun.

"The adults don't want us to know ... " A red bandana covers half of Liz's face, so her voice is muffled. "I think we're all gonna die."

She pulls the rubber cord of her slingshot taught with long brown fingers, then fires an amber marble missile. The marble's color is so shimmery that while soaring through the air it appears a flaming comet, and I think again of Jamie.

Liz is stronger than me, and her marble outdistances my cloudy topaz by a dozen feet. She's older, too, but I still feel scorned a girl is stronger than me, even if only by a little. We arm wrestled a few times before and she won all the matches, but something about the way her hand wrapped around my own made my breath stick in my throat while my heart doubled in size. I think that makes it even worse that she's stronger. Ogre and Tommy are stronger than me too, but I don't care about that at all.

"I don't understand why the council says fire would only take the old or sick anyway. Fire's fire, it burns everything," Tommy rekindles our old dispute.

"Supposedly it's like sickness. You're more vulnerable to catch pneumonia if you're old or in bad health. People who are fit don't die from being ill, unless it's cancer or something."

"That's what Ms. C. says, but Jamie was only older than us by five years. And there was nothing wrong with him, he helped fix my dad's car, lifted out the whole engine by himself," Tommy says, wiping twin beads of sweat off each cheek.

Ogre sets a chunk of rock into his slingshot and fires it straight up in the air. The rock shrinks smaller and smaller and vanishes, then reappears like a lesson in magic, growing larger and larger, 'til thunking in the bleached dirt several yards away. "My dad says we gotta get the hell outta here. It's stupid waiting any longer."

"I want to leave now," Liz says. "Stockton sucks, even worse than Tulare."

"Where can we move that's better than here?"

"North, of course. Anywhere it's cooler. Maybe Seattle, where it's supposed to still rain."

"But it's heating up everywhere, not just here," I say. "What's the point of migrating again?"

"Maybe people aren't fireballing up there like down here, 'cause it's wet."

"That's not true," Tommy says. "I heard on the radio, people in the snow are burning up too, even Eskimos in Alaska."

I don't bother pointing out that nothing on the radio makes sense anymore. Used to be, the airwaves played real music, but now with the earth heating we don't get any regular stations, but only those on CB, and all they want to do is talk and talk. One guy keys in music, but it's only religious hymns that get old real quick. Everyone else just argues. Some broadcasters say solar flares are increasing static electricity, and that causes us to fireball. Some say it's apocalypse and we're being punished for sins. Some say there's nothing wrong at all, and it's just conspiracy to frighten everyone into war. Some say the world's heating and we're just popcorn kernels, exploding one-by-one.

"It doesn't matter where we go," Ogre says to each of us in turn. "We're the strongest and we'll carry on. It's survival of the fittest. Maybe a couple young people might die that we thought were strong like Jamie, but that just proves they weren't fit after all. He could've had a heart murmur or something, maybe was a pervert or sick in the mind and hid it all this time."

"You don't fireball from bein' a pervert," I say.

"You don't know."

"Ms. Crankshaw said survival of the fittest has to do with reproducing."

"Like I said, the strongest are those who survive, and they're the ones left to reproduce," Ogre counters. "Duh."

I don't think that's right, but I don't entirely understand the theory of natural selection.

THERE AREN'T MANY unclaimed girls in camp my age besides Liz. Only Pearl and Jennifer. Pearl's in the upper kids' class with us but she's smaller and weaker than girls half her age, like if you cracked an egg against her, she'd be the one to shatter rather than the shell. If we married and had children, they'd be twigs. I want to have a ton of kids, I want to help repopulate the world, but I want them to be strong and brave, not afraid of all the things I'm afraid of. Then there's Jennifer, who's got a face like the grill of a pickup truck: hard and dented and covered in splatter as if she'd been driven down a long highway full of slow-moving bugs. I know that's cruel to say, and I would never-ever say that out loud, but her personality matches her appearance too. Ronny Jake once told me it don't matter what a person looks like under the covers when the lights are off. But you can't hide an ugly personality, even if all the lights in the world get extinguished.

Liz is dark and strong and beautiful, and it hurts me sometimes that I can't do more than talk with her or arm wrestle. I mean it really hurts in my stomach, this sense of my guts being wrung and empty. Even if I've eaten, there's still a longing inside like I'm hungry, though I'm usually that also.

But Liz and Ogre like each other, and people say they'll make good babies, and that hurts my stomach more, even if they're both my friends and I know I should be happy for them, though I'd rather be happy for myself. I'd never admit I was jealous, and I never even confessed to her in the first place that I like her because I already know she likes Ogre, and I don't want to feel any more rejected.

And Ogre's just his nickname. He's not dumb or ugly or anything. He's just named that 'cause when we were young in the lower kids' class, Mrs. Hubble read us a story about an ogre that was super-powerful and could smash anything. He (Ogre, my friend) said he wished he was an ogre and he'd smash away the sun.

Ogre said that every day for a year, like a wish that if you believed hard enough would come true. It didn't, but the name stuck.

Sometimes Liz gets in my thoughts and I can't sleep, and when I should be dreaming of water, I dream instead of Ogre being killed and then maybe I could have Liz all to myself. People die every day and no one would notice . . .

Dad says everyone's thoughts are confusing in their teenage years, and it's okay as long as you can differentiate which ones not to act upon. I do know which thoughts are *wrong*, and I'm ashamed of them, especially those where Ogre dies at my hand. I imagine that thought of Ogre getting killed and I turn it into a pane of glass, and then I imagine myself—a tiny speck version of myself, fully formed, but microscopic in size—fit inside my mind, laying that bad-thought-glass on the ground and then stomping on it, stomping over and over until the glass shatters into a billion pieces, and then I keep stomping on every fragment until those pieces are shattered into a billion more shards, and it doesn't matter how long it takes, but that I keep imagining myself pulverizing the bad idea until my head is finally clear of it.

IT'S JUST DAD and me living together. We don't need much, so we stay in a motorhome. Some of the others moved into Stockton's abandoned houses, but since Dad's on the council he likes to keep near the center of camp. Plus being in a motorhome is easier to get away if there's an emergency.

"How were lessons today?" Dad asks. "Learn how to save the world yet?"

"Ms. Crankshaw mostly talked about evolution and . . . something else . . . oh, adaptations."

"Bet you can't wait for us to evolve some fire-proof skin and independence from hydration-reliance."

"Wait, what?"

"I'm kidding, buddy."

My dad is awesome, but what he thinks of as jokes go flat. He's a lot smarter than most people and that's why he's on the council. It's also why he's constantly busy. Even now while he's talking, he's also writing in a log with jerky, harsh movements like he always does.

I try countering his 'joke' with one of my own. "Well, maybe I can mutate wings and fly to Antarctica."

"But Antarctica's melted, so there'd be no place you could land." Dad says it offhandedly, but at the same time it becomes an opening for a lesson. "And species do incur genetic mutations, but those are subtle and not related to the environment. The environment, however, dictates which of those mutations survive."

Oh God, I really don't care and want to go to my bunk and be alone, but since we're on the subject, it reminds me of talking with Ogre. "Dad, are we the fittest to survive because we're still alive?"

"Not quite," he says, flicking the pen against his chapped lips before returning to scribbling. "That's a misconception, though by reductive reasoning one could see it that way."

"Can you translate from Dad-talk?"

He snorts when he laughs, which is more endearing than it sounds.

"Natural selection is not all-determining. The more fertile an organism is within a given environment, the fitter it is to pass its genes to the next generation."

"Ms. Crankshaw says we have recessive genes for spontaneous combustion. That's why some people fireball and not others, like a . . . a *predisposition* for certain defects."

Dad snorts again. "Your teacher can make mistakes. Everyone makes mistakes."

"So she's wrong? What's causing people to burn?"

"I'm not saying she's wrong. I'm saying no one knows. She has a hypothesis. It's unproven."

When Dad talks to me, usually also he's writing or calculating or 'thinking', and he can converse at the same time, but it's like I'm speaking to only a part of him, some distracted apparition that just appears to clank chains and then vanishes without leaving any substantial impression. Tommy asked me once why I have to take lessons from Ms. Crankshaw when my dad is ten times smarter, and that's the reason.

Frustration roils up in a sudden squall, and I want to yell at him, which I know is *wrong*, and I don't know why this rage fills me because Dad already said no one knows the answer, so maybe my question is just rhetorical. I call forth that micro-version of me—my *mind-me*—and it shatters the bad-thought of my tantrum. I take a deep breath and simply ask, "But why's it happening now?"

He stops writing and actually looks into my eyes. "I don't know, son. That's the reason you go to class, to learn new ideas."

"But you're smarter than Ms. C.," I blurt. "What do you think?"

"Fifteen years ago global warming was a concern. Now it's an exterminator. The environment is changing faster than it can keep up. There are side-effects."

"Are we going to die?"

His response seems somehow rehearsed for this moment, this cue. "Eventually, yes, but not during any generation you'll know. It's estimated the human population is forty percent less than ten years ago. We're on the decline but we're resilient. Species adapt and survive, and we'll turn things around. Ultimately, however, everything must end."

I want to ask him: *Then what's the point?* But I'm afraid of how he'll respond. I'm as afraid of the truth as I am a lie or even one of his 'jokes'. I'm afraid I won't be able to tell the difference.

THREE YEARS AGO—before people started fireballing—we migrated north to Stockton. The locals didn't want us here, but there weren't many left, and there was enough land for everyone, although we had to fight for water rights. I don't mean we fought using guns, but that Dad and the council negotiated with the locals by bartering dried goods and gasoline. Like Ms. C. reminds us, this is still a democracy, still the state of California, and laws and policies remain in place, even if nobody's left to enforce them.

"Eventually, things'll turn around," people say.

It's a cycle, like tides that flow and ebb. If you throw a rock in the air, it'll fall back down. That's science: *it's observable and repeatable.*

"The laws of science," Ms. Crankshaw told us one day, "are controlling influences."

"Like Liz Delgado's boobs controlling your eyes," Tommy whispered to me, leaning across his desk.

"Shut up!" I whispered back, fiercely. But it was too late; Tommy's whispers could be my shouts, and everyone in class heard. If I thought it'd been hot before, the temperature in my face rose a thousand degrees.

"Thomas Tawny, would you like to teach this lesson?" Ms. C. asked.

"No, ma'am. You talked about 'empirical evidence' before, and I was just explaining to Kenny that it applies to him. You know, how experiments are repeatedly verified."

The room laughed.

I imagined punching Tommy in the face, and this was not a *bad-thought*. No micro-version of me came forth to shatter that idea in my mind.

"Survival of the fittest," Ms. C. said, thankfully changing topic, "is an observable and repeatable effect of nature . . ."

Dad says no matter what, education is the most critical matter, as everyone makes their own way in life, and schooling gives us a benchmark for survival. Ms. Crankshaw teaches all subjects to us upper kids, and I like it when we discuss reading and sometimes history, though more time is spent on science than all other subjects combined.

Science is most important, because that's what's going to save us.

IT'S MY SHIFT to help gather, and we leave at dusk.

The pick-up roars eastbound on Highway 120 to Escalon, and I'm squashed between Tommy and John in its cab. Tommy peels dead skin off his hands, and John sings while he drives.

"Dashing through the snow . . . "

Jingle Bells is his favorite song, and he chants it in a dry, grim voice, though Christmas won't be for eight more weeks. Couple months ago we called him, 'Loud John,' but since Quiet John died, he's just 'John' now.

I drown him out by skimming the CB channels. People argue about fireballing, though different places call it *blazing, burning men, cleansed, phoenix ash,* or a dozen other terms. Names don't matter, just facts, and those are hard to tell among the rumors and accusations. Only thing certain is it's worsening.

Tommy muses, "Maybe we'll find a hot chick, abandoned and desperate for rescue."

I snicker at the thought, but for a different reason: In this temperature, any person we find is *hot*.

"Maybe we'll find a walk-in freezer that's running on solar-powered battery back-up," I reply.

"A hot chick trapped in a walk-in freezer. *Mmm*," he says.

Today, I'd rather just have ice cream. The afternoon high was up another degree, bringing the weekly average to one hundred-eighteen. It's been nine years since I tasted ice cream.

Ogre, Ronny Jake, and Lorie Quinn follow in a second pick-up, each of our trucks towing an empty U-Haul trailer. The council says to depend on mobility and haste for protection. We have weapons, too, but rarely need them.

"*Oh what fun it is to ride—*" John sings, then cuts short. "There it is."

We turn into the entrance of a planned housing development, cookie-cutter homes that spiral around each other for miles and miles: *Amberhill Estates.*

Most people from California migrated north to Canada, where the base temperature is cooler, and few still live down here. Dad says if we stay south of the population exodus, there's less competition for resources. Dad's smart, though his philosophy of survival hinges principally on scavenging. We want to be an agrarian society, but we're reverting to hunting and gathering.

"Where'd we leave off?" John asks.

"Up Dwyer Street," Tommy answers.

A big red 'X' is spray-painted on each home's garage that we already scavenged on earlier trips. The 'X's pass by for three intersections.

We stop at the first unmarked house that looks empty. A good hint is the lump of caked fur and gnawed bones chained in the yard that might once have been a German Shepherd. Ronny Jake parks his truck across the street. They break into one home, and we break into another, entering by windows John smashes out with a hammer.

When the water dried up, most residents left in a hurry, the whole mob-mentality thing. Rumors flew about northern borders closing due to population overflow, so everyone raced each other for the safety of some fabled land that doesn't exist anymore in the way it was once remembered.

Most thought to siphon the two gallons from their toilet tanks before joining the great exodus. They don't think about their water heaters though, and when we search houses, we check the heater and there's forty to sixty gallons waiting, which goes a long way when rationing, even for a camp of over two hundred. And that's how it is here; John opens the valve, emptying the heater into portable coolers.

There're are also a few negligible sources of groundwater left in the region, too—deep wells, some muddy creeks—but we're of the mind to stockpile all we can now.

Tommy explores bedrooms and closets for clothes, camping gear, batteries, weapons, or anything else useful or tradable, while I search the pantry. Even indoors, in the evening, the bronze drawer handles could burn my fingers if I don't wear leather gloves. I find boxes of stale crackers and Campbell's soup cans and collect them into a knapsack. On the bottom shelf rests a case of Coca-Cola, which is the dearest type of treasure.

A framed portrait hangs on the wall above the dining table showing a smiling man, woman, boy, girl, and a German Shepherd. The traditional family ... How many portraits inside houses I've ransacked have I gazed upon? I wonder, every time, what became of them. Did they get out? Did they die? Did they make a new life for themselves somewhere under green trees that soak up morning dew, or did they fireball?

Maybe they're part of another camp, somewhere else, ransacking other deserted homes and staring at pictures of residents who once lived there. Certainly they just want to survive, same as me, same as everyone else. People used to say that if society collapsed, everyone would militarize and fight each other and then, truly, only the strongest would survive.

Fact is, people in dire circumstances tend to help each other. Survivors form camps like ours when times are tough. We share with each other, forage together, eat together, commune together.

"Done," John shouts, and Tommy repeats it.

"Done," I say, sparing a last look at the portrait, thinking they appear so happy, especially the man who is a husband and father.

SCREAMS ECHO IN CAMP on our return. Mrs. Rice just fireballed.

Kids and adults alike are mourning her since everyone liked Mrs. Rice, and not even us returning with food and water brings many smiles. People don't seem as hungry or thirsty when the smell of cooked human flesh hangs in the air.

John leaves to report to Dad, while Tommy and I unload our U-Haul. Mutterings sound from people all around that it's time to leave Stockton.

It's horribly hot here, but so is it everywhere, and other places got it worse. We've migrated seven times, and I don't want to pull stake and move again. We've drilled wells that still pull up marshy water, and though we never have an abundance of food, we don't starve either. We haven't tasted citrus in two years, but still grow tomatoes, peppers, eggplants, and some squash in the shade.

Used to be, Central Valley was one of the most fertile farm lands in the world. Now people call it the Mojave Desert's little sister. It's been two years since the San Joaquin River dried up, but we survive.

Liz comes over, offering to help unload.

"Hey," she says.

"Hey," Tommy and I reply.

She grabs a wad of sheets from the trailer, and when she pulls it out she makes a little squeal. "Is that Coca-Cola? Think I can take one?"

"They're supposed to be rationed," I reply, then slyly add, "But I'll arm wrestle you for it."

"Why?" she says, giving me a little knowing smile that could mean any of a dozen things. "You already know I'll win."

Tommy snickers, and I feel my face flush with embarrassment, like I just blurted a great secret.

"Never mind," I say. "John will know it's missing."

"I would have shared with you, but guess I'll wait for Billie instead." Since Liz's parents died, she's lived with this old woman, Billie Gross, who's in charge of inventory and rationing for the camp. That's how Liz gets her choice of provisions.

I think Liz understands survival better than anyone else, in ways beyond scavenging, beyond reproducing. She best understands *people*. In that regard, she may be the fittest among us.

I sigh, and once she leaves I almost tell Tommy how unfair natural selection is. For in this environment, I've become the least likely to propagate. There's a balanced number of boys and girls, and older people are always pressuring to pair us off young. Liz has Ogre, and Patrick and Susie have been together forever. Jersey was sorta odd-man-out for his age, but then Jamie died, so now he may end up with Robyn, and others are already sworn matches. That leaves Tommy and me and Pearl and Jennifer. But like I said before, if I have to marry somebody and make babies, I wouldn't want to settle for either of them.

Ms. C. said now it's an obligation to reproduce, but Dad says you still have to like someone to make a relationship work. I know he misses Mom, and I do too. Anyway, Pearl and Jennifer probably wouldn't settle for me either. When they're around, I see them both looking at Tommy instead of me.

NEXT MORNING I WAKE, and the land's as cool as it ever gets. The thermometer reads a brisk ninety-one, even though it's already 6:30 and the sun well-risen.

Dad's up front in the motorhome, writing in another log with his jerky, harsh movements. I tell him, "Good morning."

He's pale and unshaven and miserable. I know news is bad.

"Kenny, sit down."

I do.

"We had another case last night. Someone ... your age. Your friend, Osmond, passed away. I'm sorry."

I stare at him, my mind fuzzy, a million thoughts scrambling to make sense of that.

"Ogre," Dad adds.

Then the pain hits, and I say only, "Why . . . ?"

And I could've repeated that word a thousand times, but it's only rhetorical, because I don't want an explanation.

Dad mistook me as seeking answers, an opening for another lesson. "Spontaneous combustion has occurred throughout history, but the reason it's worsening—"

"Stop!" I shout, "Just stop, I don't care."

He glances at me, then his eyes avert. "You *should* care, son."

My *mind-me* shatters everything about the world, and I feel better.

Dad says, "Why don't you take it easy today. I bet class will be cancelled."

I nod. Not even Ms. Crankshaw would teach after one of her own students fireballed. I slump beside Dad while he works, and I stare out at the sun and wonder what happens to us once we burn away.

Later I go to Liz's, three rows down the camp center.

She already heard the news from Billie Gross and had cried out the worst of her sorrow. But when she sees me, fresh tears run down her face and we embrace, though all I can wonder is how her body still produces that much water. Her tears are rivers of crystalline, clear as melted glass, shimmering as dreams, and I think what a waste for shedding it away. We sit and she puts her head on my shoulder, resting under my chin, and for the first time I feel stronger than her. When she moves, her soft cheek rubs on mine and I taste those tears at the corner of my lips, and they're salty like how the San Joaquin last tasted, but still wondrously sweet.

"You're a good friend," she says.

I want to tell her I could be more than a friend, but the strength I just felt suddenly flees . . . it's hard, so hard to voice words like those... my mouth gums up, my heart starts thumping too fast for my breath to keep up. That tiny speck version in my mind screams to say it, *just tell her*! He even tries to help, laying down glass panes of me being tongue-tied and shattering them.

My mouth sticks open while I wonder at how many different ways she might reject me.

Then Tommy appears out of nowhere, walking to us down the row of trailers, and my chance is gone.

"Missed you at class," he says.

"There was still class ... after Ogre?" Liz asks.

"Most of us didn't know until Ms. C. broke the news. I'm sorry."

Liz just shakes her head.

Tommy pauses, biting his lip, but what he has to say can't be contained. "It was the best lesson ever today. Ms. C.'s finally cracked! Said she sees Jesus and wants to reproduce with him since he has God's genes and all."

"What the *eff*?" Liz says, while I just stare, my mouth agape.

"Oh yeah, and she started crying, really shrieking with hysterics and everything. She finally admitted we're all going to die."

"I knew it, I knew it, I knew it!" Liz yells.

"That's bull," I say, "My dad says it's not true. Ms. Crankshaw's out of her mind."

"Your dad's just one of the adults," Liz counters. "He's trying to shield us, trying to hide the truth like he knows what's best!"

Any trace of Liz's tears is gone, evaporated and dried like everything else. She doesn't trust adults since her parents died. It happened in an accident during our first migration to Oxnard, and adults spirited Liz away, saying her mom and dad were okay. Later she was told the adults lied for her own good, to 'protect her,' so Liz wouldn't see the mangled bodies. But false hope is the cruelest sort of lie, and all Liz wanted was the chance to have said good-bye to her parents in person.

Tommy says, "Ms. C. admitted that everyone knows we're dying, the planet itself is combusting, just a lot slower than people."

"I hate them," Liz says, "It's not fair . . . "

"It's okay," Tommy replies, "Things will turn around. They'll get better." He wraps firm arms around Liz and comforts her tight.

I should've realized Tommy also likes Liz, because what guy wouldn't like her? *Mind-me* pounds his head in disgust, and I don't know what else to do.

"Will they?" Liz repeats back to Tommy, "Things'll get better?"

"We'll make them better," he replies, giving her the *same-exact-false-hope* they claim is shelled out by adults. Liz only listens—or *pretends* to listen—because it's Tommy.

Tommy's athletic and hard-working and funny, and everyone says he's sharp and dependable. I'm sharp and dependable, too, but no one says it about me.

I think of Ogre shooting that chunk of rock into the sky with his slingshot, and I envision it as my heart. In such a moment, it went soaring high, high into the air, then suddenly turned and fell, thunking hard to the ground.

THE NEXT WEEK, three more people died, though only one of those fireballed: a council member, Mr. Garcia. That shook my dad up a lot, someone who was smart and important being taken. Then Billie Gross died naturally from dehydration and heat stroke, and Ronny Jake ate a bullet.

But after the deaths, Melody Olson had a baby, so that equaled only net two from our camp population. Dad keeps a running tally in his log. He made a graph and extrapolated it, and I saw that in seventy-eight weeks our camp would be extinct. But that'd only be if we keep the same rate of mortality. Dad says we'll turn it around.

The temperature rose another degree, bringing the weekly average to one hundred-nineteen. Used to be, late-November was a time to pull out those light sweaters from the back of the closet. Now every breath is a gasp, like choking under a blanket of dust. Your lungs burn, your eyes dry out, your head aches all day, you feel dizzy.

At least it's a dry heat, everyone's fond of saying. We couldn't survive if it were humid.

And it's my shift to help gather again. Once the monstrous sun begins melting beyond the horizon, I meet with the same group, except since Ogre and Ronny Jake died, Hester and Jersey took their places.

Liz stops by to wish us good luck, and she smiles at me, and it's sincere. But I also see her sweet fingers trail along the inside of Tommy's hand when she passes him, and I know what that means.

Wearily we pile into the pick-ups and return to Highway 120 that leads to Escalon, and John sings merrily in his dry, grim voice. *"Have a holly jolly Christmas . . ."*

I almost whisper to Tommy my grave doubts of that holiday sentiment coming true, but he's adrift in dreams, probably of Liz. I fiddle instead with the CB radio.

Less people are talking on it, and more of what they say doesn't make sense, and what does sounds violent. Everything's regressing.

Maybe I'll be the one to figure it all out in class, solve the riddle of survival. Dad still pushes education as being most important, even without Ms. Crankshaw. Mrs. Hubble took over teaching both lower and upper kids since Ms. C. wandered into the desert and never came back—

Suddenly everything changes when John stops singing.

"What in hell," he says and slams the brakes, and Tommy and me pitch forward into the dash.

There's a bus painted camouflage parked across the highway lanes.

Hester's truck is ahead, and they jackknifed when they braked so abruptly.

John slows, stops, then starts to reverse, and soldiers with flashlights and machine guns are puked up from ravine gullets all around.

"Get out of the truck!" a man screams. He's not wearing a helmet or even an officer's beret, but rather a baseball cap with the San Diego Padres emblem across the front.

Somebody fires a shot in the air, a warning, and the bullet is a brilliant comet arching across the inky sky.

A man—no, a woman—comes near and slams our hood with the stock of her shotgun. "Get yer butts outta there!"

"Give us your food!" someone else yells, and more soldiers point guns at us.

"We ain't got any," John shouts truthfully out the window, since the U-Hauls are empty. "We're searching, same as you."

"Out of the truck!" the man in the Padres cap screams again.

Another shot is fired, punching through Hester's trailer. Sweat pops on my temples, and it's not from heat. More men converge on the trucks, banging with rifle butts and even sticks for those who don't hold guns.

These aren't real soldiers, I think, then realize when society collapses, some survivors *do* militarize and fight each other . . .

The woman smashes her shotgun again on our hood. "Get out! Or I'll shoot your butts!"

I fear what awaits outside the cab, and none of us move to exit. The truck's parked, but the engine idles, a low grumbling warning.

Ahead, an arm sticks out of Hester's truck holding a pistol and fires at a man in hunter's clothes. The shot is a soft *pop-pop*, but the scream is loud. The arm moves and shoots another man who carries a crossbow, and he falls silently.

For a moment, everything's frozen and, though it won't happen, I imagine that arm just picking off all the bad guys, one-by-one, while they stand immobile, helpless.

But then they unfreeze, and the soldiers trigger their horrible weapons, and Hester's truck blossoms in a cloud of smoke and burst metal and shells and blood. I scream, and Tommy screams, and the woman with the shotgun screams, "You're dead!", and she shoots the side of our truck, and some of the pellets smash through but damage only the floorboard.

A tall man in fatigues runs in front and levels a huge pistol at Tommy and fires. The windshield bursts, and Tommy coughs out a grunt, and half his head geysers blood.

John stomps on the gas, peeling backward, and twists the steering wheel. The rest of the windshield implodes, showering us with glass. The tall man points his pistol at me and, even as we retreat, I see his eyes are emotionless. He just wants to survive, and I'm competition, and my own life is about to end.

But the man gives a tiny gasp just like Jamie Goodwin did, and suddenly he starts emitting little glints of light and then bursts into a booming, shrieking fireball. The other soldiers run from him, terrified, as the man dances in a crazy circle before collapsing.

I can't believe my luck, and John reverses us far enough down road to swing a wild backward turn, and then we're roaring forward.

The impact of small arms fire striking the truck causes it to buck and sway, or perhaps it's from the road, filled with potholes and debris that as John races over at such speed, the attached U-Haul seems to lift in the air, sailing a foot or two upward like a terrible kite, pulling us side-to-side.

Leaning over Tommy's awful corpse provides a departing view in the side-mirror of soldiers' flashlights scurrying back and forth, and the smoldering body of the fireballed man, and then—finally, crushingly—the flicker of many headlamps turning on.

John drives like never before, barreling back to camp. The only songs he sings now are curses, though there's a certain musical quality to their repetition.

And though I can't stop shaking, and my heart feels like it's going to break through my ribs, all I think about is Liz. Ogre's dead, Tommy's dead, her parents, even old Billie Gross is dead. Liz doesn't have anyone to save her, to care for her . . .

There's no one but me.

We'll have to flee, the camp must evacuate and migrate somewhere safer, maybe even somewhere wetter. Once boys used to ask girls to a school dance. Now girls are asked which motorhome they'd like to run for their lives in. *Will you be mine?*

But what if someone asks her first . . . someone like Rudy, twenty years older, but who's rugged, inventive, and good with a hunter's rifle? He can protect her, and I heard he even writes poetry.

I tear myself up inside, and we smash into the middle of camp, and John leaps from the truck without even turning it off, running to sound the alarm. People are already panicked because they're wide-eyed and scurrying, having earlier heard the faraway gunfire.

John's screaming at everyone to pack and drive north, and there's a giant church bell someone hung upon scaffolding a long time ago, and John rings it back and forth, over and over.

And then I see it true, just as I feared . . . In the distance, Rudy and Liz are leaving together for his van! A million jumbled feelings set upon me, and they must end up in the bottom of my stomach, because I feel my guts fall low with the weight of misery.

A horrible thought flashes in my mind, that I could kill him. I don't know how, but I'll kill him, I'll murder him, smash in his head, and then I'd set him on fire and blame it all on the combustion . . .

The tiny version of me leaps into my head, ready to shatter to nothingness that bad-thought, but it pauses... 'cause maybe I'd prove I *was* the fittest by killing him, I'd be the final survivor, and then Liz would want me...

But I know that's wrong, and I hate myself, and I'm lost. Tommy just stares at me with unblinking eyes as if to say he'd trade places with me in an instant, and I almost agree.

I exit the truck and shuffle home.

For once, Dad's not writing, and his face is in mortal despair, paling before me as the alarm keeps clanging. He actually lightens shade-by-shade from red-brown to baby pink.

"There's no point," he says quietly, and his attention is entirely on me. "I'm sorry, son, sorry for lying to you all this time. But we *are* going to die... soon."

I stare at him, I can't believe it.

"All I've done, all I've built, all for naught," he murmurs. "I only wanted to protect you as long as I could. But there's no turning back from where we're headed."

Dad expects I'll scream at him, blaspheme deities, cry, hit things, but I don't.

Instead I unexpectedly feel calm. I feel acceptance.

I'm going to die. We're all going to die.

"That doesn't matter," I tell him.

For that moment I realize I'd struggled against extinction all this time while still worrying that if I didn't do what people expected, I'd disappoint them or I'd disappoint myself. In the fight for survival I worried how others might judge me, and I judged them in turn, because I felt inadequate. I let little insecurities overwhelm me, the doubts, the fears, the meaningless trivialities of existence.

And it's all for naught, because we're going to die.

We only live one time, and *why-oh-why* did I fear adversity and failure, when that doesn't matter at all?

I imagine my fears all as panes of glass, piles and piles of glass, and then *mind-me* comes forth, and he is mightier than ever, and he shatters all those bad-thoughts of self-defeat into nothingness until I feel reborn, and I decide I'm going to live life for myself . . .

"Dad, pick yourself up. We're not dead yet."

He nods, dazed, but color returns to his face.

"Get the RV ready and wait," I add. "I'll be back."

I head to Rudy's van.

I never connected with Liz before except as 'friends'. And it's my fault . . . she's not just a trophy to be won or some superior vessel to wed genes. Everyone makes mistakes sometimes, even me, even Dad. Dad admitted no one knows why we're fireballing or what's going to happen to the world, and in the absence of proven theories, people hypothesize, but that doesn't make it fact. Someday the planet will self-implode, but that day has not yet come.

Education's not the most critical matter at all, though Dad was right when he said everyone makes their own way in life.

I find Liz carrying a water cooler to Rudy's van.

"Hey," I say.

"Hey," she says back.

"Can I help?"

She looks at me with another of those little knowing smiles that could mean any of a dozen things, and small-arms gunfire erupts at the outskirts of camp.

"Are you leaving with Rudy?" I ask.

"He's the first who offered."

"Would you like to come with me instead?"

She shrugs noncommittally.

"Wait, that's not what I really wanted to say," I correct. "I like you, more than a friend."

There, something so small is said, and a tremendous weight

lifts from my conscience. I continue, "You shouldn't settle for the first person who asks. You should go where you want, where you'll be happiest."

She shrugs again, but this time it feels meant for me, an opening, though she pulls back with, "Rudy's cool."

Bullets ping and echo, drawing nearer. People peel out in trucks and campers, dragging clotheslines across the dirt like the tails of slithering wardrobe serpents.

I change my earlier question to a declaration. "Liz, I'd like you to come with me."

"Kenny, you're too ... "

Too young? Too weak? Too dumb? Too troubled?

I almost falter under the resurgence of doubts, but I shatter them away myself, without *mind-me*, and it's easier than I ever thought it could be.

I tell her, "I'm going to make my own way in this world."

She nods. "Okay."

"And I'd like you to be with me. I don't want to spend another day wondering if something *could* happen between us. I'd like to take a chance and find out before it's too late. I may never see you again."

She pauses, contemplating, perhaps weighing her options, and I consider again that Liz understands survival better than anyone else.

"Will you tell me things are going to turn around?" she asks.

I think of Tommy saying those words, and of Ogre believing we were stronger than the world, and of all the adults, everyone blind to the truth, or lying to us, or now dead.

"No," I admit. "They're not. I don't know how much time we have left, but I want to spend that remaining time with you."

Someone nearby shrieks, erupting in a fireball, and the sound is mortifying. Liz isn't distracted, but searches my eyes, perhaps for traits she herself most desires.

"All right," she finally says. "I'd like that, Kenny."

She slides one hand to me, and her long brown fingers entwine with mine. We leave the water cooler for Rudy, and amidst the screams and rattling machine gun fire and people bursting to flame, we go to my motorhome where Dad's waiting to spirit us off to new lands.

Whatever awaits, I'll face it on my own terms, knowing in some way I've already survived. And I wonder: *Did natural selection predispose me to love, or do I love because I evolved?*

Though, in the end, that question is rhetorical.

LAST DAYS OF THE GUNSLINGER, JOHN AMOS

JOHN AMOS HAD FIVE CHILDREN. NONE WERE HIS by birth, but every one of them called him Pa.

In younger days, John matched shot against other men for a bounty or a bottle, and he tried not to think of such times he was called a murderer. But he'd been raised a gunslinger, and because of skills honed over thirty years of quick draws he'd been able to keep himself and the children alive, while the rest of the territory around Elmore, Arizona were killed off screaming by the *hoppers*.

Now times were different, quieter in their own way. John and the oldest boy, Lee, crouched at the edge of a cliff littered by tall ocotillo and mesquite, looking down on those hoppers. Though John saw the increasing horror of what lay below, he couldn't help but reflect: *Whereas once a man's life wasn't worth a nickel to him, every living person now had become a precious blessing.*

John and the children had carved out a life in the high mountain caves—if being trapped on the mountain could be called much of a life—while the creatures abounded in the valley below. Whether the insect-like hoppers were monsters of the earth, aliens from beyond, or demons from Hades, John didn't know. What he *did* know was that they died like anything else.

Either by his bullets or the desert heat, their number had been slowly diminishing. John's hopes had lifted at that, calculating the odds month-by-month of escape from this infested region. But suddenly, five years after the hoppers mysteriously appeared, their mating urges seemed to kick in. They bred for the first time, and John knew the whole affair of calculating odds now levied a terrible disadvantage against him and the children.

For the creatures were busy laying eggs.

Those eggs towered in great pyramid-like mounds, each bulbous shell spotted pink and purple as garish candy drops, but sized larger than a county fair pumpkin. Whereas John had prior estimated there remained only a few hundred adult hoppers in the area, that number would soon swell to the tens of thousands once the eggs hatched.

"Jesus," Lee said.

John slapped him hard across the face. "We don't take the Lord's name in vain."

Tears slipped from the boy's eyes, but John didn't know if it was the sting from his whack or if Lee just wept from the despondency of what they saw. John immediately felt guilt; he struck Lee as an outlet from the dread below, just the same as Lee sought his own outlet by cursing. Both of them were impulsive.

Nothing else was said, and they gazed across the distant desert chaparral. The hoppers couldn't sense them up on the cliffs and, even if they did, couldn't scale the sheer granite face the way a man could, climbing with hands and feet. On flat land, though—the very kind of wandering, broken desert that surrounded the mountains—it was another matter. The creatures hunted scent like a bloodhound in heat and leapt faster than a jackrabbit over burnin' coals. Years before, when the townspeople of Elmore first tried banding together, they were overrun and scattered by the creatures, then caught and peeled apart like plucked fruit. There seemed no way to outrun or outmaneuver a hopper, and the best one could do was hide or hope their bullets didn't run out.

Lee spoke, breaking the silence. He was thirteen years old, and his voice sounded a tone too deep, as if trying to talk while holding in something that hurt. "What'll we tell the others, Pa?"

"The truth," John replied. "We always tell the truth."

Far off, a desert storm began to erupt, though it was hard to believe the clear morning could be tainted by downpour. The sky shone blue as polished turquoise, but John Amos heard the thunder echo across the valley like beating war-drums of the Hualapai tribes. The spring air was warm, and the wind—often breezing through the pass—had stilled, a respite from earlier pounding squalls. Instinct told him if the faraway storm kept up, it would arrive from the east. It was the sort of peculiar weather that John once welcomed, the whisper from Mother Nature that change was coming, and not just in ways of the seasons. A long time ago, when weather like this broke, he saddled up his chestnut mare and rode far across the land searching for the things restless men dream of.

Now there was no place to ride.

John backed away from the cliff's edge on hands and knees. Lee rose to follow and knocked loose a rock that crashed into other rocks, sending several far down to the valley floor.

A hopper startled at the small avalanche. It saw them and jumped up, but was too far below to pose any danger. It let out a cackling chirrup, sounding like a cricket—amplified—and mixed with the howl of a wolf. The hairs on John's arms rose every time he heard their call.

"Careful," he said. "You've stirred them up."

Lee looked down and spat at the creature. The hopper resembled a feral ball of teeth and purple thistles as it flailed and jumped against the rise of the mountain. They grew larger than a man, and their rear legs were bulging springs of muscle and sinew, taut like the recoil of a grizzly trap. The hoppers could leap upward of forty feet in one bound, but John and Lee and the others were well over a hundred feet above, safe in the caves.

"I wish we had more ammo," Lee said, not for the first time. "I could sit up here all day long and plug away at those things."

"I wish so too, son. But we've got to conserve what we have." John flicked a green fly off Lee's shoulder. He wanted to put his arm around the boy and apologize for slapping him, but couldn't find the right words for amends.

Instead, John whipped out his revolver and fired a single bullet into the valley. The hopper that had leapt at them shrieked and fell backward, the top of its head burst open. Amber blood spilled out like glistening honey, and one of the hopper's purple legs twitched to the heavens.

Lee grinned so big that John thought his teeth might fall out. They walked back up the winding path to the caves, and more of the hoppers' cries echoed from behind.

The caves stretched deep within the Crooked Top Mountains, providing shelter and a source of food for the group who daily caught and cooked the mice or bats that lived in the crevices. There was even loose soil along one short plateau bordering the cliff's ridge, and John had taught the children how to grow vegetables.

John and Lee returned to the cave entrance where the eldest of the children, Missy, waited. At fourteen, she could hardly be called a child anymore, but adolescence just didn't seem fitting to a girl that John still remembered as holding a tear-stained doll close to her heart when he first found her.

She asked, "Anything new?"

Lee didn't reply, but took her hand and looked solemnly into her alert eyes. John knew Lee carried puppy-dog feelings for her, probably something that kept him up at night with questions and wonder. To Lee, Missy was the only eligible girl left in these parts, and maybe in the whole state of Arizona. She wore the pants of a young boy and the wool shirt of a large man—one of John's—to allow for femininity that had begun to swell from her chest.

"What's the matter?" she asked.

"Gather the others," John answered.

He scratched at sun-burnt whiskers that covered his jaw while Missy cupped her hands to her mouth and hollered. Her voice was a command the other children respected as much as John's own.

John Amos had tried to protect more of the townspeople—and for awhile he did—but the other adults always seemed to get it into their heads they could run things better than himself. Without exception, those decisions got them killed.

Children just have a different way of thinking, and that's what kept them breathing. When John told them to hide, they did it. When he told them to shut up, they did that too. And when John said to run, he could just about see sparks licking at their boot heels as they bolted. Children did what they were told. The other adults didn't and so they were dead.

By doing things his way, John had kept them alive for half a decade. But now, as hard as he tried to figure otherwise, he knew they wouldn't live much longer if they stayed on the cliffs.

The remaining children emerged. Lee's eleven-year-old sister, Ruth, carried an axe with an obsidian-blade head. Little Grace followed, freckled with the smile of golden sunrise, and holding hands with the youngest, Josiah. He clung to her like a scared nestling, unable to spread its wings and attempt flight.

"Children," John said, shifting his gun holster while the sun spilled fire onto his shoulders. "It's time for us to leave."

A wind picked up, and the hoppers' distant howls carried past.

"We've been safe here, high up, while the valley's infested with those things. We've watched the hoppers die off lately, and it's been easier to sneak down for food, even haul up more supplies from the wagons, biding our time and hoping to decamp once their number depleted. That plan won't work anymore."

The children looked around, realizing they'd be saying farewell to a home that some of them had known longer than any other residence. They'd lived in the caves for years and grown used to its musty shadows and damp earth. Besides Missy and Lee, the others hadn't left the cliff's edge since they arrived, having ridden up on wagons that stuck at the base of the mountain.

"Maybe they're on a five-year life cycle, but those things have reproduced in mass," John continued. "They're just eggs now, but they'll mature soon, and a whole new generation is going to rise. If we're here after that happens, we'll never leave this place."

The storm from the east moved in, and the blue sky turned gun barrel-gray.

"How are we gonna leave, Pa?" Grace asked. She wrung at the hem of her dress, pulling on loose threads between delicate fingers.

"I don't know yet," John replied, "but I'll figure it soon enough."

The children nodded, as if silently agreeing that John's words were satisfaction enough. If John Amos said he'd do something, they knew it'd get done.

That night it rained, and the next morning it rained harder than he'd ever seen.

John stood on the edge of a bluff and looked out over the hoppers and their eggs scattered across the valley floor. It reminded him of once finding a dead deer in the fields; from a distance the carcass looked black, but up close he'd seen the color was really just swarms of flies crawling across its pale hide. He wondered again at the creatures' origin, and then he wondered again at his and the children's future.

There was life and death and conflict everywhere. Even the land around them seemed a symbol of struggle, where cacti and sparse pine trees sprouted next to each other, jostling for resources amongst the steep adjustments of elevation. It was a strange terrain from which strange stories sprouted like wild summer weeds, and he reconsidered how much truth to them he should have heeded. Indian curses and biblical prophecies and tall tales shared by toothless old prospectors had reached his ears ever since he was old enough to hear. The legends and lore were countless, and one never knew if they were late-night fancies or moored in the experiences of those that settled the area in ancient days past. After the arrival of the hoppers, nothing remained that John thought impossible.

He heard Missy coming, but didn't look back. The rain masked most sound, but long-ago he'd learned to tune in any noise that sounded out-of-place, such as approaching footsteps from behind. John's wide-brimmed hat drooped under the heavy downpour, and he lifted it off and flicked away the water as best he could, handing it to her when she was close enough.

She took it. "Sure is coming down."

He nodded, feeling like they'd moved beneath a waterfall.

"You come up with a plan yet to leave?" Missy asked.

"No, but I prayed on it. The Lord will give us a sign."

A fork of lightning flashed across the morning sky, followed by the crack of thunder.

"We always thought we'd be rescued, Pa. The cavalry or some posse would come riding in and clear out a path for us. What if the hoppers aren't just in the valley? What if they've taken over everywhere?"

"There's no creature that can take over *everywhere*, not folks, and not those things. There's safety out there somewhere, and we'll find it."

"I believe it. You've always kept us protected."

"You can't count on me forever," John said. He turned to face her, and she held his gaze. Her eyes shone green as dew-touched leaves and reminded him of his wife, Belle, from long ago. The only time he ever thanked God for Belle's death was the day the creatures appeared. It had been terrible enough watching tuberculosis slowly eat away her life, but he couldn't fathom seeing her get torn apart by the hoppers, as what happened to most everyone else from their small settlement. He patted Missy's arm. "The other children look up to you. If anything should happen to me, you've got to watch out for them."

"Ain't no hopper gonna get you, Pa."

"I can only handle what I can handle."

The rain fell harder still, like hammering fists, and the wind picked up, slapping waterlogged sagebrush across their legs.

"Guess we should tie tarps over the garden?" she asked.

"About that time."

"Maybe the rain will wash those monsters out of here."

John smiled at the thought. He was about to respond when a low, steady rumble erupted. He recognized the sound, and his brain started calculating, like the greased-cogs of a wound clock.

"Missy," he said. "Go tell the others to get ready. We're leaving."

She looked around. "Now?"

"Now, child! The Lord has given us his sign!"

She turned and ran up the path to the caves.

The rumble grew louder, and John closed his eyes, listening to where it came and the direction it headed. The valley below was a channel, surrounded by mountains on both sides. Roughly four miles west, it emptied out like a funnel onto the desert plains, southwest of the mining town of Florence and twenty-five miles from Phoenix. It might be a running fight from there, but it was a start.

A flash flood was headed their way, and John knew the only way through the hoppers was to jump in and ride it out.

He returned to the caves and found the children grouped together, waiting for him.

"Weapons only," John said. "And the clothes on your back. There ain't nothing else we can afford to bring."

The children nodded at his words, but their eyes were dumb, unable to imagine escape. Rain fell harder, pelting them like needles, and the wind whipped their faces. John waited to tell them until a tremendous roar rushed past. When it broke, Josiah flinched and covered his ears. Water crashed across the land below, and the screams of hoppers mixed with pounding thunder.

"It's a flood," John said, "and the valley's filling. I don't know how long it'll last, and I don't know if it'll get us past the creatures, but it's a chance, and we've got only one."

Grace shivered. Lee gulped. John turned his palms up, fingers splayed. "Gather and hold hands."

The children obliged, and he called up to the wild sky, "Lord, deliver us from these sons of bitches. Amen."

"Amen," the children repeated.

Missy held his Winchester rifle. John asked, "You got that loaded?"

She nodded.

"Good girl." He motioned to Ruth. "Hold on to Grace and Josiah. Keep 'em tight."

"Yes, Pa." The two youngest moved to her, clinging at each leg.

"Lee," John said. "Get the axe. We're going to the wagons."

The wagons were a pair of pine buckboards that John and some other men had managed to drive partway up the mountain until the incline became too great. This occurred years before, during their dismal escape from Elmore, when the hoppers first began hunting. Of course John and the others didn't understand what was happening then, only that they were surrounded and the creatures couldn't climb, so they sought the mountain top for escape. Only afterward did they realize they'd trapped themselves on an island of refuge surrounded by a stormy sea of monsters. John doubted they would have made it through the valley anyway during their flight, but sometimes he wondered what the purpose of their escape had been. The horses they used were gone—as were the other men—taken as food by the creatures. The wagons had proved invaluable though, filled with the trappings of society. Clothes, blankets, guns, food, seed, and loose trinkets that reminded him they weren't reduced to savages. Most of it had been carried up to the caves, and the buckboards had since settled from disrepair, leaning against each other.

Fighting the downpour, John and the children climbed down a network of ladders and footholds to the shelf of land the wagons sat upon. The flood already rose to lap at the wheels. The mountain descended another twenty feet beyond to the valley floor, but now it was only a raging gray river, foaming like a rabid beast and filled with the debris of land.

A hopper rushed past, caught in the powerful current. It shrieked and struggled against the deluge, but was helpless. Like a rabbit, it could not jump in water, for there was no solid surface to leap off. It splashed and screamed and sank.

John took the axe and positioned himself next to the wagon closest to the water. With a mighty strike, he cleaved one wheel off its wood axle, then moved to the others and severed them, until the buckboard fell flat to the ground. He chopped off the two front shafts used to harness horses, then shortened each shaft to lengths of eight feet apiece with another round of swings.

"Push!" he ordered.

They lined up at one edge and shoved the wagon into the water's shallows.

A thunderous clamor sounded, and John turned to it. Upriver, a side of the mountain peeled off, crashing into the flood. The whole valley shook, and boulders dropped all around, tumbling past on waves before sinking into the darkness below. For years, the mountain had been their refuge, sheltering them from the monsters' reach. Now that haven was crumbling. He imagined the caves above shifting until their ceilings collapsed, the home they'd built returning to that shapeless mass of shattered granite they first discovered. Though John was desperate to flee, he felt a twinge of melancholy, too; the time spent living in the caves had not been completely awful—he'd enjoyed a sort of fatherhood in looking after these children, an experience he never had with Belle. But they were cut off now, and there was no going back.

"Get in," he said.

The rising water picked up the wagon and he struggled to hold it in place while each child climbed inside. Without wheels, it resembled a low-lying box, rectangular with three-foot-high side walls. A bench and single chair mounted on the front, where once John rode, driving a team of horses. He would ride it now as a captain, trying to navigate the churning currents. He pushed the buckboard from its rocky perch with one horse shaft, while Lee pushed from its back with the other. The battered wagon was built of white pine, a light wood that could float while dry, but once enough water soaked through the grain, that'd be the end of their sailing.

And it wouldn't take long, John guessed, for the unsealed wood to become waterlogged as such. But neither, he also reasoned, would it take long to sail out of the valley.

The wagon shot into the flood like a greased arrow.

"Yee-haw!" Lee shouted. "Like breakin' in a new horse!"

John was about to warn off his arrogance when the wagon slammed something underneath, knocking John's legs out from under him. He struck his head on the bench and landed in a tangle of limbs with the children, and found all he could do was curse.

More of the mountain fell around them causing the river to rise and sink in giant walls of water. The buckboard lifted and turned all the way around in the currents, so the back became the front. Lee pushed his pole against an outcropping, and they spun again.

Grace screamed, and Josiah followed suit.

"Pa, look out!" Missy lifted her rifle and fired.

A hopper collided against them and the waves almost shoveled it inside. Her bullet went wild as the wagon dipped, and water poured in over the lip. The hopper's teeth snapped, and its legs flailed, trying to dig claws into the wood to climb inside. John whipped out his pistol and shot a round through its face spraying amber blood in a great arc. The creature tumbled backward, and the river took it away.

"You three," John said to Ruth, Grace, and Josiah. "You've got to bail out water. Use anything you can, your hands, shoes, hats."

There was a sharp smack, and a saguaro cactus snapped against the wagon's front, its razor arms swinging wide overhead. "I can't shoot and steer," he added and motioned to Missy. "You've got to cover us, Lee keep steering from the back."

Hauling himself into the bucket seat, John poled them away from a spiraling whirlpool that formed amongst broken trees. Bulging hopper eggs bobbed up from the water and shattered against the mountain walls. A grin crept over his face in spite of their circumstances; fragments of spotted pink-and-purple shells showered the water. The creatures wouldn't be multiplying anytime soon after this. The air stank of wet creosote, and the valley boomed in rolling thunder. John's grin flipped as the buckboard lurched, then sailed faster through the current, gaining momentum.

A crack sounded from Missy's rifle, then another, but he didn't look behind to see what she shot at. Ahead the valley narrowed between shaking mountain outcrops, and he saw a dozen hoppers crawling up the broken rocks like soggy beetles. The wagon aimed to sail right amongst them, and he imagined the things leaping down into the buckboard as they passed through.

He pulled his revolver and fired. Two of the hoppers fell in noisy somersaults, showering purple thistles to mix with the rain.

I can't shoot and steer, John remembered saying. *Well, I guess I'm learning.*

Missy stumbled to the front and fired the rifle alongside him. Another pair of hoppers were picked off.

The buckboard tilted and shuddered, and John began to feel doubt it could hold up long enough to ride out the flood. The wagons had been left to the elements for five years at the mountain's base and there was no telling how the bolts and joinery would hold up under these conditions.

John and Missy fired again at the creatures on the rock face, but the river spun them, and the craft tilted, taking more water. The shots flew lost into the rain. More cacti erupted from the river, their spines lashing in all directions. A dead hopper floated by, impaled on a saguaro's limb. The youngest children bailed frantically, but it was a losing effort. Already, gray floodwater sloshed above their ankles.

The valley trembled and the mountain outcrop broke free, collapsing in great explosions of rolling granite. Slabs of rock beat against the river, and the flood grew more frenzied. The hoppers shrieked as they fell, sliding off the boulders into watery depths.

At least timing is on our side, John thought. *If we'd been any earlier, the collapsing rocks would have dropped right on us.*

Dust billowed up from the avalanche, filling the air, though John still heard things breaking and falling around them. They sailed blind through the murky grit hoping the river would carry them through safe. Half a dozen rapid heartbeats later, they were on the other side, roaring along at breakneck speeds.

The flood had risen farther, so the towering pine trees now looked stunted; only their tops were visible above the water's surface. The buckboard skipped across curling whitecaps then crashed down into a black eddy. Josiah flipped in the air like flicking up a coin on your thumb and forefinger. He came down at the same place he'd gone up, but the wagon had already been carried away. The boy dropped smack into the river's frenzy and vanished. Ruth howled, and John scrambled to the back. The wagon bounced off a submerged boulder and almost flipped up too, the way Josiah had.

"Lee," John shouted, "take the front!"

He strained to see sign of the lost boy. A tree top whipped across as they sailed past and slapped John's face. He saw flashing stars instead, and then he saw a hopper pop up from the water like a cork that's pulled down and released. Josiah's arm shot out from the torrent behind it.

John dropped his pistol and dove in, immediately buffeted in cycles the way it might feel in the midst of a twister.

He thought for a moment he should have pulled off his boots and belt, but knew there wasn't time. Just as quickly, he sank under the crushing waves, then struggled back to the surface. The flailing hopper lurched at him with spiked claws, but didn't have any better control in the water than did John. The creature was pulled under and John thought he could swim past. Something horrible sliced under the cap of his knee and he screamed until he was sucked under again, the icy rainwater filling his mouth and lungs.

Underwater, the black shapes of trees and rocks and moving things blurred in an aquatic nightmare. John felt he might pass out right there from the pain in his leg, but he managed to force himself to swim under the current, his limbs weighted by clothes and burning from the strain. The river seemed to change directions at impossible angles, and he recalled a time long ago, when he was once caught in a stampede: The sensations were alike, unseen things cutting and pounding him as he got pulled along. He was dragged faster and faster downstream, but finally broke surface gasping for air, then coughing out water, then gasping again. A massive tree trunk sailed past and John grabbed hold, using it as a float to regain his senses.

"Pa!" Missy shouted.

John turned and saw he trailed only a few feet behind the wagon.

"Grab the pole!" She held out the wood shaft, and he reached for it.

Then Ruth bawled and pointed, "Josiah!"

John swung his head the other way and saw the boy's arm again rise through the river right behind as if he'd been the one chasing after them all along.

John tried to turn the tree trunk perpendicular to slow it against the river's flow, hoping the boy could catch up. Something rattled like clattering dry beans, and even over the roar of the storm, he recognized the sound.

A huge rattlesnake rose from a knot in the tree, its copper snout only a foot from John's face.

He cursed three shades of blue and eyed the snake as it rose closer.

Another sound, a cackling chirrup, as if a monstrous cricket mixed with a wolf's howl, rushed toward him. The flood pulled a hopper along, its cry growing louder like a boiler riding the tracks straight at him.

The rattlesnake struck at John's head and he dodged out of its way more by luck than anything else. He let go of the trunk as the hopper collided against him. Its force struck him so hard that John felt his ribs nearly cave in, and he rebounded back against the tree. A bullet whizzed by before he realized a shot sounded, then a wave covered them all. John would have been sucked back under the water, but he grabbed onto a limb from the tree with one hand and held on as they all spun around in a swirl. The hopper gnashed its teeth and tilted its head to snap at John. Another gunshot, and the creature was knocked aside with a hole in its shoulder.

Missy's aim was getting better.

The snake swiveled and lashed out again. In the matter of survival there wasn't much John Amos wasn't willing to attempt. Never though, had he considered snatching up a rattler by bare hand. One wrong move and a snake bite would send him to Belle quicker than he would've preferred. But he let that ghostly guide of reflex take over, and when the snake struck, John reached up and caught it under its neck. The serpent's rattle went crazy like a chain of Chinese dynamite ripping through the earth. He sensed movement and turned, seeing the wounded hopper surge forward again, its jaws stretching open to tear John apart.

In that instant they could have kissed, their heads drummed so close to each other. The hopper snapped its teeth shut twice, and John came an inch to being decapitated, but he knew the way the monsters lunged, head-first in a corkscrew motion with neck extended, and he ducked underwater just in time to avoid it.

Along the way down, John pressed the rattler against the hopper as hard as he could. The snake caught the beast's mandibles and sank its fangs into that wiry purple fur lining the hopper's jaws. The hopper shrieked and sank under the tree trunk taking the snake with it.

Clinging to the trunk, John pulled himself hand-over-hand to its furthest point just as Josiah soared past. He caught the boy under one arm and pulled him tight to his chest, feeling how icy-cold they'd both become.

"Josiah," he said. The boy was limp and his eyes rolled up.

John sensed his own strength fading fast from the broiling water and debris hammering at them. His legs weren't working right, and he was trapped against the tree, unable to let go and swim in the river while holding Josiah. A crash jolted him and, looking up, he saw the wagon. Lee had maneuvered it alongside the trunk, and Missy leaned over.

"Hand him to me," she said.

He lifted the boy up with one arm and Missy caught and pulled him in. John followed, pushing off from the tree and grabbing the buckboard's side. A hopper's egg bounded through the waves next to them. Even in desperation to get out of the water, he couldn't help but feel disgust at the thing. Part of the shell was cracked, and something was trying to push its way out. An ebb of strength welled within, and John reached over and punched the egg. The shell shattered, and its contents were taken by the water.

He began to pull himself over the side of the wagon and paused. *Something was wrong.* His arms trembled, his vision was darkening around the edges. He couldn't get in.

Lee caught him under his arms and heaved, and John finally tumbled back inside. The buckboard rose high in the air on a wave, then sank just as quick, and he felt his guts get left behind. The wagon was half-filled with water and the two youngest girls tried desperately to bail it out, but they could just as easily have been swimming in it. Everyone's eyes were on different things.

"How is he?" John asked wearily.

Missy held Josiah over her knee and pounded on his back. The boy vomited gray water and coughed. "I think he'll be okay."

"Where's my gun?" John asked.

Ruth had it tucked into her belt. She pulled it loose before looking at him, then shrieked.

Half of John's left leg was gone. Below the knee—where he'd felt the hopper slash him in the river—there was nothing attached, just hanging red streamers of flesh and ligament.

"Pa!" Missy cried.

Blood poured from the stump, mixing with the wagon's rainwater. John glanced down at it and was almost relieved to at least understand why he felt steadily weaker. The adrenaline rush while fighting in the river had kept him going, but now he just wanted to close his eyes and dream of a life gone by. An avalanche of rock and pine trees collapsed behind them with a thunderous peal. A hopper's howl chased after. The wagon spun again, though lazy, as a spinning top begins to slow.

"I said, where's my gun?" His voice had gotten quieter, but it was still not to be argued with.

Ruth handed it to him, her eyes growing big. John checked the chambers. She'd loaded it with the last of his spare cartridges, five in total.

"Good girl," he said.

The darkening of John's vision spread until his peripheral sight was gone. He looked at the world as if through a pair of opera lenses; everything seemed larger than it should and focused only on small circumferences.

But it was enough.

He swung the revolver and fired once into the water. A hopper's head split in two.

Ahead, the mountains opened up, and the flood waters dispersed into the plains. The river slowed and shallowed.

The rain began to lessen.

Lee took off his leather belt and wound it around John's upper leg, cinching tight. Like the river, John's blood flow slowed, but it still pulsed in spurts. "You're going to make it, Pa. We're almost there."

"Less talking," John said. "You need to steer us through."

Already the flood level had dropped to five or six feet deep, and the wagon descended halfway into that, sinking steadily lower from the waves breaking over its sides. Had he two legs, John would have jumped out and pushed them along. Now though, he wanted only to lie there, floating. His eyelids weighed half a ton each, and his head drooped like his neck didn't work any longer.

At the final mountain pass, and before the flood poured onto the empty badlands, a tight bottleneck had formed of trees and rubble and drowned hopper corpses. Lee steered the buckboard past shattered cacti and pine limbs. Egg shells covered in mud broke to pieces, oozing amber residue like rotten molasses.

Josiah sobbed. His eyes were bloodshot and puffy. He attached himself to John like a layer of sad clothing, chanting, "Don't go, don't go."

Something moved under the mud, and the buckboard tilted. Missy swung the rifle toward the muck, but the movement subsided and they passed over.

"Get out, stay together, and run," John said. He lay back so the water flowed over his hair.

"You're coming with us," Missy told him. She spoke it as an order, though the question of her own words was plain across her face.

"I'm not."

"We've got wood, I'll make you a crutch or stretcher," Lee said.

"I'm bleedin' out. Those creatures are still around, and I'll slow you down," John replied, then gasped. He cleared his throat and his voice cracked. "There's not much left for me . . . I just want to know you've got a chance. Get out of here and hope the hoppers haven't infested the next town."

"We're not leaving you here!"

"How do you stay alive?" John asked. He looked at each of them hard as he could.

Grace whispered, "We do what you tell us."

"And I'm telling you to leave."

A splash and howl clattered toward them. A hopper was trying to jump through the water, but unable to get far enough above the surface to leap; it looked almost like it bounced in place. John shot it through the neck, and it sank.

The wagon rocked against the bottleneck, unable to move forward, just bobbing up and down over debris. Dozens of eggs floated against the pine board sides, and hundreds more seemed to be riding the flood straight to them. Many were cracked or punctured, but there were enough eggs that seemed preserved to give John great worry. Some of those eggs pulsed, like something inside was getting ready to break out.

A hopper lay tangled in cacti and boughs only twenty yards away. It was alive and moaning, but unable to jump. One leg was snapped, jutting at an impossible angle over the hopper's head. It clutched a single egg with insectile claws against its abdomen, the way a mother holds a bundled baby.

Missy raised the Winchester to it.

John gently pushed her arms away. "Save your ammo," he said. "That one's no danger."

No one else said anything; they didn't have to.

"The Lord will guide us all," John said. "Now get the hell outta here! *Go!*"

He took one of the poles and smacked it against Lee's head, prompting them to move. Each child embraced John Amos and said they loved him. He promised he'd find his way to meet up with them another day. For the first time, none of them believed it. The pooled water in the buckboard was crimson, and John was pale white.

"I'd give you the pistol, but there's only three bullets left. I'll put them to better use keeping those things from following you," he said.

The children nodded, and finally they left, picking their way over the bottleneck dam. Missy led, holding the Winchester. On the other side of the river, John saw them find footing on the beginnings of solid ground, wending from mud to desert sand. They walked slow at first, as if a terrible pressure fought to hold them back then, as they moved farther away, that pressure seemed to lessen, and their pace quickened. Except for Missy, each one looked back.

John watched them go with mixed feelings of pride and loss.

His senses were dulling, like being under a bout of three-day drinking, and the sorrow of his circumstances was only a distant sensation, though the stump of his leg screamed fierce.

He lay on his side and used the wood pole to smash every egg within reach. As the broken shells sank, more eggs took their place, pushed against the wagon by the current, and he broke those too. John's strength dimmed like his sight, but it didn't take much energy to whack them.

The last of the rain stopped. Though the sky was still murky as the river, he watched a single shaft of late sunlight break through, and it was enough to feel satisfaction.

Movement to his right, and John rolled over. It was the hopper with a broken leg struggling to rise. It still clutched the egg, which seemed a strange thing to him. There were thousands of eggs, and each female creature seemed able to lay hundreds. Was that the sole survivor of this hopper's clutch that it cared for so desperately? Did the monsters love their brood the way John loved his own children? He remembered thinking how his perception of life had changed after the hoppers' arrival: *now every living person was now a precious blessing.*

Did the creatures feel the same way about their own kind? Maybe that flood completely destroyed them ... at the least, they were gravely weakened. This hopper must have watched in frenzy as John smashed the eggs one by one. As the creatures' numbers decreased, did they consider each of their own remaining to be *a precious blessing*?

The wounded hopper gave up its efforts to stand and fell back, half-submerged. John contemplated it for a long time: that one-legged, half-drowned horror, and that he and it were similar, just wanting to survive, to see their offspring persevere.

Only he wanted it more. The shaft of sunlight vanished.

And to hell with it all, he thought.

John shot a bullet into the last egg, and it burst in a runny mess. The hopper tried to rise again, howling, and John shot his second bullet between its eyes.

The world turned black, and he didn't know if night had fallen, or his vision gone out. He prayed for forgiveness of all he'd done wrong, and he hoped he'd find his way home to Belle.

The third and last bullet John Amos turned on himself.

MOMMA

MOMMA ASKED, "WHERE'S WILLIAM?"

"He's visiting Poppa," Daniel replied.

Momma smiled, thin lips straining upward like a rusty lock that turns in creaks. Poppa died twenty years ago, said to be murdered during the night by a man of town who was never named. So it was true, in a way, that William *was* visiting Poppa. William was Daniel's brother and had been caught in a fire that burned him so bad, he died a week later, coughing out the ashes of his lungs. That was six years past, when Momma's illness began, when her memory began to falter. Even *she* was unable to save him.

"It's strange, the things that come to me like ghosts in my mind," she said quietly. "They appear and vanish with a whisper, as if apparitions of something I once knew. I search for them, but I don't know what I'm looking for. I don't remember what it is I've even forgotten." Her eyelids fluttered and sagged over milky eyes.

Her mental clarity was better today than it had been all week. Daniel thought he should feel relief, even some joy, at her cognizance, but instead felt only melancholy. He could not decide which was preferred: To dream blissfully unaware of what you have become, or to have recognition of the slow death sentence, the incurable disease that sweeps away your faculties.

Momma sat in a wicker-back chair under the afternoon sun. Her eyes closed, and a drool of pepper-flecked saliva leaked from the corner of her mouth. It dripped slowly down her chin, following the canal of a wrinkle, like a drop of molasses seeping from bark. Such was her mind, too, like a reservoir which leaked the sap of life, drop by slow drop, until one day it would be left as only a dry husk.

That day was soon to be coming, and Daniel felt conflicting sorrow and relief.

He kissed the top of her head and hobbled through the screen door into their house. The sounds of wood flies and cicadas followed inside. The house was dark and old, an intimate realm of musty dreams and stale woes. He walked upon its cracked linoleum, some sections missing entirely to reveal the charcoal-brushed timber underneath. In the kitchen he boiled Momma's tea, as he did five times a day. Into it he soaked wood root, gathered from mangroves out back, and added a teaspoon of pepper and a pinch of ground calcite.

He retraced his steps across the cracked linoleum and returned outside to give Momma her tea.

"Lucas, you spilled my gum oil," she said, her words slow and unsteady.

"It's me, Momma. I'm Daniel."

"I know who you are, Lucas. Get your brothers, it's bedtime."

"I will. You know they can't sleep until they say they love you."

She smiled at that and sighed, the sound like wind blowing through dead stalks of wheat.

"Drink your tea," Daniel said. He held her shaking hand in his own and guided the cup to her mouth.

She drank, and they were silent for a long time. There were no other brothers left to say they loved her. Daniel tried to make up for it, and often he would say *I love you, Momma* seven times, once for each of her sons.

Momma suddenly remembered. "They're all dead . . . " she said. "God, why have I lived so long?"

Daniel squeezed her shoulder with his good right hand. His left arm was shriveled and hung loose, like a parasitic thing sucking at his shoulder. The afternoon sun began to fall and the sky darkened, indigo blue, streaked with cherub-red.

He was the youngest son, born last and born deformed and weak. Each of his six brothers had been beautiful and strong as the wild sycamores that blossomed on their land. It were as if by the time Daniel was birthed, all the resources which went into making flawless children had been used up by his siblings; there was little left, and he was cobbled together with the scraps of placenta and hope.

But as each brother grew into manhood, he left their home to make his mark on the world, only to be stolen away by a great divine theft. William, the eldest, was first. Ezekiel was next, crushed by falling rock from a mudslide. Aaron was mauled by a wild animal. Lucas, struck by lightning. Henry, pulled under the dark currents of a river's undertow. Orlie, infected by raging fever. The brothers died one per year, in the order they were born.

Momma stood abruptly and hurled her cup of tea across the porch. It shattered midair into flying ceramic bits. Daniel winced. She spun at him and her milky eyes turned black as oil.

"It's the townspeople's fault. I'll get them, Daniel, every one of them," she said, her voice rasp with growl. The exertion made her faint, and she collapsed back into the wicker chair just as quick as she'd stood.

Daniel bent down and wrapped his arms around her tight. He rested his head against her breast and said, "I know we will."

She looked at him, her face sagging. "We will what, Lucas?"

THAT NIGHT TURNED COLD, a brush tipped with frost flicking over the wilderness. Daniel sat alone on the porch in Momma's chair and watched the moon cast shadows across near trees. Night birds and frogs sounded, calling and answering each other. *Their songs must be what music is like*, he thought. Momma used to sing when she was healthy, but she told him there were also man-made instruments which could produce song. She used to dance and sing and make music with others, long before the townspeople settled the land.

The townspeople were out there, somewhere, and Daniel narrowed his eyes as he looked carefully at each shadow in the surrounding woods.

"It's funny, I've never even seen a townsperson before," he said. "Momma says to stay away from them, but I don't even know who *they* are."

A cicada rested on his shoulder. It chirped into Daniel's ear, sounding like raindrops batting on the tin roof.

Daniel replied. "I *know* they must look like the rest of us, but I wouldn't care to meet them, seein' as what happened to Poppa."

The cicada extended its wings and chirped again.

"That ain't true about Poppa and you know it," Daniel said. "Momma says he was murdered, and this world is a cruel, cruel place."

The cicada climbed over his shoulder and went up his neck.

"Quit it, Ezekiel. I've told you before that tickles me."

It flew off and circled around to perch on Daniel's outstretched hand.

"Momma's real sick, now. I don't think she's going to live through the week. I'm going to be the last of the family . . . I'll be all alone."

The cicada rubbed its antennae and chirped a series of quick, rising tones.

"Thanks," Daniel said. "That's not what I meant. I know you and the others will still be here."

"DANIEL," MOMMA CRIED OUT.

"Coming," he said.

Daniel was in the kitchen brewing her morning tea. He

shuffled to her room, a small space separated from the main parlor by a faded sheet filled with red-and-gold images of mythical animals that stood upright in tunics. He sometimes wondered if Momma were as old as the images on that fabric.

Behind the sheet she lay in bed, staring at him, her eyes open wide and aware. A spiral of blood and snot hung from her nose, and drops splattered on her nightgown. She spoke in a voice which sounded clear and strong. "I'm dying."

"I know," he replied. He felt honest at saying those words out loud. He understood she'd been dying for a long time, but they lived their life together as they always had, without ever speaking of it.

"I haven't much time," she said. "My mind plays tricks on me, little pranks I once would have laughed away as a child. Now though... I don't know what's real, or dream, or memory. I've been asleep for so long..."

Daniel gently handed her the cup of tea and kept his hand placed over her own as she drank.

"I had a dream, son. A vision of the holy land." She coughed, then wheezed, and Daniel could hear the death-rattle, like pebbles grating in her lungs. "Your Poppa was there, waiting for me. He said he's happy, but it's lonely without us. There's a place set for me at the golden table, and all my sins and black transgressions will be forgiven if only I undo the evil I have wrought."

"You and Poppa back together?" Daniel squeezed her shoulder and his eyes widened. He only knew Poppa from her stories and the sad oil painting that hung crooked in the parlor.

"But first I've got to free the spirits of the townspeople I've bound to this land."

"You're going to let them go?" Daniel asked. She once told him that she kept their souls trapped in the woods like moths in a jar. He'd asked what that meant, but she never chewed over details. *Knowing too much leads to wicked ideas*, Momma had told him.

He continued. "But all my life you said there's nothing more important than revenge on Poppa's killers. We still ain't ever found what happened to him."

"There's no peace found by keeping a grudge," she said. "I realize that now. The townspeople know I'm dying... I hear their whispers in the wind. They hate me, and they're waiting..."

"How could anyone hate *you*, Momma?"

"I cursed them... all of them. I cursed the earth like an ulcer, oozing cancer to rot the town. I wouldn't let the ulcer heal, and it spread. I cursed everyone, so they'd die and their spirits could never find rest 'til I found what happened to your Poppa. It was a curse that took everything out of me and it made me sick." She turned and buried her face in the pillow. She spoke again, and her muffled voice broke in a sob. "I filled myself with black magic, more than I ever had before, and it poisoned me. You were inside of me still, and it poisoned you too. That's why you don't look like your brothers."

Daniel felt a sharp sting, as if the flying bugs from the marsh crept inside and bit his heart.

"We've got to leave this dead land in our own ways. I'm sorry—real sorry—I've held you back... I've kept you hidden from the world, 'cause of my fears, my hate of the townspeople." Momma turned back and her face was wet. Blood smeared her lips. "Lord, my poor, poor boys. Your brothers weren't meant to suffer, but the curse didn't discriminate. It seized them like the others... I thought I could control it."

"But they ain't suffering. They're all around us," he said.

Her face crinkled like a dried flower while confusion washed upon her eyes. She opened her mouth to speak and stayed like that in silent pause before responding. "I've done wrong. I've got to free them, if it's not too late yet."

"I love you, Momma," Daniel said. "I don't want you to leave."

She shook her head, as if clearing cobwebs off her thoughts. "It's time for us to move on. Your brothers and me . . . we'll all be a family again up in heaven. All we have to do is get there."

"But this *is* heaven, Momma. We can all stay here."

"Honey, this world is a cruel, cruel place. Nothing is as it seems."

"No," Daniel said suddenly. "I'll be all alone. You can't take them with you."

Her eyes turned oil-black in rage, a flash like colorless lightning. "Boy, you do as I say!"

Just as quickly, the black dissipated and her face fell slack, the weight of anguish dispersing the rage. "I need to make one last spell . . . to release them. You must gather things for me, roots and spiders and water hemlock—I'll tell you a list. You understand . . . Lucas?"

DANIEL WALKED THROUGH the woods pushing aside Spanish moss and batting at mosquitoes and snakeflies that hovered with each step. He carried a wicker basket yellow as a summer daffodil and, as he hobbled over wet ground, he placed things inside.

"Ezekiel, why don't you talk to Momma like you talk to me?" Daniel said. He'd asked that question to each of his brothers many times, never satisfied with their lack of explanation. "It's never made sense I can hear you just fine, but she can't."

The cicada hovered in the air, wings buzzing close to Daniel's face. Ezekiel spoke in a series of clicks and peeps like the warble of a whippoorwill.

"Momma doesn't believe you're with us," Daniel said. "She thinks everyone's trapped in some limbo, like ghosts walking the land."

Ezekiel chirped and settled on Daniel's disfigured shoulder.

"But how can you be a ghost if you're a critter?" Daniel asked. "You got flesh and blood like me. Even though we look different on the outside, you and me is the same on the inside, just like Momma always told us growing up."

Ezekiel chirped again, its tone rising like a brewing storm.

"All of Momma's children living around her and she don't even know. She wants to make a spell to kill everyone and take you to heaven with her," Daniel said.

He stopped under a black cypress that leaned to the earth, burdened by half-dead limbs and clumps of beryl lichen. He peeled off lichen by the handful and set it inside the basket, held in the crook of his limp arm. Ezekiel jumped into the air and started to speak, but Daniel interrupted.

"It's murder, and murder's bad, just like what happened to Poppa. Momma's so confused now, she don't know what she's saying."

Ezekiel flew to face Daniel and they stared deep into each other's eyes, searching tenuous boundaries to find some compromise. The cicada clicked rapidly, telling old stories from the shadows of perpetual dusk.

Daniel listened and nodded when he agreed, and shook his head when he didn't. They were silent awhile, and he moved onward, deeper into the marsh, gathering lilac root and hideous spotted beetles, fleshy mushrooms and poisonous crabapple fruits from manchineels. The farther he travelled from home, the colder the air turned, as if he sank slowly through a river into depths that sunlight could not reach.

Ezekiel hopped to a branch and raked its legs through hanging ivy. Daniel turned, alone, to see the purple-striped blooms of water hemlock growing next to its look-alike kin, the parsnip plant. One was harmless, if not edible, and the other a slow death. When he was a boy, and Momma could still walk, she showed him the woods' great mysteries and taught him the secrets of the plants.

Once she caught him about to pop a leaf of hemlock into his mouth and slapped it from him so hard he thought her hands were made of mountain.

In appearance, the two were nearly identical, and he thought she wouldn't notice the difference now in her fugue state. He plucked a sprig of parsnip, and Ezekiel saw him.

BY THE TIME he returned home, the sun sagged behind a latticework of cypresses that surrounded Daniel's home. Things he picked nestled and crawled in the wicker basket, and Ezekiel sat on his shoulder chirping rapidly, its series of clicks sounding like a lecture that was half admonishment and half plea.

"My mind is made up, and it don't matter what you say," Daniel muttered. "I won't let her take y'all away."

He reached the porch, ascended its rickety stairs, and walked through the kitchen into Momma's room.

"I'm back," he said. "I gathered what you needed."

Momma lay stiff in bed with her mouth hinged open. A bramble fly dipped down into her gullet and flew back out, its wings buzzing across cold lips.

"Momma, no—" Daniel fell to her side and a weight of loneliness and remorse sank upon him. He suddenly didn't care if she was half out of her mind, or if he had to fetch her tea five times a day, or oblige any of her strange whims. He just wanted to hold her body and feel her hold him back. He wanted to tell her again that he loved her.

Ezekiel leapt off Daniel and chased away the bramble fly.

Daniel knelt by Momma's bedside and caressed her face, wondering how many times had she done the same to him? He remembered as a boy, lying on a plank bed with each of his brothers curled around him, and Momma stroking his cheek, whispering that he was beautiful and would one day be stronger than them all. He wished more than anything for that moment with her to last forever.

He heard a quick clatter from the porch, as if spindly legs ran across the weather-beaten boards and then darted off.

"They're coming already, ain't they?" Daniel asked. "The townspeople are here, just like she said."

Ezekiel clicked and flew out the room.

Daniel squeezed her hand. It was cold, and he felt strange to hold the limp weight. He gently rolled down the lids over her empty, white eyes.

The clattering steps from the porch grew louder and spread into the parlor, accompanied by the loud buzz of a thousand wings. It sounded like a nest of rattlesnakes in dry grass.

Ezekiel flew back into the room, followed by their five brothers, colored orange and copper and mint-green. The cicadas lined up in order of age next to Momma on the bedside.

Daniel kissed her and stood up. He spoke as if in eulogy. "It's better this way. You thought you cursed the land but, the way I figure, you've blessed us to stay together. We'll never die, forever."

Swarms of cicadas began to pour into the room, jostling between the sides of the sheet and doorway. There was a smell to them that Daniel had never noticed when around only a few at a time. But, in mass, he was struck by their musty odor, like old moth balls left too long in a sealed closet. Their droning wings filled the air with a wild clatter, and he almost had to cover his ears as they flew to Momma, covering her body with their terrible roar. Soon she could not be seen at all, and instead there appeared only a mountain of writhing insects, fluttering and spitting out syrupy secretion from their proboscises.

Daniel's brothers joined them.

Daniel had never seen the transformation before—Lucas tried explaining it to him one evening, but it was a thing which Daniel could not understand. The closest he imagined was a butterfly emerging from the cocoon it cast, but that was only similar in terms of the physical impression, rather than the physiological process. He watched the cicadas climb over her and over each other, emitting sticky residue like golden honeycomb until Momma was immersed in the secretion. It hardened and cracked, as mud does under the sun, until she looked like a great rigid pod, the features of her bones pressing up from beneath.

Moving as one, the insects rose from her in a dark, glittering cloud and flew from the room. As they left, the cicadas introduced themselves to Daniel, those long-ago townspeople he had never before met.

It was true, they told him, that they once hated Momma. But her curse caused their rebirth, and they cherished her as that herald of immortality. She was the mother of them all.

MOMMA'S SHELL LAY in bed for several days, a frozen monument to her majesty. Her remains mummified, turning to a rigid, brown mask of hard lines, so unlike the soft flesh that once dimpled with each smile and laugh. Daniel sat with her, stroking the calcified husk and talking to her as he did all his life.

"Orlie says he sure misses your singing. I reckon I do too."

He traced one finger along a hollow knot that he thought might have been her mouth.

"Your voice was beautiful, Momma."

A wind blew through the trees, sounding like distant murmurs. The house creaked on its foundation.

Daniel cupped one hand under his cheek and leaned in closer. "I wish I knew Poppa. Ezekiel says he wasn't killed at all, just ran off one day with sights set on a new life. I don't know why Ezekiel says that; wouldn't nobody abandon *you*, Momma.

"You were so powerful. You bound the souls of the

townspeople to this land so they couldn't leave. But the thing is, they don't *want* to leave. They say Poppa's trying to trick you, and there ain't nothing after death but lonely cold shadows. It's a good life to remain, when your friends and family are still around. That's why I'll never leave you. We all love you, even the townspeople. They just want to keep you right here with them."

The shell quivered.

Daniel ran his finger down the ridges of her neck to the pitted hollow of her chest. Between the bulging remnants of weary breasts, a thin crack split.

"Don't be scared. C'mon out," he said.

The split widened like a yawning mouth and a pair of pale green legs poked out. A mass pushed from underneath the shell and the chest broke open as if poking up through a piece of wet paper. A cicada emerged, glistening and trembling.

"I'm sorry, Momma. I'm real sorry I was gonna fix it so your spell didn't work."

He extended his open hand, and the cicada climbed up his finger, probing tentatively with bobbing feelers. Daniel carried it to the parlor and set it on the kitchen table. Poppa's portrait faced them.

"But you see, we're all here, we're a family again. Here comes Aaron and Lucas, and there's Henry and Ezekiel and Orlie and William."

Six cicadas flew to the table top, landing with taps and chirps.

"You said this world is a cruel, cruel place, and maybe you're right. Maybe you're right, too, about Poppa at the golden table. But maybe the townspeople are right. Nothing is as it seems. I remember your list, Momma, and maybe one day, when I'm tired and can't go on no more, I'll go out and pick those right ingredients."

The cicadas circled her.

"But for now, I think you'll be happy. Like you always said, *heaven is family*."

He leaned down and whispered into her ear. "I love you, Momma."

Each of her other sons repeated the sentiment, and six more times it was said: *I love you, Momma.*

FOOTPRINTS FADING IN THE DESERT

THE FOOTPRINTS IN THE SAND SHOULD NOT BEEN possible. And yet they were. They were here, in the desert, the imprints of bare feet . . .

The survivor, Lisa, shook her head, troubled by this.

She first thought it must be a hallucination, an early morning dream or desire for rescue projected onto this desolate land. But then she crouched down and ran a slender finger through one of the shallow marks. The soft ravine her finger carved in the sand crossed over the footprint, disrupting the indentation of its heel before curling up to the toes, each remarkably preserved in that coarse, white grit. The tracks were human, someone's feet just a little bigger than her own. The left footprints stepped in a normal gait, but the right prints were turned slightly inward, with scuffing, dragging marks at each step, as if that side were lame. The prints were fresh, and she scanned the wide desert for their source, but saw the steps only shrinking away, fading into the soft line of the horizon. Conversely, searching for a destination in the other direction led to the opposite horizon.

Lisa's vision had never been good, and she normally wore gold-rimmed glasses, which were now gone. Her view, already fuzzy, was further hampered by the constant blowing sand, tossed howling and furious through the sky by a hot wind that rarely lulled. Could there be refuge nearby? Some place just beyond her field of vision, close enough that someone could romp about this expanse of barren earth without shoes? She couldn't fathom that was possible, yet those footprints came from somewhere and led elsewhere against all common sense. Lisa considered the chance of those tracks passing by and then wondered if it were not just someone else stranded in this wasteland as herself, a misplaced socialite plucked from hotel-top cocktail parties in an irony of the cosmos.

Lisa decided that whether the person was lost, crazy, or just enjoying a midnight stroll while she'd slept, she must find the walker. Anything was better than withering away alone under the wreckage.

Fifty feet away lay the twisted and burned remains of the Cessna 172 aircraft. The shattered rear fuselage, resting underneath the shadow of one severed wing, had been her home for the last three days. Away from that (*not far enough away, though she had been too hysterical to go any farther*) were two mounds, covered with sand and rocks, each projecting a pair of feet like grim armaments. One grave contained the Cessna's pilot, a salty old redheaded man with bristly whiskers and stagnant breath. He was brought on as a replacement for the regular pilot, who coincidentally also crashed in the desert just the week before: a bad omen indeed for Lisa's flight. The second grave contained her husband, Phil Strancell, entrepreneur and owner of Strancell Technologies. The impact of the crash had split Phil nearly in half, from crotch to neck. Somehow, he lived for almost a full day after the accident, strapped into the co-pilot's seat looking like a snapped turkey wishbone, his organs and arteries held together miraculously by the same portion of torn fuselage that had also performed his grotesque bisection.

Lisa knew she was in the Great Basin Desert, somewhere between Idaho and Nevada or, as Phil likened it, *halfway between Hell and Hades*. The Cessna had nosedived into an ancient fissured lakebed, blanketed under wind-swept sand. There shouldn't have been a mark of civilization for hundreds of miles around to disturb the dotting sagebrush and rolling dunes, yet, looking down at those footprints, Lisa saw hope. Whoever left those tracks came during the night, walking obliviously past the wrecked plane. The desert night was as dead-black as the Cessna's melted tires, and it was impossible to see more than a few feet away.

Now, within that forsaken land, she'd discovered that another person existed, one who limped past while she fitfully slept. Each night since the crash, she'd rolled back and forth in haunted slumber, dreaming of rescue from her worsening nightmare... though the actualization of her dreams had all the substance of a mirage: The trail of a barefoot man or woman wandering the desert through the dead of night? But the prints were fresh, and they led away from her aircraft crypt. To Lisa, that was motivation enough, and she knew she must follow them.

The morning was young, but time was against her. Lisa would have only a few hours to pursue the tracks until the summer sun began to crush her with its choking, heavy heat. She lacked a thermometer but guessed the daily temperature rose above one hundred ten degrees, and her only comfort was to curse each searing day with a creative lexicon she didn't know she possessed.

She dashed back to the mangled Cessna and packed to leave. Fashioning a hobo's knapsack by looping a cloth seat cover around two broken poles and tying it in place with electrical wire, she filled the sack with the meager food and clothing she'd been able to salvage. She also carried a thin blanket and, most importantly, two plastic eight-ounce water bottles, the last of her one-a-day rationing.

By the time Lisa returned to the footprints, they were already beginning to fade, melting to ghostly imprints that cut into the flat, gritty earth. Wind blew a steady mist of sand, covering the line of tracks as it covered everything else. Lisa jogged quickly along the trail, each of her footfalls leaving marks that mirrored the ones she followed. She looked back only once at the wrecked aircraft, bidding a silent farewell to the graves she was forever leaving behind.

It had been only three days since Lisa's life was split abruptly apart, much as her husband's body had been split. Three long and desolate days of cooking under the desert sun, her skin once moist and fresh, now turning brown and cracked like dried jerky. Before the crash, she'd been napping quietly in the rear passenger seat until a sickening drop in the plane jolted her awake, and her face slammed against the metal ceiling. The plane fell, and she bounced backward behind the seat in slow motion while trying to remember how to scream. She saw only the backs of Phil's and the pilot's heads. Like herself, Phil was silent. He was frozen, and his hands clenched into claws upon the armrests of the co-pilot's chair. The pilot screamed into the radio, "*Oh crap, oh crap, oh crap,*" as if that were the latest lingo for a mayday request. The plane shook apart as it fell from the blue sky. The pilot pounded on dials and struggled with the throttle and almost seemed to bring the craft under control, just before it slammed into the sandy earth below. Lisa blacked out.

Waking groggy, she found herself buried under her seat, a cushion of space surrounded by crumpled metal and fiberglass. Her left shoulder was sliced to the bone, her body a map of swollen bruises. Pulling herself up, the first thing Lisa saw was a large hole in the plane's windshield. The pilot had ejected through it, leaving behind streamers of red flesh across the jagged shards of glass. Her husband still remained, buckled in, and Lisa crawled slowly between the twisted alloy tubing to his side. In shock, she found him alert and staring at her, his chest cleaved into two halves. Even through his injury, Phil could speak and calmly inquired as to Lisa's own health, before politely asking for a drink of water. She tried to unbuckle him, but the crevice in his chest began to split wider open. The seatbelt running crisscross over Phil's body acted as a tourniquet, holding his torso together so its insides didn't spill out like a burst sewage pipe. When he drank the water Lisa brought him, it bubbled out from under his shirt. She shrieked, and Phil spoke, calm and reassuring to the end. Clenching her hand, he declared that someone would come for her, she would be rescued . . .

Lisa shook her head now, telling herself to focus on the footprints. They were becoming fresher, more pronounced in the sand as she shuffled across, although after hours of walking, her stamina began to falter. She grew weak while the sun grew strong. Heat waves rolled upon the land, blurring her thoughts and vision in watery mirages. The wind, too, punished her, a ceaseless beast that gusted in unnatural flurries like small dervishes. It was not a strong wind, but it blew enough to fill the air always with sand, to scratch her face and dull her vision, and to produce strange ghostly images. The wind was also enough to blow away the footprints she followed, if she did not hurry.

Lisa staggered farther until exhaustion forced her to rest. Three days since the crash, with little to eat or drink, had crippled her vigor, while despair chipped away her resolve. She'd followed the footprints into the roasting afternoon, but they still cruelly outpaced her; she couldn't catch up to whoever left them. She wondered if they might stretch forever across that forsaken land, one mysterious leg dragging tirelessly behind the other.

Scattered along the trail, thick sagebrush sprouted from the searing desert, and Lisa selected the largest one to rest beneath. She draped the thin blanket from the Cessna atop its gray-green needle branches, creating a semblance of shelter, and collapsed under it. Sipping a water bottle, she moaned lonely bleats and closed her eyes remembering . . .

Phil's final hours after the crash had been ones of agony. Not agony for Phil himself, who bore his death sentence as serenely as a Zen monk, but agony for Lisa, who helplessly watched her husband fade away. She wept and lashed out at the wreckage in frustration, and imagined that the vultures circling high in the sky were helicopters searching for them. Phil and she each had cell phones that were shattered and useless, and the plane supposedly contained an emergency beacon that transmitted in cases such as this, but what that really meant, or if it even worked, Lisa did not know. All she knew was that no one came for them. Dying, Phil drifted in and out of consciousness, repeating the same simple message, urging her to stay calm.

"Someone will find you . . . you will be rescued," he whispered between gasps. "Just stay here. Someone will come to you. People don't go missing in the desert forever."

Phil had said someone would arrive to rescue her, and he'd been right.

As Lisa lay under the sagebrush, a veil of shade passed above her, blocking the burning bright light. Her eyes fluttered open, blinking at the shadow's unexpected presence. Before her stood a man dressed in ragged clothes, tattered as if he'd been pulled through a cyclone. His pant legs were ripped at the knees in long drooping angles, and his waistband held up loosely by frayed suspenders. He wore a button-down shirt, once white perhaps, but now torn and blackened from grime and age. A wide-brimmed hat drooped over the man's head, casting murky shadows across his face. The hat was pockmarked with holes, as if chewed upon by worms and moths.

The man stared down at Lisa, the features of his face fuzzy under the brim of that rotting hat. Sand coated his skin and seemed to float off him like drifting snowflakes. He spoke to her in quiet earnest, his words monotone, yet sincere in their desperation.

"My family needs help."

The man's plea left Lisa feeling sick. It was as she feared: the walker was as lost in the desert as she herself. She replied, "I'm sorry . . . I'm lost out here, too. Our plane crashed and my husband is dead. What—what happened to you?"

With a slow shake of his head, the man spoke in a whisper. "We lost the trail. We was travelling to Oregon territory from Missouri. Gonna farm wheat in the Multnomah Valley, but got turned sideways in a great sandstorm. That was a long time ago. We ain't got no water left, and my children are thirsty."

The man's voice drifted as if borne upon the wind, and dissolved across the vast expanse. Each word formed slowly and creaked from his mouth with a rough texture like coarse gravel grinding upon itself. Lisa shuddered, bewildered. She thought of the impossibility of two lost people finding each other in that desolation, and a sobbing grimace broke free as she imagined the answer.

"Oh, God, am I dead?"

"Dead? No, Miss, sunstroke must be getting to you. Please though, I need your help. My family needs your help."

Lisa coughed hoarsely, feeling foolish now for having asked such a thing. She uncapped a water bottle and took a tiny sip, sucking tenderly at each drop. She looked back to the man, struck again by his face, fuzzy and dark with dirt, outlining foggy eyes that gazed upon her with such appeal. Hesitantly, she offered up the bottle.

"I just have a little bit left, but you can have a drink."

"No, but thank you, ma'am. If you can spare some, please save it for my children."

He stood there, solemn and motionless, staring at her, and she stared back at him, confused and contemplating, until he reached a hand out to help her stand. The movement made Lisa flinch. She declined his assistance and stood on her own.

"Come with me," he said. "They're this way."

The man set off, walking through the sand, and only then did Lisa note his feet. They were bare and gnarled, blistered from treading unprotected over the burning earth. He walked with a limp, and she observed as he strode away how each footprint in the sand was formed. The thousands of empty prints she had followed were now filled. The left leg stepped strong, compensating for the weaker right leg, which twisted slightly and stepped at an odd angle. After several yards he paused and turned gravely back to her.

"Please, we must hurry."

That voice again, gravelly and hoarse, flat as the desert land, but whispered light as the air. Apprehensive, Lisa followed.

They walked for hours. Lisa proceeded slowly, staggering under the pounding sun. She needed to rest often, and the man always waited for her. He never seemed to need rest of his own, and only after several minutes of her sitting motionless, would he quietly urge her on again, pleading that she must hurry. They continued hiking under the blazing sun and through the clouds of sand. Lisa followed each footprint that formed in front of her, until fatigue wore her down.

"I can't go on," she panted.

"We're almost there. They're waiting over yonder."

He pointed to a steep dune rising before them. Lisa grimaced, but commanded her legs to keep moving, forcing each to lift just one more time, and then once again after that. She plodded up the dune behind him, trembling in exhaustion.

Rising over the crest of the dune, she saw wagons below. They were skeletal remains, as if beached whales had inexplicably rotted away in that dry land. Bleached bows rose like arched ribs above the desert floor, their wood cracked and withered from exposure to the elements. The wagon carcasses sat in a semicircle, three of them decaying in unison, with each frame tilted low and borne by many-spoked wheels. Lisa knew those wagons were very old, like the Conestogas pulled by oxen or horses she often saw in spaghetti western movies. The man walked down the dune to the nearest one and motioned for her to join him.

Lisa trailed him to the wagon and saw four skeletons propped against its slumped sideboard. Each skeleton was smaller than the one to its left, as if a row of children were lined up in successive ages. She cried out in sorrow.

Nearby, another skeleton, this one full-sized, lay sprawled on its back and half-buried under the drifting grit. It wore the tattered remains of a calico dress, and Lisa could only imagine the mother's grief of watching each of her children wither away and die like poisoned flowers. The skeletons were rotten and crumbling with age, but each skull was positioned so that it looked expectantly at the dune Lisa and the man had just climbed over.

"Please, can you help them?" he asked. His voice sounded again as a haunting whisper drifting on the wind.

"Them?" Lisa replied, pointing in horror to the collected bones waiting in the sand. "This is your family?"

"Yes, they need help. They need water. I swore to them I would come back, that I'd bring help."

Lisa covered her mouth to stifle a rising scream and backed away from the strange, pleading man. Past the first wagon's remains more battered skeletons lay in similar postures of demise. They wore chaps and boots, all with hollow eye sockets staring sightlessly at the crest of the dune, waiting for the man's return.

She staggered from the wagons, struggling through sand that sucked at her feet and blew into her eyes. Clawing at the air, Lisa tried to flee, only to abruptly trip upon something half-buried in the earth. The scream escaped then, as she fell. Her ankle twisted with a sickening pop and, attempting to rise, she found her leg could no longer support her.

When Lisa saw what tripped her she screamed again,

scrambling at the ground to crawl away.

Another skeleton protruded from its grave of sand, although it was not as ancient as the others. Aviator goggles hung around its serrated neck and a torn leather cap adorned the skull, resembling a World War One pilot. Like the dead of the wagon train, this corpse stared toward the crest of the dune, one bony white arm raised above its brow, forever shielding from the sun's blinding rays as it lay waiting.

Lisa wailed at her crippled ankle while a gust of sand blew past, then cleared. She dropped her head and crawled on hands and knees from the pilot's bones. She moved like this until her hand pushed upon another skeleton half-screened by the bleached earth. The sob that broke free as she jerked away was equal parts disgust and despair. The carcass was dressed in high-waisted jeans, with chains and cuffs rolled up to showcase two-tone Keds sneakers, baking under the endless sun. Patches of its crisp dark hair remained, piled high in the style of Elvis or James Dean.

A wild frenzy overtook Lisa. She wanted to flee, to escape this scene of horror, though her impulse for flight was immediately countered by a sense of submission, as she wondered where she could possibly go. Behind her, the strange man did not give chase, but remained motionless by the first wagon, watching her without expression. Lisa's mind raced to understand, to unravel this puzzle. How could an aviator and a 1950s greaser be found amongst a wagon train from the 1800s? Had others become lost in this terrible land by coincidence and wandered upon the wagons' remains, only to perish there themselves?

As if in response, the wind calmed and the flying sand cleared, and she saw there were many more . . .

Beyond the Elvis-kid's remains lay another skeleton, this one slender and wearing lime-green pedal pushers and a tarnished peace symbol necklace. Past that were row upon row of the dead, circling around the wagon train. She saw one corpse finely dressed in a tattered pinstripe suit that fluttered in the breeze to reveal an old gangster's revolver. Another body wore the unfortunate attire of a Victorian-era's stiff velvet dress. To wear drapery like that out here was madness ... yet nothing about this desert made any sense. The next skeleton wore the fatigues of an infantry soldier, while beside it lay bones in a prisoner's uniform, serial number etched across its breast.

The worst was a dead man in Bermuda shorts and polo shirt sprawled on his side. He was not a skeleton yet, and Lisa could still make out mottled features, partly hidden underneath Oakley sunglasses. The corpse was in the process of decomposing, and the rotting flesh cooked under the sun while insects and lizards feasted on it.

All the dead stared at the crest of the dune, each waiting for the man she met to bring back help. He calmly appeared next to her, his quiet stride betrayed only by clouds of dust kicked up by each step.

He asked, "Please, can you help them?"

"I can't help them, I can't help them!" Lisa sobbed. "I'm dying too ... I need help, don't you see? I'm dying out here, like all of them—" She broke off with a wail.

The walker's expression changed. He looked down at Lisa in grief, sympathizing at her incapacity. She too needed help, and her words repeated the unendurable plight of his past. His sinking eyes flickered black and white, and he knelt to her. The man took Lisa's hands solemnly into his own, so that her fingers buried deep within his firm and gritty grasp. She felt sand moving beneath his skin, flowing deep through the veins and arteries of his being. It was cold, unlike the sand of the desert that burned hot to the touch.

"Please, then you must wait here. I will go out and find someone to help us." He brushed back a loose lock of hair that had fallen across her brow. "I make this oath to you, that I will not rest until I have found rescue for us all."

Lisa nodded, gazing into his face, her only hope.

"I must leave now to search. Wait here. I'll be back, and I will bring help. I'll return over that rise." He pointed at the dune's crest he'd so recently led her across.

"I swear it," he whispered solemnly, and Lisa knew he was a man who kept his promises.

The man stood, sand dripping from his arms, dust floating from his mouth, and turned to trek back up the dune. Lisa wondered how many times before had he left? How many times had he sought rescue in others, only to find they too were lost and wandering in hopeless despair? How many years of searching the desolate wasteland had it taken to wear off the very boots he once walked in? Someday he would find help, he would never cease until rescue was brought to her and those others lost in the desert.

The man walked away, slowly and eternally, his twisted right leg dragging with each limp step. He left a fresh set of tracks in the sand as he departed, rising up and over the dune's crest. She lay there waiting, as the sun melted to moon and was born back again. She lay there staring at the dune and watched as his footprints faded in the desert.

THE HOUSE OF THE RISING SUN, FOREVER

THERE IS A HOUSE IN NEW ORLEANS, THEY CALL the Rising Sun.

And those who enter this house... well, it ain't the same experience for no two men. This house, see, it's a way of escape. And each man or woman, rambler or fool who passes 'tween its heavy oak and iron doors is searching for something they think is unique to them, some fucking iron chain that no one else has ever bore, and they alone got to find the key to unshackle it. It's an escape from loneliness, from despair, from abandonment, regret, or ruin, though the freedom sought from these things is abject in its own way, like hating yourself for a certain weakness, then swearing to overcome such weakness, only to fail in the attempt itself. In this way, you've proved the weakness even stronger. Such is sorrow, friend, such is sorrow.

But there inside the Rising Sun, right when you enter, waits a fine woman, and you know for some fleeting time, some goddamned too-short winks, those weaknesses will be stayed, the holes in your soul plugged as neat as copper pipes by jamming that last smudged penny into the ragged break and welding it shut. You were a metal worker in the ship yards once, so welding should be easy. And they've plenty of pennies here, near as many as you've got holes.

Now imagine for a moment your name is Lincoln; it ain't tough, since your name could be anything. Lincoln (you) has been through these doors before, these very same doors of the House of the Rising Sun that I'm telling about. And Lincoln knows this fine woman before him, has spoke to her every single time without exception that he's entered.

It's a funny thing, Lincoln thinks, *that the woman is delicate and fair in a way no woman in no house like this oughta be, and especially not for so long.* It's been, what? Four years, Linc's been coming here, five? Ten, twenty, a hundred? One half hour here, and your life's lost a month. Time's a jade, and she wears you out faster than any mixed-Creole whore.

Jeannie Ja says, "Hello Lincoln Brown."

Linc hates when she calls him by his full name, but that's how she greets everyone, all those other Lincoln Browns waiting in the front room upon couches that were carved in the reign of some wizened old Han king, and Linc's displeasure is tempered anyway and immediately by the way her algid green eyes flutter at him, sort of how a chip of jade sparkles beneath melted snowcap. Linc's displeasure never even has a chance when she cocks her head, just that tilt she always does, and thin light from the red globe bulbs high above catches the smile at her lips; it's not a happy expression. Jeannie would never be so vulgar as to look amused, but it's the damned finest smile you've seen a fine dame ever smile, a look of *knowing.*

As it always is.

Linc's heart kicks a beat, his mouth turns a little dry. Jeannie Ja ain't a woman you have to tell what you want. She just knows. And a woman who knows as Jeanie does . . . well, as I said, it ain't the same experience for no two men in the House of the Rising Sun.

"This way, Lincoln Brown."

And don't all the other Lincoln Browns in the front room get up and follow at her word, those ghosts, those blind shadows who were of the chances Linc squandered, the choices ill-made, the oaths broke, the loves debauched, the gambles lost?

Yeah ... yeah.

Linc doesn't like himself, doesn't like the things he's done, but that's a given. He follows at Jeannie's heels too close, way her raven-black hair sorta rises and flits back with each footfall to tickle his face, *come along*. In it, he smells incense, cinnamon, sulfur.

In this way they pass behind a screen of drapes, through a silent couloir, enter a set of doors that look like two beckoning hands. Now looms a hallway seeming to stretch on forever, and the doors leading off it are innumerable.

It don't make sense, Linc considers. From outside, this house sits in a choked quarter of French gothic façades, crammed into a lot no larger than a fishing ship's berth, the moldering wood shingles masked by gilt pink and turquoise and sapphire. Inside though ... well, the eye fools a man sometimes.

Jeannie opens a door off this hallway with no end, and they enter. It's a real small room, a boudoir refashioned to a cell, filled with a narrow bed, a sheet of silk, some kind of pillow like a soft log, sable blue wound by gold fancy. She takes him in hand, lays him on the bed, opens the button at his collar. When the backs of her enameled nails trail down his cheeks, it reminds him of falling tears. A chill melts the hard lines forged on Linc's face from squinting under sparks and torchlight too hard, clenching his jaw too tight, pummeling men with fists like iron pistons while they pummel him in return.

She undoes the next button. The air is warm and languid. The ceiling, high above, painted in stars. Linc can't help it, he trembles.

Jeannie Ja pretends not to notice. Next to the narrow bed is a card table, and she turns to it. On the table is a lacquered tray, inlaid with iridescent shell. On this tray is a choice: porcelain, sugarcane, or bamboo. Linc prefers sugarcane. Jeannie knows this.

She rolls a little ball that looks like clay, skewers it on a long needle, rolls it some more, now it's the shape of a pill. The pill goes into an earthenware bowl that's glazed crimson and decorated with the Endless Knot, a Buddhist symbol denoting infinity. The bowl connects to a pipe, and the pipe's other end fits to a brass saddle connecting to Linc's preferred sugarcane stem. The stem will then fit into his mouth.

But first, the pipe-bowl must be heated over an oil lamp. This is what Linc stares at with an affection like love, this lamp impeccably designed for the slow vaporization of opium. Its funnel-shaped glass begins to billow with clouds and whorling promise as it channels heat upward as a chimney. The glass is clenched in place by taloned prongs to a bronze base with openwork motifs that scroll in perpetuity like a merry carousel. The motifs are of birds, bats, fish with great eyes, serpents that coil and strike. The motifs are of men: the rooster, the dog, the rabbit. Himself, overlaid by jeweled cloisonné.

Lincoln doesn't know when Jeannie Ja has left, but it's only him now in this tiny room in the House of the Rising Sun, and he softens his lips with flicking tongue, he swallows, gently touches the mouth of the sugarcane stem with his own mouth just as he did with Purity Jones whom he loved so long ago, and he breathes in deep. Holds. Exhales. Breathes deep again. And again. And the opium smoke fills him . . .

The stars in the ceiling high above glitter and flash, they dance a trot. The stars are eyes peering from behind curtains of ebony hair, the stars are fertile grain, sprouting in infant fields. The stars are dragons, each stalking him with long reptilian tails that comet through the cosmos and with whiskers that reach from murky depths as the tentacles of rising leviathans. The stars are eyes, they are dragons, they are seeds, and he flies to meet them.

And what are the stars of the universe but hopes for us all? What are the stars but dreams of new lives, dreams of existence, brought of mortals, of ancients, of children never born, of elders who have seen the rise and fall of a million universes from their chariots of muck?

The stars, too, are portals, each pressing behind a locked door from the endless hallway Linc once walked. As he soars, they spring open to new worlds, new joys, the flowered and untrampled fields a colt is born to, its supple legs young and ready to run farther than any colt has ever run.

Man, it's a fucking rush, I know that much . . .

Lincoln Brown goes through one of those doors.

O'ER A VAST DISTANCE he hears the screech of birds aloft, and for a time Clayton Winfield thinks of gulls soaring past the docks lining the Mississippi River, but that wouldn't be right. These were hawks, the ones with red-shoulders, his grandfather (who had been interested in such things) once told him. Red-shouldered hawks are gulls of the prairies, Grandfather quipped, since the birds sound the same. There aren't seabirds around for hundreds of miles, nor has Clay ever seen the sea.

His grandfather had been a cavalry captain in the Army of the Potomac, riding for years along the Eastern coast. Afterward he settled in Wichita and oversaw the rail yards that accommodated mass deportation of wretched cattle. Grandfather's hands were stiff, roughhewn things like the boiled leather of saddles that crack and peel under hard riders, his hands so unlike his laugh at puns and gags, a sound as buttery soft as his skin was broiled tough. When his heart gave out in 1893, people said he'd done all right for himself.

Clay's done better.

Clayton is none of what was his grandfather, and all of what his grandfather was not. He'd taken to schooling and numbers with the frightening obsession of a flagellant, whipping himself not with needle-pointed barbs, but by the lashes of Gordian economic theories. Should the thought arise, his eyes reflect an almost indignant look upon his Winfield forebears for not bequeathing him the higher social status he rightfully deserved upon birth. Clay's hands are soft as a baby's cheek, and his humor a stiff, roughhewn thing that's cracked and peeled not from use, but from neglect.

The screech of distant birds passes—whether gulls or hawks, it does not matter to him—driven off by a mélange of far-flung horse whinnies, a rumble of locomotives, the thick murmur of voices from the street below. Upon his balcony six stories high, he glances over Wichita as a king would the empire he has conquered, with a sigh and righteous satisfaction. He turns away and passes 'tween bright silk and gemmed drapes into a marble-walled salon. There he is met with cheers.

"Here is to acumen, to prosperity, to decency, and to the man who courts them all."

"To Clayton!"

"To Clayton, you bastard!"

"To Clayton, you rich, lucky bastard!"

The others laugh.

Clay does not. His smile shows no warmth, but he lifts a drink to them in return, and through its dimpled glass he sees the distorted shapes of two dozen men: top hats that swell upward like tall mushrooms, waist coats that waver, pale heads with faces bulged out like the multi-lensed eye of a housefly. He replies, "To my friends."

They applaud. There are more cheers, more toasts. Clayton Winfield has love, he has wealth, and the day is a grand affair.

Men mill about him, grazing at the fertile pastures of commerce. There is his vice-president, Pritchard Digby, leaving the salon. There is Jacob Luggenheim entering. There are other bank presidents, the city's mayor, aldermen coming and going, their faces commutable, as if siblings all weaned from the same mother of capitalization.

He wonders where is his wife, but she has vanished. Jacob takes her place by his side.

"The city's son," Jacob says. "If we had a golden key, it'd be dropped in your pocket."

"If the city could afford a key of gold, I wouldn't bother buying the Rothschild building."

Jacob bellows, ruddy-faced. One eye is glass and it stares at Clay unmoving, while the other winks. "And I thought your humor was locked in the vault with all that money."

"It's a funny thing," Clay says, his own eyes darting almost in surprise at his surroundings, "the old adage is twisted. Money doesn't buy you levity. But happiness? That's earned at two percent of every new client."

And Clay gives another cold smile. Grandfather said he'd been born to scowl. It wasn't for worriment Clay guarded his mirth; he actually felt quite chirpy most days, but decided long ago that severity reaped prestige tenfold over jocundity. Look at Grandfather: he'd done so much, yet left nothing behind but tall tales and a collection of dime store novels. Clay would leave an empire.

"You're doing splendid, Clayton. We all are your proselytes."

"As I am yours."

"Well met. But by that coin, I feel I must also gently admonish you."

"Really? Then forgive my rebuke as serene as it may be."

Jacob's face loses its ruddiness. "Mr. Pendergast wants his money."

The glass in Clay's hand seems to double in weight. "What's this about?"

"You're bright as the sky, Clayton, and know full well what this is about. Mr. Pendergast asked me to remind you the consequences of nonpayment."

"You . . . you're with Jim Pendergast?"

"I come from Kansas City. Before that I was a Chicagoan, a financier. Part of National Bank of Illinois. I invested all my capital in a 'sure bet', the silver reserves, which had a double digit inflation rate. That was 1896, just before it all collapsed."

"'96, the year of the panic," Clay says, feeling the beginnings of that very emotion. "It must nearly have bankrupted you."

"It did, in fact," Jacob agrees. "I lost everything, and now I am Mr. Pendergast's. I did not *diversify* my holdings across multiple investments. Got greedy, all my eggs in one basket, as the adage goes."

"I see . . . "

"Here's another adage, my friend: Never do like I have done. You've put all of Mr. Pendergast's money into this new bank. You haven't diversified, and now when the note is due, you're caught somewhat short."

"More time, Jacob, please. The railroaders flatter me each day with gifts, earmarked by proposals for capital to lay tracks or roll stocks. Men are indebted to me, even those in Senate."

"The speakeasy men are more dangerous than Senate men. I know. It's Mr. Pendergast who assumed my debt."

Clay clenches his teeth. "I have no liquidity at the moment. My own bonds are lent out to others upon favors. Men are eager to borrow but reluctant to repay."

"Do unto others," Jacob says, "and you'll be fleeced as a sheep. You ever wonder why I have a glass eye, what happened to my natural one?"

"I thought it improper to inquire."

"Mr. Pendergast took it for missing payment." Jacob hurriedly lifts the drink in his hand and drains it in one hard gulp before abruptly turning away. "It's not all he's taken. You have two weeks."

Clay's good life suddenly feels sick at the edges, blackening in ash like a photograph set alit in the corner, and the flames spreading downward. In two weeks, all could be lost.

Yet two weeks is the lifetime of one and a speck of sand to another. Time has a queer habit of speeding past when a man is exuberant, though while a moment is loathed to come, one may creep toward that dread with the deceleration of lurching through stank mire.

So it happens by dread that Clayton has time to reflect upon all—who he is, what he loves, what he hopes, what he's done, what he might lose or give up—and he charts course through unexplored probity.

He has wealth and he has love, but Clay accepts he may lose the former and still carry on, if with her, for what Clayton loves more than riches is his wife. He must only tell Evelyn the truth, prepare her for slight privation.

Clay married the first girl he ever kissed—and the most beautiful girl he'd ever lain eyes upon. Evelyn née Winne was also the *richest* girl he'd ever lain eyes upon, and he, the grandson of a rail yard overseer, who lived comfortably and enjoyed a moderate respect by way of his grandfather's name, could never hope to satisfy the airs of the vaunted Winne house of Kansas City . . .

Now it is dark night, but electric light fills their parkside mansion as if the sunniest of day. Evelyn stares past him, gazing at the painting of a great ship in harbor, or perhaps staring only at the blank wall that surrounds it, her hands clasped tightly together in a twice-robed lap as they recline in bed against a pyramid of pillows.

"My dear," Clay says cautiously. "Our finances are out of order."

"I'm told," she quietly says.

He opens his mouth to reply, but pauses, wondering from whom she's heard this report . . .

Clay first met Evelyn on a spring fling while in youth, and she enjoyed him, and they parted. Nothing could come of it, for even in girlhood she was promised to another. But the infatuation he felt over the years burned bright as rushing summer; each day dawning hotter than that before with thoughts of her, until he scorched from it.

Clay is not otherwise a passionate person and because of this, perhaps, the effect of love is like a mythical beast; once encountered, proof of its existence changes a man irreversibly. Whereas others who love as one encounters ants marching daily across the road may trample a colony without passing thought.

"My dear," Clay continues, his face impassive, his face a mask concealing the wounded animal's terror, its fury at defeat. "It is only a temporary setback. I'll double our holdings within five years."

"Why even think of the future, Clayton? All we plan for, all we're promised are lies." She unclasps her hands and reclasps them with the opposite hand on top. "What is to come but ruin?"

By their wedding, he was not Evelyn's first spouse, nor even her second: She married and lost two husbands long before she aged thirty, aristocratic men with titles and lands that she was rumored to have devoured like so many midday aperitifs. Evelyn's inherited wealth was indeed stately but also declining, so much did she hazard in wanton expense.

And yet for her flaws, against the disapproval of her family and in the face of loathsome rumors that he courted only for her affluence, Clayton loved Evelyn as purely and innocently as the moon loves the sun: galactic opposites so far in distance as to never collide, but always one in motion around the other, hurtling and lost, and powerful and revered, one body turned hot, the other fallen cold.

"Don't be so fatalistic," Clay says. "I've strove to succeed, and I will persevere. Before we're forty, I'll own this town."

"I want only what I can take today," she replies. "Tomorrow is hopeless. The pledges you made have already worn bare. I have no children, I have no boat. Where is happiness if I fear the future, rather than delight for it?"

By their wedding, Clay had made his own fortune. By their wedding, he could meet the Winnes on level grounds of finance, though by social standing he was much the disadvantaged. Evelyn's family, however, was distressed over her twice-widowed position and they were near-frantic at the emotional catastrophe of her sense; she was already delicate, but after doubly-marred by the guilt of survival, Evelyn took to embarrassing conniptions and demeaning immodesties. Only in the throes of self-indulgence did she seem distracted from sorrow.

And none other than Clayton Winfield proved willing to forgive her advancing capriciousness.

But all the while, Clay wonders: Does she love him as thoroughly as he to her? This he does not know, can never in self-certainty claim, regardless of the ends he procures, the undertakings he employs, that damned gnawing doubt always vexing him.

"The bank has lost money already," Clay tells her without emotion. "I had to sell the East Bay partnership. Mortgaged the steel cars. But those are trifles to be collected like marbles. We will fill our pockets with them again."

Evelyn seems not to hear, her eyes still fixed on that far wall, lost in reminisce. She speaks in a faraway voice, "First was Franz, and the promises he made were glorious. Then he died of cyanide. A suicide, doctors proclaimed, but I don't believe it. Then was Balthier, and the future was brilliantly assured. Until a hunting accident felled him, and his business partner a seasoned marksman, and in debt at that. And now you lose all that we have, stating with a brave face our very home will not be foreclosed while we slumber under its roof."

It's true I overextended, he thinks. Bought when I should have sold, traded up instead of down, made promises I could not fulfill, but done to restore Evelyn's happiness, to keep her draped in *Revillon Frères* fur stoles and *Aimé Guerlain* parfums. I've invested all my holdings in a single asset: *Her*... as Jacob Luggenheim warned against. What have I but my wife and my monstrous debt? And for Evelyn, I would do it all anew...

I'd have them killed again and again, a hundred times over: Franz, Balthier, and any other man she wed in my place, for what is love but the fortitude to meet its challenges, proving one's heart true by rightful conquest? Must she know what I have done to match her love as could no one else? And now the extortion, the blackmail of those Kansas City assassins... their services have cost more than a few bank notes...

"My love for you knows no ledger," Clay says, trying to please her. "If we must peddle in the streets, I'll place each penny to your palm and say it is all for you. Only believe me, another day will come that we'll have more than your family's ever known."

"No," Evelyn says with a terrible finality. "I no longer believe in the vagaries of tomorrow. I will drink and dance for today and the rest of the world can wallow in their morrows."

"Then will you still love me today, should my coat change from silk to stained wool?"

After an awful pause, she answers, "Yes. I will love you as much as today allows."

And he is still unsmiling, but his heart swells. He wants to tell her more, to release the ardor, the anguish, the elation and grief and pride he's kept quelled for so long, but it's like trying to inflate a shriveled, crumpled toy balloon; with time it may expand, but at first the rubber is sticky and tight and shrunk.

"I'm so tired," Evelyn says suddenly, and she feigns sleep.

Clay clenches his jaw and lays there until slumber overcomes, which is in surprisingly little time. And more surprising is that he slumbers in rare peace, a respite from decimal marks and menacing debts and ill-made friends.

It is from this rare, peaceful slumber he is woken by a faint ringing: two shorts bursts, then a long. He's want to ignore it, but after a silence seeming louder than the rings, the telephone calls again. He sits up, rubs his eyes, notes his wife is no longer in bed. The electric lights still fill the house; Evelyn does not like the dark.

Again the phone stops ringing, again it starts. He stumbles into a large room filled with tapestries and accolades. There is an enormous pigeonhole desk topped by a French handset that jangles anew.

Clay picks up the handset and a click sounds as the operator connects the call. He says methodically, "Here is main line 185, Clayton."

A tall clock chimes for midnight, and two things occur as one:

A man's voice on the other end tells Clay, "Come to the bank now, into the salon."

And, at the same time, Clay sees on the desk a sheet of pink notepaper scrawled upon in Evelyn's script by three cursive words: *Today has ended.*

He is now awake, so alert the other receiver hanging up cracks loud as a gunshot.

Clay remains in his dressing gown, in his slippers, but dons his grandfather's cavalry revolver, which he's hired another man to oil and maintain. He slips the gun into his pocket and charges from the house.

Clayton owns the finest automobile in the city, and he races it up Douglas Avenue, praying the engine should not combust as he pushes it to a blistering thirty miles per hour. *Where is Evelyn? What does this mean?*

He arrives at Winfield Credit Bank, parks half on the

sidewalk, fumbles with his keys before realizing the front door is unlocked. There is a manual elevator, but no operator at this time of night, nor has he the patience to regulate its heavy levers and cables, so he dashes up the stairs.

Inside the salon is Jacob Luggenheim. In Jacob's hand is a small pistol, and he holds it as one does a champagne flute, as if to make a toast.

"I have the money," Clayton blurts. "I have it all, sold my holdings, I have only to transfer it to Pendergast."

"I am sorry, my friend," Jacob says. "You do not have it."

Clay's impassive face cracks. Something twitches at his lip.

"Your vice-president, Pritchard Digby, has been embezzling from you. The money you liquidated is lost unfortunately, though Digby was found with some petty cash on person. Your wife was complicit, advising him where to plunder, in fact."

The crack grows, the twitch convulses. "Impossible. You're mad."

"They met here tonight," Jacob says, and to his credit, his face is strikingly mournful. "I discovered them, preparing to decamp. A lover's rendezvous, pillaging the last of the bank's funds, and then off on a White Ship line to globetrot."

"No," only, "no."

"Here is their passage," Jacob sets the pistol onto an ornate sideboard so as to unfold a sheaf of documents. He hands Clay the papers. "An agent has already booked them First Class by rail to Galveston and then by liner to the world. Evelyn and Mr. Digby, your second, apparently, in more than signing deeds."

Something in Clay's throat is torn free, and it is a sob.

"Unfortunately, the damage is done, Clayton. You are now even further at odds with Mr. Pendergast—"

Clay shrieks, "To blazes with Jim Pendergast!"

Jacob's single eye widens in surprise. "We have staunched an ulcer for you, caught the inside perpetrators who were robbing you—*us*—senseless."

Clay makes a strangled sound, clenches his jaw.

"It's not so terrible," Jacob continues, "being Mr. Pendergast's man. Once an understanding is reached, you know what is expected. There is a certain... *security*, a lifestyle you may maintain. It is better than the alternative."

The words come out, barely a whisper. "I want to speak with her."

"I'm afraid that isn't possible."

Clay pulls out his grandfather's revolver. "I think it's quite possible."

Jacob tenses, surprised, his own pistol that he'd set down now out of reach. "No, you misunderstand, dear friend. I'm sorry... they are dead."

Clay feels the floor tilt under him, he wavers, stutters, "No... where?"

"They are on the balcony where I found them, wishing upon stars."

"Damn you, goddamn you," Clay says and pulls the trigger at Jacob.

Jacob gasps, steps back. His scare at Clay's act is involuntary, though there was no shot, only the dry click of the gun's hammer against its firing pin. And Clay looks wonderingly at the gun: *I forgot the ammunition. The revolver is maintained by another and not loaded*... The ineptness of it all is too much; a tear slips down his cheek, hot and alien, as much frustration as it is anguish.

"I thought you an imperturbable man," Jacob chastises, retreating to rearm himself with his own gun. "Acting upon practical tacts of a matter, not sophomoric emotions. It's what Mr. Pendergast admires in you."

Clay steadies himself, says nothing more. There, cut into the far wall, are the bright silk and gemmed drapes leading to the sixth story balcony outside.

He passes 'tween them to find the bodies fallen side-by-side, his wife and Pritchard Digby. In death, Evelyn seems to bear a strange smile that Clay could never quite bring about, not since they first kissed so long ago. He kneels and cradles her head, and a streak of blood smears his sleeve, and another tear slips past his guard.

There is a hollowness now in Clay, as if he could step into the sky and float away, for the means of the world are what bind us here, and having nothing left, one is set free.

"I must say, there's a certain disappointment in finding we've misjudged you so severely," Jacob says, having joined Clay on the balcony. "Mr. Pendergast will not be pleased. You have quite a bit of work ahead of you, dear friend, work that requires steadfastness."

Working for debts I should not owe, under the man who has killed all I hold dear, and to what avail?

Clay looks up to Jacob Luggenheim, and it is Jacob's face peering back, but there's someone else, another face overlain, a fine woman with algid-green eyes, and raven-black hair, and a smile says she knows, and so swiftly does all we have fall to dust.

And the stars overhead are a ceiling painted by other stars that glitter and flash; they beckon with the promise of more doors, new ways . . . *come again, come again* . . .

Clay stands, staggers away, Jacob—or the woman—just watching, knowing.

He retreats until the balcony ends and its iron railing presses against his back. At its touch he recalls with grief the voice of his wife: *What is to come but ruin?*

He retreats farther, pushing himself backward out and over the railing, falling and falling. Before his impact on the street below, what Clay hears last is the screech of distant birds, and he knows them true for the gulls of the Mississippi River.

AND ANOTHER DUSK, Lincoln finds himself walking New Orleans. Up Chartres Street, down Conti, Royal, Bienville, they blur as he turns and cuts through alleys, ducks beneath wash lines, bisects cobblestone arteries that pool with piss and rain and gloom, pulled by an urge as strong as the current of the waterways. It's no time at all he finds that house, that very same House of the Rising Sun he's visited too oft before.

'Tween its heavy oak and iron doors he passes, and there inside, right when he enters, Jeannie Ja is waiting, and in the front room, a group of Lincoln Browns numbers one more.

She says, "Hello, Lincoln Brown."

And he knows soon everything will be fine, that for some fleeting time, some goddamned too-short winks, everything will feel all right.

But it's never enough, and each time one hole is plugged, another rends open ... the rot spreading elsewhere, the flames reigniting, blackening all to ash.

Just one more chance, Linc thinks. *One more chance to make it last ...*

One time he was Albert Acton, an oil tycoon's son on the edge of inheriting an empire. But in his prime he travelled to Paris and caught a French malaise from the gartered tarts of Pigalle, and ruinous sores formed on his pecker and on his brain, all incurable but for *la fin.*

Once he was Tommy Moore, a boxer on the floating rinks in the Hudson. Fans called him 'The Monolith,' 'cause he wouldn't fall, before a knockout blow broke his back and paralyzed his legs. The Monolith did not rise again, but wheeled himself through gutters, begging handouts and recognition.

As Lafayette Carr, he was paramour to the high ladies of Boston until a wronged husband had him imprisoned on trumped-up charges, and he turned paramour instead to the greasy mill men and cutthroats at Charlestown Prison.

He's sang grit in the honky tonk jooks of Nashville, murdered trees in the lumber yards of Tacoma, driven trolleys in San Francisco, robbed men on the waterways of Green Bay, all miseries, all miseries.

And before that Lincoln Brown beat steel in the ship yards of New Orleans, while *Vieux Carré* still entertained aging pirates and sulking spirits and dark Vodou queens, and the city electrified its streetcars and birthed jazz in crazed dance halls . . .

And he loved Purity Jones, and he drank, and he gambled, and he wept. And Linc lies on the narrow bed in a room the size of a cell, and Jeannie Ja rolls a new little opium ball and skewers it on a long needle, and such is life, but to be rolled and skewered.

That's where he is still, trying to plug those holes with the promise of the Rising Sun, near worthless as that last smudged penny, 'cause the holes Lincoln Brown's got—the holes *you* got—don't seem like they can be plugged by anything else.

I know it's so fucking difficult, while everything good in your life seems it's rotting away, everything good in all those lives, rotting and rotting 'til you can't take it no more, and you think the only way of escape is here in the House of the Rising Sun trying for that final high.

But it ain't, friend, it ain't. 'Cause if you've a glass that's cracking, don't matter what you fill it with—sour mash whiskey colored like hot bronze, bijou rum and gin, absinthe with a dash of burnt sugar, a hundred casks of wine—it all leaks out 'til you're empty inside.

And you think that's a ball and chain, how 'bout a bottle of Eli Lilly rat poison to take away the pain? That's how Linc first ended it in a wharfside room along Canal Street.

In Paris it was a pistol. In New York's Hudson he took drowning.

I know a time Linc realized what he'd done, what he'd

become, and tried fighting his weakness, really fought that fuckin' rot so hard he placed his hands around Jeannie's neck and tightened until her eyes popped from their sockets and her black tongue unfurled from the mouth. Jeannie's face was Linc's own. In such a way, Linc died as Lafayette Carr, his hands a bed sheet noose in a prison cell in Boston. Time after that he lay down before a speeding train. There have been others; once you're hooked, you won't ever escape.

So never do like I have done.

See, Lincoln is you, friend, but it don't have to be, 'cause Lincoln Brown is also me, and that ball and chain is dragging me down the mountain I climb every day, dragging me back to where we're all dyin' inside the House of the Rising Sun.

And Jeannie Ja's right there, 'tween those oak and iron doors, knowing all you gotta do is step through, just step through one time and you're hooked forever.

Jeannie Ja's always there, whether you're a son or a daughter, a banker, a boxer, a paramour, a welder. Jeannie Ja's always there with that slight tilt of her head, that smile says *she knows*, waiting for all who're led astray.

So hear my tale, I warn you never do what I have done, spend your life in sin and misery, in the House of the Rising Sun.

This I plead, don't you ever go inside. Shun that house in New Orleans they call the Rising Sun...

But you won't listen, will you? Folks like me, folks like you, never heed the warnings, searching that escape we think leads somewhere better... it's a sad fucking thing.

We're all fated thus, gonna spend our wicked lives beneath that Rising Sun.

The Inveterate Establishment of Daddano & Co.

WE HANDLED THE UNDERTAKING ARRANGEMENTS for them all: Bosses, capos, killers, tough guys—once you reached certain levels in a family, it was known you'd be cared for when the time came, like part of a benefits package. And we were strictly neutral territory, no affiliations. We didn't take sides, didn't ask questions, didn't exclaim how it was that some poor schlep had his kisser blown off, how we'd have to pack the skull with sawdust like a punching bag just to keep its shape, and cover it with a wig and more makeup than Carole Lombard so his mother could hang rosary beads over him one last time. We did good work and we earned respect. Every outfit came to us over the years: the North Siders, the South Siders, the Circus Cafe Gang, Egan's Rats, the Forty-Two Gang, I could go on.

Daddano & Co., that's our signage, been there near a century. My father was in the funeral business for forty years until his heart went kaput while sitting on the crapper one mornin'. His father started the business in 1872. Grandfather Daddano apprenticed for an Irish prick who made him dig graves from sun up 'til sun down. Nothing but gravedigging, fourteen hours a day, earning twenty-five cents a week.

"Hell with that," Grandfather said. He figured digging was the hardest part of the mortuary game, and he was doin' it already on his own. The easy part was rolling in bodies. So he set up shop on Halstead, and his first service was for the Irish prick, if you catch my drift.

"Simplest business in the world," Grandfather said. "Everyone dies. Ain't no shortage of that."

From day one, he never had to go seekin' clients, either, and that goes for all us Daddanos. People got a way of knowing who to do business with, who they can trust, who can get the job done right, and in that way Grandfather's name got passed around.

But I'm runnin' my mouth the wrong way. You don't wanna hear about my family's history. You wanna hear about the Massacre.

It's all people want to hear about these days. Thing is, everyone else died that morning, so who's gonna buy the word of some old funeral man over what the coppers trumped up? Not even you, I bet …

I was only fifteen at the time, my father still alive, running Daddano. Al Capone and Bugs Moran were warring all over Chicago, which meant a boon in business for us. I dropped outta school to work full time with Father, and that pleased him a lot.

"Education is for the phonies," he'd say.

Anyway, I'd been helping him around the funeral home since I could toddle. As I grew, so too did my responsibilities, and while other kids in the neighborhood were playin' ball or lifting pockets, I was doing autopsies, embalming, going out to pick up stiffs in our stake bed delivery truck or maybe the old hearse if it was someone important. Sometimes he'd go with me, sometimes one of the other help went.

One of those help was a mortician named June whose hair was whiter than a snowstorm. June was maybe fifty, sixty years old though his hair had been colorless since birth, one of those pigmentation defects, I heard. June also carried a knife scar like a big crescent moon running under his right eye down to the corner of his mouth where a tooth was missing. My whole life, he'd been working for my father, but me and June barely ever said more words to each other than *mornin'* and *night*.

That day though we were together, taking the delivery truck to make a pick-up, and June outta nowhere says to me, "Johnny, you wanna know about death?"

I'd been helping my father so long I could tell you where the renal artery ran through the major calyces and whether a hematoma expansion was two hours or six past its onset. I'd seen a thousand dead faces wearing every ghoulish expression that would cause your nightmares to wake up crying. So I answered, "What's there to know? We're livin' now, and then we ain't. We got it better than most, then someday it's all over."

His voice lowered then, and he says quiet, "I mean real death, Johnny. Not just seeing the shell death leaves behind, but the act of dying. You never seen a man really die, have you?"

And that was true, though I never thought about it before. Every mutilation, every disease, every murdered dame and run-over kid and suicide and accident had come to me after the fact. It never struck me that the moment of transition was important. Just like waking up, I thought. One moment you're sleeping, then you're awake, and in the end, it goes the other way.

He nodded when I said nothin'.

"You're going to see it today," June whispered. I remember his breath stank like wild onions left in the ground two seasons too long, and when he paused between words, he chewed on the side of his tongue the way other men might roll a toothpick between their teeth. "You're gonna find out plenty, Johnny."

Those few words sent a chill so far down my back I could've pissed an icicle. My father liked June 'cause he worked hard and never said "no," but that cinched it why I'd kept my distance in the past. The old man was creepy as a sewer bug. And, Christ, the way he had to say my name in every sentence!

Though I had a thousand things I wanted to say, I kept 'em to myself. That was our business, remember? We didn't ask questions. June closed his eyes and went silent, as if the exhaustion of talking to me called for a nap. Which was fine, since I was driving and preferred my own company. In those days it didn't matter how old you were to operate a vehicle. If your feet could reach the pedals and you could see over the wheel, you could drive. And, friend, I started drivin' fast.

I probably looked like one of those little wind-up toys, my shoulders hunched and head craned over the wheel, arms jerking left and right as I veered around slow-poke traffic. There wasn't no rush otherwise, but I was gettin' edgy.

Then outta nowhere, June's eyes pop open, and he begins muttering some gibberish words I never heard in my life. I thought maybe he had Russian or Bulgarian family, and that's the language he was speaking, on account it sounded almost lyrical, the way monks might chant down in the bowels of a relic monastery.

I noticed too, while he mumbled, June kept looking behind us, his eyes darting from the rearview to the side mirror. I followed his gaze and thought I saw the flash of something darting in the street after us, flitting along the storefront walls where shadows were deepest, growing long when the street gutters ran into sewers, receding when the sunlight bounced off windows. Boarding houses and coffee shops blurred as I sped by, but that sense of something chasing after us kept pace just fine.

June's muttering changed back to words I was plenty familiar with, and I almost drove us into a light pole when he said, "Don't ever fuck with me, Johnny."

"What're you talkin' about? I thought you and me were on the level."

June eyeballed me strange. "Maybe we are, maybe not. I heard you all those nights, whisperin' I was a loony."

My heart could've hauled itself outta my mouth and swan-dived into my lap, and I wouldn't have been more surprised. "I never said anything like that!"

"You've been warned, Johnny. Oh, yes, warned I ain't loony at all."

"Yeah, okay, I've been warned."

I thought to ask if he'd been drinking a Mickey Finn of formaldehyde, but the way June's pallid forehead popped beads of sweat in the cold air made me keep my tongue.

I ain't told you yet, but our pick-up that morning was to be in a mobster's mechanic's garage. See, we were going to a warehouse owned by Bugs Moran for his hatchetmen to use in chopping up hot cars, fencing stolen booze, turning stool pigeons to sausage, whatever . . . and here I was, more nervous by the old man sittin' next to me.

It was Father who'd taken the phone call last night, though when June heard about a pick-up at the garage, he offered to do the job with the haste I never seen a dog beg for porterhouse steak. Father said fine, but to take me along, I needed more field experience. June might have nodded his assent, 'cept you could tell he wasn't happy about it, way his lids slitted down the tiniest of bit.

Father didn't tell me squat about the pick-up, just gave me the address, and said to let June do the talkin', and for us to use the truck, so I knew it as another backstairs affair.

Reason we used a stake bed delivery truck instead of the hearse was that it blended in with the city, nothing memorable about it, just a rattletrap rusting at the edges of its doorframe, could have been a regular delivery of lumber or some hayseed cartin' his wares to market. Half the corpses we picked up, the men who hired us wanted to keep the matter quiet. Forget about the movies, nonsense like 'sending a message to the enemy'; that only inspired guarantee of reprisal. It was better an unliked man simply vanish, and no one knows nothin' about it.

So here comes the brick face of our destination, S.M.C. Cartage Garage. I slowed as I drove past, to make the first right into an alley and circle around to its rear entrance, while that impression of being shadowed still lingered ominously, like something leaping through the air after us, one leg at a time, the way a child takes great strides over cracks in the sidewalk.

Halfway down the alley, June says, "Stop the truck," and I did.

He climbed out, clenching his fists. "I'm going in the front."

Once he left, I didn't feel that sense of being followed anymore, and only later did I consider it was waiting for June.

At the time, I was nothing but relieved to be rid of both him and that spooky vibe of bein' watched. June walked toward the street past moldering tires and bags of trash, and I continued through the alley to park in the garage's dingy rear lot, backing up so the tailgate faced the rear steel door.

Since the door was closed, I stayed in the truck, checking things out through the side mirror.

My father usually did all the talking with customers, me and June and the other help doin' the legwork, but I got to know our clientele by face, by name, by rep, even if they didn't know me from Shinola. Like I said, sooner or later every outfit came to do business with Daddano & Co.

Which is how I recognized the man right away who opened the garage back door: Al Weinshank, one of Moran's men. You see a mug like that, ya don't ever forget him. He was a gorilla, near six feet and a couple hundred pounds of muscle, with a towering pompadour of oiled hair that added another half-foot in height.

I got out to meet him.

He says, "Kid, you with Daddano?"

"Yes, sir."

"Truck ready?"

"Yes, sir."

"All right."

Then a fat guy dressed to the nines comes to the doorway, smokin' a snipe. Weinshank turns to him and they whisper to each other. The other guy nodded.

Past them, through the open door, I could see inside the long narrow garage there were four or five other men, only one of whom looked to be doing any actual mechanic's work, his head concealed under the hood of a dismantled coupe.

Weinshank and the fat man whispered something else, and I overheard a bit, "...comin' here to booshwash with Kachellek."

Kachellek.

Like I said before, we ran a tight operation at the Daddano business. We kept our mouths shut, did our part, and people knew to come to us for *sensitive* disposal matters.

But that don't mean business was always hunky-dory, either...

Some months back, Weinshank and a Moran lieutenant, Albert Kachellek, had cornered June in the stairwell outside our shop.

They pushed June around, slapped him, affirmed the usual threats for a debtor to pay up. Seemed June had run up some gambling dues with Kachellek, and the tardiness in payment turned issue.

I saw the fracas through a window and told my father, and he went out and ran them off. Not that I bore any love for June's well-being, but it was bad for business. And not that the men feared my father so much to scram, but they respected him enough to not worsen the scene.

Before they left, I overheard Weinshank sayin', "Don't make us open the side of your face again, Juney. And Al Kachellek's still got your last tooth."

Then they had a big laugh.

Is this what June was talkin' about, getting *fucked with*? Was he in over his head with debts? Were the threats gettin' to be too much? I wondered why in hell he'd *want* to come here, if he knew the garage held men who were leaning on him . . . I wondered too if the sick feeling rising in my guts meant every guess I made about that question ended in a bad way . . .

Someone from in the garage shouted, "Close the goddamned door, Frankie, whyn't you give the world an eyeful!"

"Aw, loosen your girdle," the fat man shot back, with a hint of foreign accent, before returning inside, slamming the door after him.

Weinshank came to the back of the truck, inspectin' within.

"All right," he says. "Your pops does good work."

Then he walked to the alley I'd come through, peering both ways to see if anybody'd been watching.

The garage door opened again, and a new guy comes out, half-readin' a newspaper. He was slim, balding, normal as any Joe accountant. The door closed automatically behind him. "Hey, your father said you need something?"

"My father? He ain't around. He's back at the shop on Halstead."

Accountant-Joe lowered his paper. "Old man you came here with, white hair, chews on his tongue real funny-like. Said you're his son?"

I made a face at him, confused, and maybe it's 'cause I didn't say anything back that the guy felt obliged to add, "I dunno. Old man said, 'My son is coming for us.' Took that to mean you were lookin' for something . . . What the hell's he got me runnin' around for?"

I shrugged, like what-the-fuck was I supposed to do about it? Though the next thought crossing my mind was a given, that because June told me *not* to think him loony, I immediately started judging he really had cracked a lid.

Weinshank comes back around the truck, as if readin' my

mind. "Who you talkin' about, Adam? Loony Juney in there givin' you crap?"

It was then the first scream roared so suddenly from the garage that my heart almost burst outta my ribs. The other two men's eyes went big as dinner plates, and the one who looked like an accountant dropped his paper. He pulled back the lapel of his suit coat and out came a revolver from his shoulder holster, though he didn't look in any hurry to go use it. That scream sounded... I don't know, *unholy,* pitched-too high, too gurgling, and finally cut off too quick. The ensuing silence pretty much seemed as terrifying as the scream itself.

Weinshank shoved past us both as a second scream erupted. There was this barrage of submachine gun fire inside the garage, shouts, curses, the slapping sounds of revolver slugs hitting cement. Weinshank flung open the door and bolted inside.

The garage door hovered open just a second, before closing again on its own. And in that one glimpse, I saw the closest to Hell I'd ever care to know.

My impression of the scene was a raging whirlwind, one of those small dervishes that blow up off the lake sometimes, swirling leaves and shit into the air, only here it was blood and shell casings and a couple severed heads, all of it fuzzy, like how a blob of dust and grime clumps together. You ever look real close, there's no hard edges to dust, it just seems to fade in and out of existence at the edges.

Now imagine that fuzzy dust being in the size and shape of a man, but every part of it always moving, as if an invisible wind blew over it from every direction at once.

Yeah... it was something like that.

The fat man who'd come out with Weinshank—Frankie— was squirming over the hood of the dismantled coupe, only it wasn't really Frankie anymore, but a severed gut spilling its insides and a pair of legs kicking up like a Rockettes routine.

Someone fired a Tommy submachine gun at the swirling dust man, and the roar was deafening, louder than a factory of dames at their Graybar sewing machines, just *rat-a-tat-a-tat*. The bullets ripped into it, passing through without doin' jack squat, like you're shooting at air. Someone else stumbled past, minus a head, his arms flailing around like all he'd done was lose balance.

I'll give credit to Weinshank, he must've seen the same things as me, and he didn't even blanch, just rushed right at the... *whatever it was*... his gorilla hands curled to battering ram fists, though I knew exactly the fate awaitin' him.

And I ain't even told you the worst of it. June—June was just standin' there with blood raining over his face, watching the whole thing and laughing and laughing, a horrible shriek you couldn't ever imagine coming from someone's voice. And that look of goddamned *glee* on him... it'll haunt me the rest of days.

Then the door closed shut.

I backed up real slow, and this panic took over. I turned alongside the tail of the truck, and all I wanted to do was hide, I couldn't even make it another ten feet to the cab to drive away, so I just dropped and crawled underneath between the tires.

Meanwhile the balding normal guy—*Adam*, Weinshank had called him—stood there, pointing his revolver in two hands at the door.

The shooting inside abruptly stopped, the screams, the cries, all those sickening sounds ended like a switch got thrown off.

I thought the machine gun fire had been loud, but that was nothin' compared to the *rat-a-tat-a-tat* of my pounding heart, and we're not even done yet. A voice calls out to me from the garage, and my nuts just scrambled up into my stomach.

"Oh, Johnny-boy, where are you? Johnny, come meet my son—"

The door slammed open. There stood June in all his loony

glory, that snow white hair now soaked red and standing on edge, his eyes glaring near to poppin' out of his head, and him chewin' on the side of his tongue. Blood and gore splattered over his coat and his face, and his arms were outstretched like he thought I was right in front of him and he was gonna grab me up in an big happy embrace.

I don't think he even saw Adam; the gangster pulled the trigger of his revolver—*Pop! Pop!*—and June's eyes went bulging even more. His legs sorta gave way real slow, and he dropped to his knees in the doorway, two neat little smoking holes added to his chest. The life seemed to fade from him real quick as his mouth went slack and his head rolled down, and a bubble of blood popped at his lip right where the crescent moon scar connected . . .

Then *it* came out.

The whirlwind was silent as clouds, but if it had a voice, I knew it would've been howling. It twisted around June, straight at Adam who fired the pistol again, each shot carefully aimed into the center of the dust man. For all the good it did him, he might as well have been slappin' it with a wet noodle.

That swirling form of soot and grime sorta surrounded Adam, and then it expanded outward, and took Adam with it, expanding him I mean, so he came apart at the seams as if nothin' but a rag doll, his legs and arms and head all pulling off in different directions. Adam's gun fell to the ground inches from me, though I knew it didn't matter if it landed right in my hand and the trigger under my finger, cocked and loaded; it wasn't gonna do any good. I stayed where I was, frozen.

After that, the whirlwind kinda slowed, hovering there awhile, gazing down at Loony Juney's corpse, and it almost seemed like the wind holding it aloft began to soften, as if some despair got the better of it. I took a closer look than I would've wanted . . . the swirling dust was still in the form of a man, yet seein' it nearer, I realized it wasn't just any man, but a thousand men, ten thousand men, a horde of faces all sifting and overlapping each other, layer upon layer upon layer that you could see through, but fuzzy too, and mucky and wet and ethereal, and Christ, it's just so hard to explain, y'know?

It wasn't no ghost, not like that, but it wasn't no human either, and it didn't seem right for a demon or some boggieman . . . It was something else entirely, which even now I still only vaguely comprehend.

See, there was somethin' fluttering around in that whirlwind's figure, and I don't think anyone else would have recognized it, though bein' raised in a mortuary I knew right away the small string-wrapped slip of cardboard for what it was: A toe-tag.

And after all these years tryin' to settle it out, the best I can tell you is it's something there ain't a name for. It's the little scraps of death and residue that accumulate together the way motes of dust collect to form clumps under the hutch, or the way grit always seems to build in the same board cracks until it overflows to spill across the floor. Give it chance, and that buildup keeps going, those dust clumps grow in no time at all.

You ever neglect sweeping beneath a couch or bed for awhile and then amaze at the mass of gunk that's festering down there?

Think of that gunk in your home, how it happens to us all— dust bunnies you might call it. Now think of that gunk in *my* home, Daddano & Co., decades upon decades of death filling our halls, and the worst kind of it: The remains of mob men and pushers, wife beaters, assassins, pimps, whores, thieves, and all their ilk and leaders. Flakes of their skin, drops of their blood, strands of their hair, remnants of their hatred, their viciousness, their corruption, all slipping under a loose floorboard and *growing together*.

Looking back, I think it's June all along, hardworkin' employee that he was, stayin' late and closing up the doors after me and Father and the others gone to bed. June found that mass . . . or maybe it found him. A gust from the fan, a dropped nickel rolling past the crack . . . a scent of something moldering, or maybe June lookin' for that lost toe-tag, whatever it was, he found the creature, made cause with it, and tried to control it like a pet dog. Loony Juney who'd probably been beaten down all of life had found his chance to rise up, as fleeting as that chance was.

Anyway, my story about the massacre that day ain't even finished yet. 'Cause I was still cowerin' under the truck while watchin' the dust man continue to swirl over June's body. It hung in the air a few minutes, kinda circling June, touching him, waiting for I don't know what. Then real carefully, like trying on a new suit, the thing sank down into June and filled the old man back up with itself.

There was a twitch of limbs, a fluttering of eye lids, and June pulls himself up, as if he'd been faking death all along. Only those two bullet holes over his heart don't lie.

He opened his mouth, and a little puff of dust billowed out, and he only says one word, "*Johnny . . .* "

It was June's voice too, but aloof, like our work here was done, and we needed to get back to the shop, bein' on the clock and all . . . only it wasn't June's voice either, 'cause it was dry and wispy as bones rubbing against each other. June began to walk toward the truck, so as he got closer, my perspective of him changed by scale, my line of sight falling from his air-holed chest to his waist, then his legs, and finally just a pair of scuffed black loafers a foot from the fender.

I was tryin' not to cry or piss myself, when I heard sirens in the distance, gettin' near fast. June's feet turned away, hesitated, and he—*it*—walked off down the alley.

Afterward, the police didn't have any clues, never mind what I told 'em. There were seven dead men torn to pieces, and I mean literally, a hand here, an ear there, a pile of guts draped over someone else's legs.

So they framed it all on Al Capone. It was convenient since him and Moran had been warring, and the coppers wanted him bad. Capone was a thorn in everyone's ass back then, he was so popular with the public that judges wouldn't sentence him 'cause fear of backlash. Capone gave people jobs, donated to schools, set up soup kitchens for the poor, all out of his own pocket, for God's sake. Chicago loved him, all except the cops who knew where he was getting all that money from in the first place.

Yeah, that garage massacre pretty much put Capone outta business, ironically blamed for something he wasn't responsible for in the least. He was never convicted of it or anything, but the media crucified him, and people began riding him for the crook he was. The federal government took notice too, and they're the ones who ultimately got him, trumping up tax offenses.

I'll tell you somethin' else too, that I don't hardly tell anyone. To this day I see fellas lookin' like June once in awhile, out of the corner of my eye, never aged, just blending in with the crowd but for that snow white hair and crescent moon scar, and I don't like to think where they're going, what they're doing...

So there's my story, friend. Take a look at the pictures that day in the Cartage Garage, why don't ya? The real pictures, I mean, if you can find them, not those staged phonies, the ones where Hollywood actors were brought in and laid on the ground with a daub of blood at the corners of their mouths. Anyone with a nickel's worth of sense can make those out as shams; the story that each mobster was riddled with at least fifteen bullets apiece on Valentine's Day don't even match the images, let how alone how they *really* ended up lookin'. Anyway, it is what it is, I guess, and folks say history is only what we agree it to be.

And I don't know any more than that. I'm just an old mortuary man.

LAST NIGHT . . .

LAST NIGHT, THE MOON TURNED FULL.

Last night, the world stopped turning.

Last night, the cosmos froze, like the slow-moving cogs of an ancient clock that finally grind down. Perhaps the great horologist of the universe simply forgot to rewind the mechanism of its gears. Perhaps he will appear at any moment to lift the stop lever and turn back its counter wheel. Perhaps he has decided the clock is broken and not worth his patience to tinker with any longer.

The earth hangs motionless now, peering to the sun from one face which, presumably, must begin to burn. Is the other side of the planet in flames or is it simply cooking like a slow-roast oven? I cower in North Vancouver, across the Burrard Inlet and, here, it is only night. My own watch has outlasted the mechanism of the universe and ticks away, telling me it's three in the afternoon. The sky shows otherwise, black and interrupted by a soft moon which rests high above like a pool of cream.

The temperature had fortunately been warm, golden months of Canadian summer that were just beginning to fade into autumn's auburn embrace. But I feel it cooling already. The red mercury on my thermometer outdoors drops steadily—forty-eight degrees and slowly sinking. The electricity is still on to generate heat but, once that goes out, there will remain nothing to warm this part of land relegated to nocturnal shadows. Lest that great horologist return, I can only image the arctic wasteland all of Vancouver will soon become.

If the sinking cold were not grim enough, the howl of werewolves chills me even more.

It's true they exist, but they've been of little consequence. One night a month, they transformed and ran wild through the piney wilderness above Lion's Bay. Their victims were homeless vagrants found sleeping in ravines or drunken hunters, piss-proud they killed a rabbit with a shotgun. Poetic justice, if you ask me, and their deaths unmourned. We all knew of the creatures and simply stayed home those nights with doors locked and shutters bolted. The werewolves were people of the town, members of families with long-standing roots to the indigenous men and women who first settled this country. When the time of month came, they did their business elsewhere, and we let them be.

Now, however, the moon does not fall. It no longer cycles the earth, while the earth no longer cycles the sun. That beguiling orb in the sky has petrified and casts its strange call permanently over mortals who would transform into howling beasts: those mortals who will never be mortal again. As the cosmos are stuck in their current alignment, so too are the creatures stuck in their transformation. The moon may stay full on this part of land for the remainder of eternity, and the wolf-men will run wild.

LAST WEEK, the moon turned full.

Last week, the world stopped turning.

Last week, time fell meaningless as calculations based on the rotation of the planet ceased. My watch ticks onward, the quartz crystal in its center vibrating at a steady frequency to tell me the hours, the days that have passed. It matters not for, outside, it is still midnight . . . always midnight.

I look out the window and see the dark ocean far away, its surface illuminated by the moon's reflection. Burrard Inlet is motionless, flat as a sheet of glass. There are no tides to pull the waves in or out, motions I once let myself be hypnotized by, dreaming upon their quiet, steady roar. Little moves outside, except for glimpses of fleeting shadows that dart across the hills—shadows that quickly melt into darkness and, once they are gone, cause me to wonder if they were ever there to begin with.

The werewolves have grown bold. In the past they relegated themselves to the wilderness, but now they roam the city. Their number is multiplying. I hear howling often, and screams too, but can never tell where the sound comes from as it echoes in the cold, still night air.

I have gone outside my house only twice since the world stopped moving.

The first time, I sought my neighbors to exclaim the wonder, the terror of what occurred. I am old and lonely and fear, most of all, enduring the end of life by myself. I thought unity, companionship was crucial for us all—the catastrophe of what occurred too great for anyone to bear alone.

Those I visited, however, were already touched by hopelessness, searching in their own ways for acceptance of the event.

I visited the cottage across the road first. Mrs. Gordon sobbed when she saw me, and her voice choked when she spoke. "My marigolds will die."

I embraced her and said I would replant them next season.

She smiled and nodded. She wore a pink bathrobe with images of angels playing lutes, and she wiped her nose on its sleeve.

"Thank you," she said. "Perhaps you may come back tomorrow when I prune the daffodils."

"I will," I quietly replied.

The next house down the road was Jim Franklin's. He sat on a rocker on his porch, swaying back and forth in a parka. He stared at the moon with a shotgun on his lap.

"The Mayans were right," he told me.

"I think we should band together, share resources," I said.

"What's the point?"

I couldn't answer. He kept swaying, and I left.

I went to other houses as well, knocking on doors while nervously looking over my shoulder. Families were either missing or they chased me away with curses and guns. I have always believed the full moon has a strange effect on people, whether they're werewolves or not.

I returned home, and later that night the electricity went out. Most of the older homes out here have backup generators, as do I, and I know to use it sparingly. Everything is turned off, except for the heater. Outdoors, it is nineteen degrees and so cold.

Sometime later I went outside again, my second time, to check on the neighbors.

Mrs. Gordon was gone. The door to her house hung open, and her marigolds were torn up and flung across the yard, as if a wild animal dug in her garden.

At Jim Franklin's house, I found him lying in the yard on his back.

"Jim, are you okay?" I whispered.

He lay naked and mauled. Fresh wounds channeled across his chest and arms, and torn strips of flesh revealed imprints of teeth marks. His skin shone mottled blue-gray from the frost, though patches of fur began to push through. He convulsed with transformation, and veins bulged as if rope coiled under his skin. At sight of me, he growled deeply and slowly rose.

Across the road, I caught glimpse of a great beast dart between trees. It stood upright and was covered in dark hair. In that moment I saw the beast's eyes glow like sparks of fire and, I saw too, it wore a tattered pink bathrobe.

I fled home and barricaded myself inside.

My house could be considered cozy and safe, a historic marker, dating to the late nineteenth century, built of thick stone and brick. The windows are glass though, and that worries me. I've moved furniture and nailed planks across the panes, but for how long it will last, I don't know. Not much longer, I suppose, and then I will retreat to the wine cellar beneath the floor. I mostly stay down there anyway, bundled in bedding and thick coats.

I listen to the ticks of my watch counting away moments that have no meaning and wonder at the world. I think of the small stockpile of food and water down in the cellar and wonder how long it will last. I wonder how I will die.

I have a prescription bottle of sleeping pills, should I decide to end this nightmare on my own terms. I wonder if there is someone left who will judge me on the choices I make.

LAST MONTH, the moon turned full.

Last month, the world stopped turning.

Last month, the human race began to die. Whether by climate-induced chaos or the wolf creatures' advance, I have seen nor heard anything evidencing mankind as I once defined it. Day-by-day the lights of mankind extinguished. The sky turned dark and then, for me, darker still.

I long for the moonlight now, as I cower in the shelter of the wine cellar. Down here, it is black as the shadows of dreams and cold as the realization I will never wake from them. When I leave my bedding, I crawl blindly on hands and knees to feel for the shrinking stockpile of food. I shiver as much from terror as from the cold. The werewolves are above me, and they smell my fear down here. They bang on the iron door overhead and howl in frustration, vicious snarls that slash at me almost as painfully as their claws surely would.

As I suspected, they came in through the windows. Three of them broke through, baying in unison, and leapt at me. One of the creatures was missing its left ear, and I think now of Max Everman who ran the Shell gas station and had his ear blown off in a hunting accident back in '87.

When the werewolves attacked I escaped, barely, into the cellar, screaming like a child. An hour later, the generator went out. That occurred several days ago.

I don't know how cold it is, because I've never experienced bitter chill like this for such an extended length of time. My teeth chatter and I feel the puffs of frost exhaling at each breath. I sleep intermittently until howls and scratching claws wake me, like raindrops of horror splashing on my brain. When I wake, I try to rub the numbness from my feet and hands so frostbite does not set in. How much longer can I survive? How much longer do I *want* to survive?

How much longer will it take this part of the world to freeze completely? Another month? A year until we slip across a mantle of solid ice?

The creatures do not seem affected by the biting cold, as if they've adapted like arctic wolves. Whatever viral infection or evolutionary mutation caused them to transform to beasts in the first place, bred the means for survival in this new world, evolving appendages with massive leather pads and coating skin in thick blankets of fur. Perhaps it was arranged all along, evolution working to modify us for survival as it sensed the slowing of the universe. Perhaps other species in other lands have been slowly developing adaptations for this event, hiding mutations in their DNA. I think of fish that live far under the glaciers of Antarctica, where no plant life or sunlight ever reaches. They flourish below, while perhaps the werewolves may flourish above. For all I know, the demon dogs have been slated for the top rung of evolution's master plan all along.

I wonder at these things as I lie alone in the dark, in the cold.

My watch still labors onward and, if I listen closely, each second sounds a quiet pulse, a bond for my own heart to beat: tick, tick, tick... If that watch should cease, I know I would, too. I wind my watch each day, in consideration of that, and I pray the great horologist of the universe should do the same just one last time. My prayers are not answered. It seems futile of me to continue winding my watch as the seconds of my life count down. Maybe that horologist thought the same as he lay trapped and dying in his own wine cellar, or maybe I *am* the horologist and the microcosm that considers me their center will perish, wondering *why*?

I believe madness seeps into my brain, carried along by flurries of terror and chill, and I wish desperately to see the radiance of the beautiful moon again.

I blindly feel around the floor until my hands grasp the bottle of sleeping pills. I shake them and listen to the rattle of capsules against each other like the dry seeds of a gourd. The werewolves howl and pound at the door. I could consume the pills and be done with it all; peace would whisper upon me and perhaps a final moment of warmth. I would die alone in the dark of the cellar.

I curse the absurdity of it all and wish suddenly: Oh, to be a wolf-man now and live free under the full light of the moon, to run wild in the companionship of a pack! To no longer wonder if death would come from frost or starvation or worse.

Would they devour me, should I give myself to them? Or would they be merciful, my neighbors and friends, and turn me to one of their own? Do they know more than I?

Perhaps they recognize who I am, and the beasts are only trying to help, to save me. They pound on the door calling for me to come out so they may rescue me from this dying human form.

Is madness deceiving me or has my watch already stopped

ticking? Should I take the pills or go outside? I gasp and my muscles spasm as the cold constricts with icy fingers. I would weep, but the tears turn to icicles on my lashes. I think of the dark and the light beyond.

LAST NIGHT, I opened the cellar door . . .

THOSE WHO WATCH FROM ON HIGH

THE BOY LOOKED UP TO THE SKY AND SMILED, AND it seemed to Lee that the boy looked up at him, smiled at *him*.

The boy's teeth were white and perfect little squares like the teeth you saw on a poster in the orthodontist's waiting room: *Trust us to make your teeth look like this!* But Lee doubted this boy had ever been to an orthodontist. Lee doubted this boy had been much of anywhere, outside a few miles from his mud-brick shack. The boy was just blessed by nature with a beautiful smile.

Lee came down closer, closer still, nearing the desert, nearing the shack. He reached for the ground. His boots made contact. He took a tentative step, then another, impossibly feeling solid earth. He began to walk. The boy wasn't far away, and Lee watched him play. The boy rolled a ball into a skirmish line of toy soldiers, and they toppled over. He charged with a thrusting gun, dueling invisible opponents. He climbed a rock. Chased a lizard. Drew a picture in the dirt with a stick. The boy was happy, and this made Lee happy.

Lee's son, Jacob, would have been about the same age as this boy, and it reminded him terribly of all the lives that are taken too soon. If circumstances were different, it'd be Lee in that shack in

Afghanistan, playing with his son, trying to survive from one day to the next. The boy with perfect teeth was about eight years old and had two siblings that were both still infants. That was a large gap in age between the children, and Lee wondered if there had once been others. If circumstances were different, Jacob would have had siblings. If circumstances were different, Jacob would still be alive, and Aimee alive, and they'd have three children by now. Three . . . just like the family he watched.

"Stand by for orders."

The voice came to him, filling his head, but he couldn't make sense of it. The words didn't fit with his surroundings. Lee felt the uneven ground beneath his feet, one step sinking into white sand and the next step stumbling over ancient stones. The region was so rocky that danger of misstep loomed greater than snipers' bullets; out here a snapped ankle could be a slow and lonely death.

Desert heat swirled against Lee, and a line of sweat ran down his temple. But the boy was close, so close . . . Lee wanted to run to him, touch him, tell him to take his happiness and flee everything.

"Check the angle, Bruce. We're tracking insurgents, not sand dunes."

Again it felt unnerving, like someone speaking in a dream, and Lee only wanted the voice to leave him alone so he could remain with the boy. Instead, the voice seemed to pull him back, seemed to lift him in the air, and the boy and his desert home fell away like a sinking marble.

"Bruce, you with me?"

The dream voice was louder, and the wasteland faded below. A computer screen coalesced over it, like overlapping frames of film. *He wasn't there.* He, *no*, it—the Drone—was there, following the boy and his family, but he—Lee—was in a trailer on Nellis Air Force Base. He was First Lieutenant James Lee, and he was on duty.

"Bruce, report!"

Reality came back fully, and he remembered that it sucked.

He was an Unmanned Aerial Vehicles operator. Six computer monitors glowed before him, jostling for attention with moving images, scrolling feeds, changing numbers, things blinking, red, green, eighty-four, nine, radius, lock, C2, surge. It was a child's room of toys, messy and random, too much visual stimuli going on at once. He operated half the cockpit of a remote aircraft on the other side of the world. Watching, ready to fire a missile anytime onto unknowing targets.

Lee adjusted camera #3, and the video feed panned back to widen its scope.

"Roger that, sir. Adjusting angle," Lee replied to Disick, the other half.

"I don't know how you made it through the academy, Bruce."

Bruce . . . He hated that nickname.

Never mind he was blue-eyed with hair fair as butter, or that his family were English-settled coal miners from the Appalachians and the farthest one could get from the Orient, Lee had been christened 'Bruce' upon assignment to the squad, no explanation necessary. It was just funny to the rest of them. He'd grown up trapping and fishing, an outdoorsman before he could say *da-da*, yet zit-faced Captain Disick called him Bruce while coining his own unlikely nickname of 'Hunter.' The irony went unheeded. Disick was built soft as a wet cow pie and looked like he'd be better suited playing *World of Warcraft* than soldiering. Of course, in current confines video gaming skills were traits superior over machismo. Plus Disick was his commanding officer, so Lee didn't say jack or shit back to him. They flew together which was supposed to inspire camaraderie, though Lee detested his younger co-pilot; Disick loved the power play one increase in rank held over him, and he hid behind it like a shield while picking apart Lee on a basis as punctual as cadence.

Captain Disick flipped a switch, taking over from the

automated control pilot. He sat to Lee's left less than five feet away, in front of his own bank of computers, though still speaking to Lee in a headset, never turning to face him. "Disregard and disengage. Colonel Brown just ordered we bring the craft home. The next shift can watch the hajjis sleep."

"Affirmative, Captain," Lee said.

"That's *Hunter*," Disick said. "Remember, Colonel Brown says it's good for squad morale to use our code names."

"Yes, sir." Lee replied, deadpan.

"That was an order, *Bruce*."

"Yes … Hunter."

TIME TO LEAVE.

The trailer door opened from outside. The next shift of drone operators waited to enter, faces already dull, already exhausted, the look of adult children sentenced to twelve hour detention and dragging their feet to begin.

Lee went to the door and nodded at them, but said nothing. On the other side, the sky was bright, colored as pale water, colored exactly as the Afghani sky. He expected that once he walked out, he would see the boy's mud home in the distance. There'd be a picture drawn in the dirt, a lizard on a rock, toy soldiers lined up in battle. There'd be someone high above observing *him*.

Twelve hours. He'd been on duty, staring at a patch of desert the size of a football field for twelve mind-numbing hours. His night shift began at seven p.m. and ended at seven a.m., and when Lee went into the Air Force trailer it was day and when the door was unlocked to allow him out, it was a new day. Flying over Afghanistan occurred during *their* day, opposite hours of Pacific Standard Time. It seemed to Lee that night no longer existed; he saw only desert sun at all times.

No wonder he couldn't turn the visions off so easily. When you hyper-gaze too long into a television screen, the afterimage haunts you, that sense of disorientation. Though he existed here at Nellis, just north of Las Vegas, half of every day was spent in Afghanistan. Half the day he *felt* he existed in Afghanistan. It was not something he could easily reconcile, the *here* and *there*, every day, looking at two worlds which were so much alike, but were not.

"Christ, Bruce, move out of the way. You're blocking our egress."

Disick was behind him. Lee blinked and exited the trailer. Three metal steps down and he was on a cement lot. The Mojave Desert surrounded Nellis Base, glints of quartz and mica sparkling from its golden sand. Like the sky, Nevada's desert appeared identical to Afghani desert.

We're the same all over.

Disick plodded past, and the other operators went inside, door closed on a time lock, unable to reopen until the next shift change for security reasons. All routine. The trailer was just a souped-up shipping container, ambiguously known as a Ground Control Station. But inside it was filled with death rays and mad scientist diodes and buttons that caused people to explode.

And there were several dozen trailers here, each ready to obliterate, each part of the 29th Attack Squadron. That's who he was attached to.

He knew somebody he'd like to attack . . .

ANOTHER DAY.

Lee flew the UAV drone far above, where air was too thin even for clouds to form. The ancient village of Oraza Zaghard sat below like a pile of ash dropped upon a beautiful quilt. Lee had once tried a *Google* search of the village to supplement the demographics the military supplied. Although it was highlighted on the Air Force map, he found no reference to it on the internet. The village was insignificant to the rest of the world; only those who lived there, and those who watched from on high, seemed privy to its existence.

Lee directed the cameras downward. The Multi-Spectral Targeting System streamed color video back to the Air Force trailer, and as the sensors zoomed in, so did Lee. He felt like he was soaring, then diving, straight down through the sky. Zooming in, zooming in. Afghani desert swirled around, and he moved through Sar-e Pol Province, past Oraza Zaghard, and to the mud-brick shack at the end of a winding footpath. Back to the boy . . .

The boy who had no name. He was only 'Son of Mullah Hamid Zadran, suspected insurgent.'

The camera lenses were so high-powered that Lee was able to pick out the scars on the boy's arms and the cowlicks in his hair. The camera lenses were so high-powered he felt as if he were there alongside the boy.

The family had a goat, and the boy ran to it, circling with waving arms. The goat stood there, staring plainly, then suddenly turned and darted away. The goat was too quick, and the boy could not catch it. He sat on the ground and laughed.

Lee was quicker than the boy; he reached out and caught the goat by a rope tether around its neck.

The boy looked at Lee and smiled, and Lee saw again how perfect those teeth were. The smile was honest, relieved, as if the boy expected him to be there all along, to watch over him.

TIME TO LEAVE.

The trailer door opened from outside. The next shift of drone operators waited to enter.

Lee went to the door and nodded at them, but again said

nothing. On the other side, the sky was bright, colored as pale water, colored exactly as the Afghani sky. It was all so familiar. He expected that once he walked out, he would see the boy's mud home in the distance. There'd be a picture drawn in the dirt, a lizard on a rock, toy soldiers lined up in battle. There'd be someone high above observing *him*.

"Rifle!"

Lee vaulted to the ground, sprawling. Only he was three metal steps above cement, so rather than vaulting, it was falling, hard and fast. He hit concrete, bruising his knees and elbows, but that didn't matter. Roll up on reflex, one hand over the back of his head, the other hand covering behind his neck.

Disick laughed. There was no *rifle*, the term for incoming missile.

"Just keeping you on your toes, Bruce."

The other operators laughed too.

"What the hell, Disick?"

"Have to live up to my nickname. I was *hunting* you." He laughed again.

Lee stood, balling his hands to fists. But he didn't react the way he wanted, instead turning his back.

Disick knew somebody high in the chain of command. That's who watched over *him*. That's how he got his Captain's bars so young. But Disick didn't know his ass from his double chin when it came to real hunting. It was all a video game to him.

Someday, his superior by one rank would get his due.

"Lighten up, Bruce," Disick said. "It's only war."

IT WAS DIFFICULT trying to sleep during the day. The blinds of his bungalow were drawn and it was dark inside, but Lee's brain knew the sun was up, and his body's rhythm fluttered anxiously as if he'd grossly overslept something important. He could never grow accustomed to nocturnalism, the knowledge that it was nine in the morning outside, and he was only now trying to fall asleep, trying to get in a good eight hours before tonight's shift began.

Eight hours... who was he kidding? He'd be lucky to get four. Lee had taken a couple sleeping pills, but those never seemed to work, instead just muddying the line between wakefulness and slumber even more.

Everything—day, night, Afghanistan, Nevada, here, there—was a blur, a series of memories of what may have occurred and hopes for what *could* occur, playing side-by-side, like viewing two videos simultaneously...

...Lee's thoughts interrupted. He'd returned to the trailer. Disick sat next to him and said something, and Lee responded by reflex, and that was it. They fell silent, having nothing more to say for hours while stationed alongside each other.

Lee felt himself drifting. Again. His face hung slack, his mind numb, conditioned to study the target on the ground, watching, just watching. The computers around him had long ago fallen into the backdrop of his mind, filed as forgotten thoughts. He felt dull and tired like sitting inside a car on a road trip that goes on too long. Sweaty, grimy, breathing each other's air, each other's smells. Did Disick ever bathe? Come to think of it, when did he himself bathe? The world outside the Air Force trailer seemed dim, speeding past on simulated auto-pilot just as it did inside. He couldn't remember much of it. He couldn't remember the last time he'd washed, the last time he'd slept, eaten, or felt happy.

No, scratch that, he remembered that last time he was happy. Watching Jacob play...

...Lee had been married once. Had a son once. Spent six years as an enlisted man in Air Force logistics at Edwards Base, dreaming of the day he'd transfer out of low-grade clerk's activities. He wanted away from the rote routine of uniformed paper pushers. He wanted some action, to reach the combat zones, kill the bad guys like his father. So Lee pushed himself, got accepted, and then finished Officer Candidate School third in his class. He could fly a Raptor or a Lightning II high above the world. He was going to be *badass*.

But then everything changed.

Aimee died. Jacob died.

It had been nighttime, cruising down Interstate 15 to visit her parents in San Diego. A drunk driver hit them. He came out of nowhere, *absolutely nowhere*, no lights on, no warning, just one moment Lee was driving their leased Corolla while Aimee and Jacob snoozed, and the next they were blindsided. All Lee could liken to the impact was that of a missile slamming into the side of their car, and he hated himself for that comparison. The Corolla was knocked through the guardrail, tumbling in catastrophic rolls down a ravine that sliced through the Clark Mountain range. Lee didn't have his seatbelt on. The others did. Lee was thrown from the car with barely a scratch. The others were burned alive in the ensuing fire.

Though he survived unharmed, part of him still died. Life became that car wreck, confusing and pointless. He was evaluated as mentally unfit to fly a jet. Inexplicably though, the next week he was transferred to Nellis and assigned to fly one from behind a desk, even though military psychologists claimed it was tougher to pilot a drone than a real plane. The work was time-intensive, vigilantly staring at the same plot of earth through cameras for months on end. Watching, just watching, just another rote routine like when he worked as a logistics clerk.

It's not the planes that are drones. We're the drones, filling the monotony of our lives with buttons and monitors.

Lee lay in bed dreaming of Aimee and Jacob, dreaming after the accident, after the fire, of their melted stick bodies that looked as if they'd been doused in tar . . .

. . . And he knew somebody he'd like to attack. Hadn't he been tracking that person for a long time, *hunting them?*

The drunk driver who rammed them off the road. *Lee could fire a missile anywhere in the world.* To kill the bad guys, he had only to watch and wait . . .

. . . And he watched the boy in Afghanistan play with toy soldiers. They were cheap plastic men, molded in olive green that every toy aisle in every drug store carried since toys and aisles and drug stores first came around. Even there, in that country, some sales clerk had gotten his wares dispersed all the way to the mud shack at the end of a winding footpath outside Oraza Zaghard.

Lee had played with those exact soldiers when he was a boy, and his own father played with them before him.

"Yup, same poses, same faces," his father once said. His father died in Iraq.

The green solider frozen with a bayoneted rifle swung overhead. The solider with a deadly flame thrower. The one with a far-reaching mortar. The one with a pistol and binoculars which, though no insignia was present, was always assumed to be the unit's officer.

Jacob, too, had played with those soldiers . . .

. . . Lee walked through the desert in Afghanistan, feeling the hot sand even through his combat boots . . .

No, he was in Nevada. Nellis Air Force Base. He walked through the sand of the Mojave desert . . .

But the mud shack was there.

So, too, was the UAV trailer, alongside, but not, like viewing two videos simultaneously ...

Both screens went black ...

THERE WAS SOMETHING watching him.

Lee stepped to the side of the trailer, his back hugging its wall. The sky was bright, colored as pale water, colored exactly as the Afghani sky. He looked to it, searching for the drone. He blinked. He blinked again, a hundred more times. Though it wasn't visible, he *knew* something was up there ... somewhere, someone watching him ... *targeting him.*

He was alone on the ground. Lee suddenly wanted to run back into the trailer where it was safe, but the next shift was already inside, door closed, locked.

He dashed across the lot, past the other trailers lined up like desks in a classroom. The red crosshairs of a target seemed to hover over each of them, but the biggest target followed himself. His squadron fired missiles like video games onto other countries, and someday those missiles would be returned.

Even now, satellites had watched him exit the trailer, knew *he* was the one pushing the button. Satellites, drones, cameras, eyes, all watching ...

Was the boy watching him on his own monitor, inside a mud shack in Oraza Zaghard? Or was the boy inside the trailer and he, Lee, in Afghanistan?

UAV operators weren't supposed to experience the same effects of post-traumatic stress as those pilots actually flying jets into global combat zones. But he grappled daily with the hazards of depression, insomnia, and anxiety.

One time, Lee had even been so unnerved by these ailments he'd worked up the courage to approach Captain Disick outside the trailer.

Back then, Disick wasn't so overweight as he was fleshy, the way a linebacker may look: solid, but with those too-plump curves, like being swaddled in extra layers of clothing. Now Disick was just 'fat-ass fat' and Lee wondered how he could ever pass a fitness test. Or did it matter? After all, the future of wars was only button-pushing.

"Sir, can I ask you something?" Lee asked.

"S'up?"

"Do you ... well, ever come out of there and feel like you're losing track of where you are?"

"What?"

Lee knew Disick heard what was asked, and that he understood it, so the curt response meant he was more baffled as to *why* Lee would ask such a thing.

Lee tried again. "Disassociation. That's what the doctors call it. Does it ever get to you, so you're not sure if we're here or still staring at another land?"

"Don't tell me you're ready for the shrinks already," Disick replied. "Long enough day without dealing with your bullshit."

Lee never told Disick about Aimee and Jacob. Maybe their relationship would have been different if he had. Maybe Disick would have understood why his co-pilot was a glum, tightlipped burnout. But Lee never told anyone about Aimee and Jacob.

Lee just rubbed his eyes, playing it cool. "Sorry, Captain. Like you said, it's been a long day."

"Then go get some sleep. Tomorrow will be another long one." Disick walked away, probably to pound beers at the Officers' Club.

And now, something—*someone*—watched Lee from on high. He'd had this sense before, often, but it'd been growing stronger lately, slowly stronger, like zooming in and refocusing. Were they tracking him like the insurgents? Did they know of his plot? Did they know about who he wanted to attack ... ?

'Cause he'd found that drunk driver, hadn't he? One push of a button, just one push, and Jerome Anderson of 3145 Wingate Avenue would be blasted to Kingdom Come. In the land of dropped bombs, could it be so inconceivable if a drone missile happened to defect and land at that very address?

Lee could not see them—you could never *see* the drones—as they were a quarter mile high in the sky. But he knew better than anyone else, *they were there*, watching, waiting. They watched everybody.

Just like Lee had watched Jerome once he returned home from Chino Prison. A lousy two years was all he served, reduced vehicular manslaughter charges for the deaths of Jacob and Aimee. But Lee tracked him down with a reprogrammed missile at his fingertips.

Lee could do it. The failsafe systems were overridden, the drone armed, the target locked in. He could even find a way to blame the wayward missile on Disick. He could do it, all he had to do was push a button . . .

But before Lee acted, Jerome Anderson of 3145 Wingate Avenue died suddenly of circumstances unrelated to Lee's doing, run over by another drunk driver, such is fate's irony. Lee had waited too long, the opportunity for revenge snatched from him as unexpectedly as the lives of his own family.

That was over a year ago, yet something still watched Lee.

ANOTHER DAY.

Lee was on duty. He sat before his bank of computers watching the same football field-sized patch of desert. Watching the same mud-brick shack of Mullah Hamid Zadran.

On this day, Lee was alert. His nerves tingled as if they caught fire. Abu Ayyub al-Husseini was en route, a target considered 'high value,' this being a term which always reminded Lee of video games where the *Bosses* were worth the most points.

Lee's monitors flashed more images than normal, more lights blinked, more numbers scuttled past. A multitude of voices filled his head, Intelligence Analysts chattering back and forth. *Observe, confirm, report.* They patched into a team of Information Officers inside another trailer, maybe next door to Lee, maybe on another planet. He never knew where the rest of the squad was. *For security reasons.*

"There he is, Bruce," Disick said, his voice nearly in glee. "There's al-Husseini. We're gonna nail that bastard."

Onscreen, a Mercedes Benz slowly drove up the winding dirt road to Zadran's mud shack.

Colonel Brown joined the teleconference. Whenever he spoke, his voice was garbled with static, as if he spoke far, far away, in an underground bunker. Lee had never met the Colonel, but he knew that static-filled voice would haunt him the rest of his days. Colonel Brown was the great decider of who lived and who died.

Today, it was thumbs-down. Colonel Brown said, "We have a high value target arriving. Prepare to prosecute."

An analyst added as an afterthought, "Confirm clear of civilians."

Lee felt sick. They were going to bomb the boy's home. *He* was going to bomb it, was going to be *ordered* to bomb it. He didn't want to—God knew that—but he was merely a drone. A voice he barely recognized as his own replied, "Only Zadran has been observed on premises in the past hour."

"Good," Colonel Brown said. "Killing two bad birds with one big stone."

Zadran stood outside the shack, talking animatedly on a cell phone. He was alone. *Should* have been alone. Earlier, a neighbor had driven to take away Zadran's wife and children. The boy *should* have been with them ... of course the UAV Predator had banked left at a moment the family entered the car, which had been on the blind side of their home, so it wasn't certain. And heat signature didn't do squat during the day, when the desert sand cooked hotter than the readout of anything alive. But Lee hadn't seen anyone else since, couldn't *prove* to the others anyone else since.

Military intelligence had been tracing Abu Ayyub al-Husseini for weeks. He was supposedly plotting some sort of attack, and Zadran was supposedly working with him. al-Husseini was one of the bad guys. So was Mullah Hamid Zadran.

Lee was never privy to the validity of such charges. Proof was classified on a 'Need To Know Basis.' And Lee didn't need to know. He only needed to push a button when told, so someone could die on the other side of the world.

The Mercedes Benz arrived at the mud shack, and a static-filled voice ordered, "Prosecute."

Time to push the button. Time for Lee to launch death from on high. Zadran and al-Husseini would have no warning. To them, the missile would come out of nowhere, *absolutely nowhere.*

Lee hesitated. A line of sweat ran down his temple, as it had when he walked in the desert.

It didn't matter if he'd seen the boy or not in the last hour, because he knew, didn't he, just knew something was wrong . . .

"Prosecute."

This is what he trained for: there should be no emotional attachment to the enemy.

He wouldn't do it. They'd court martial him, but he'd have a clear conscious.

"Prosecute."

It was only a duty. Only reflex. Only rote routine. And if he didn't bomb the target, Disick would.

Disick would enjoy it . . .

"Prosecute."

"Rifle," Lee said, and an AGM 114 Hellfire missile was set loose.

It was twenty-five seconds until 'Splash,' when the payload detonated. Lee had a window of time to maneuver the missile away, if any non-targets approached the area. But the monitors were clear, only the intended targets visible, only Zadran and al-Husseini.

The missile soared down, down, down.

Still there was time to maneuver the missile away, but no reason. He had the controls and the authority to do so, until seven seconds before impact when it turned too late.

The seven second countdown came and passed. Six seconds until impact, five—

Disick whispered the numbers in reverence, "Four, three—"

Lee knew, without knowing how, what was to happen, and it did. It happened just as he knew: the boy exited from inside the shack. The boy flew a cardboard airplane in his hand.

"Abort!"

Two-too-late, one-too-late, detonation.

A flare of white bloomed on their screens, a silent, beautiful flower.

"Where'd that kid come from," Disick said. "I didn't see him before..."

"Confirm target." Colonel Brown's voice came online, barely understood over the static.

"We might have got a civie," Disick admitted.

"The boy," Lee whispered.

Brown was silent. Static filled Lee's ears.

"Sir, sir," Disick asked. "What do we do?"

"Return to base, gentlemen. Good work. Target eradicated."

"But the boy—"

"It wasn't a boy," Brown said. "It was a dog."

The voice clicked away.

"You saw it," Lee told Disick. "A dog doesn't walk upright in sandals."

"Colonel Brown said it was a dog, so that's what it was." Disick sounded relieved, detached.

"You saw it—"

"It was a dog, First Lieutenant Lee, and I don't want to hear another word about it!"

The use of Lee's proper rank and name unnerved him. It made the matter official. *A dog.* In records, the boy would never have died, would be living, indeed, in the ruins of that mud shack forever.

He wished Disick would have instead called him 'Bruce.'

FOUR SLEEPING PILLS that morning, and he dreamed between there and here.

Lee walked in the desert, sand crunching beneath his combat boots. It was rocky and hot. Some of the rocks were black and shaped like crumpled leaves, and it took awhile to realize the black rocks were debris from the mud shack. He kept walking and found a single wall that still stood, precariously truncated and shorn off smooth at each side. In the center of that wall, a door hung canting from twisted hinges.

He wanted to cry, but nothing came out. It was a desolate land, a dead land, and he belonged here. He dropped his head to his chest, eyes cast to the ground. Something white glistened there like a chip of porcelain. He bent and picked it up.

A tooth. A small, perfect white tooth.

Lee's cry had no trouble coming out now.

Another tooth lay three feet away, and Lee picked it up also. He searched the sand for more teeth, an idea forming in the back of his mind to reconstruct that which he'd destroyed.

He found fifteen. But that wasn't all, was it? How many teeth fit inside a boy's mouth? He seemed to remember there should be twenty . . .

The door in the ruined wall creaked open. Lee looked up. The boy stood there, visible within the doorframe, and this did not surprise Lee.

The boy—*it*—now appeared as a charred monster, a skewer of steak chunks dropped and forgotten in the broiler. Or it could have been the sculpture of a thin monkey built from wire and car parts, then sprayed matte black, though it moved like a living thing with half its bones snapped apart. There was just enough support left for the boy to walk in a feeble, lurching stumble toward Lee though, with every movement, something shifted loose under its charcoal skin, something that appeared ready to break free with a hollow crack and a poof of ash.

Its feet dragged slow, leaving long charcoal smears with each step like skid marks of a hot rod that's peeled away on asphalt. That same *smell* of hot rod was there too, burning rubber and gasoline fumes that caused Lee to gag.

Closer it came, until halting before Lee, looking to him expectantly from hollow eye sockets. They remained this way, the child's head upraised to him, patiently waiting. Lee held the child's sightless gaze for ten long seconds before he could take it no more.

Lee held out his hand, opened it. The boy's perfect teeth rested on his palm.

The child took its teeth one by one and replaced them back into the horrible gummy blackness of its mouth. One by one, the teeth resumed their place, like connecting a jigsaw puzzle. First a molar, then a canine, another molar, then an incisor, pearls in a pond of tar. There were a few missing—Lee hadn't found them all—but by the time it was done, the boy's perfect smile had mostly returned. It flashed that mostly-perfect smile to Lee, happy again.

The boy stumbled to a large boulder, where a melted mass of

plastic army soldiers lay like green bubblegum that's been chewed and stretched apart. The boy pulled some of the soldiers free; they were ruined, formless, like the boy, but the boy played with them. Grating commands given from binocular-wielding officers to mortar and flamethrower-armed troops came from the boy's throat as it played, sounding like the dry *whisk* of sandpaper rubbing against rough wood.

Some of the sounds were even recognizable. *Boom, whisk. Pow-pow, whisk. Rat-a-tat, whisk.*

Lee went to the boy . . .

. . . Only now it wasn't a dream anymore because he and Disick were flying over Syria. Of course, Lee was still in a trailer in the Mojave Desert outside Las Vegas, but he *watched* over Syria.

After Oraza Zaghard, Lee and Disick had been enthusiastically congratulated. Oraza Zaghard was a success. But then the minor city of Saraqeb, located in an insurgent-filled corner of Syria, had been assigned as the newest directive of high value. They flew there post-haste to watch over another patch of desert the size of a football field.

Lee directed the cameras downward, and they zoomed in. The sensation was like falling face-first from the heavens: down, down he fell, and the ground rushed up to meet him.

Zooming in, but another image coalesced over it, like overlapping frames of film. It was Afghani desert that swirled about—not Syrian—and he returned to Sar-e Pol Province, passing Oraza Zaghard, soaring down to the ruins of the mud-brick shack at the end of a winding footpath. Back to the boy, waiting for him . . .

. . . And a new image coalesced over that, of another computer monitor, watching himself, and Lee saw that he sat inside the Air

Force trailer and the little boy now sat on his lap, a little charcoal boy who'd returned with him from Afghanistan, a boy with limbs that stuck out in all the wrong directions, but who had the most beautiful teeth he'd ever seen . . .

. . . Heat smoldered off the boy, and Lee felt it warm his chest as the boy snuggled into him. Brittle edges of its charcoal skin scratched Lee's neck, but he didn't mind. Lee was happy.

Because the boy was dead—even *he* knew that—but the boy was also here with him now, and if the boy could be with him didn't that mean that Aimee and Jacob could *also* join him?

Lee glanced five feet to his left, and saw Disick slouched at the controls, eyes half-shut, staring at nothing. The drone was on autopilot. Disick never looked at him. Lee flipped a switch.

And another image coalesced over that, and he saw Aimee and Jacob as very small drones. They were the ones watching him from on high, and he wanted so desperately to fly up and join them.

And another image coalesced over that, like looking through a stack of transparent negatives, and Lee saw the Air Force trailers, each with a red crosshair hanging overhead.

He knew somebody he'd like to attack . . .

Lee pushed a button.

"Rifle, *whisk*," the boy said, though it was Lee's own voice he spoke through.

And suddenly Disick was awake, screaming about '*What had Lee done?*' and something else about him going '*Batshit-crazy!*'

Lee wanted to say something clever about how he was *hunting* Disick, but then he realized his co-pilot's words didn't make any sense to him; they had a rough, baying tone, as if he barked like a dog . . . yes, that was it. *Disick was really just a dog.*

Disick tried to push his own button, to counter Lee's, but Lee had fixed that already.

Then Disick was running to the door of the trailer, but couldn't get it open, because it was locked, and his hands were paws, and he was barking something else unintelligible. The boy smiled to Lee, and Lee smiled back.

"Lighten up," Lee told the dog. "It's only war."

And then Lee was back at the mud-brick shack, and it had been rebuilt, and the boy was there and Aimee was there and Jacob was there, all the charcoal people, with overlapping images of how once they looked, and they welcomed him, and somewhere he heard a countdown with a *whisk* after each number, and then he heard a final bark.

VANCOUVER FOG

THE VANCOUVER FOG ROLLS QUIETLY IN, AND I think of Laura.

I think of her laughing. I think of her dancing in the forest, darting between trees. Her smile was so brilliant and she laughed and skipped, the spirit of a carefree girl preserved in her heart. She teased me to catch her. I did, and we rolled amongst the leaves and flowers, and I promised I would never leave.

I think of us lying in bed as I combed her hair. She laughed so wonderfully as I ran the brush through her glassy raven locks. Such a small act, but she adored it. She delighted in my attention, and I delighted to hear her laugh.

I think of the Vancouver fog that rolled quietly in the night Laura was killed. Because of me, she died, never to dance in the forest again. We had argued that evening as I drove down the highway, fog closing in on my speeding car. I was upset. I turned to her and cursed, and her eyes widened. She saw what I did not, and I drove us off the road. The car did not dart between the trees as Laura oft did, but collided instead with the largest one.

I woke to her silent corpse, and I wailed and wept through the night. The fog thickened, great pools that we slowly sank into. I cradled Laura's head and pled for her to laugh again.

In the morning, as the mirage of the moon faded, I carried her body in my arms. I carried my love up the road for miles and miles, walking stricken, until our home appeared over a dark rise, materializing from the fog.

I laid her in bed and kissed her lips and whispered to her. I pleaded for her forgiveness, to never leave. I yearned for her laugh. I combed her hair.

I combed long, loving strokes, brushing gently. I combed to bring out the shine she adored so much, the luster gleaned from glassy raven locks.

Her hair began to fall out, but I combed still.

Laura's features melted, a sigh of the wind and the world turned. I combed her hair, and the Vancouver fog rolled quietly in.

I now hold her loose hair wrapped in one hand, so that it does not spill away.

Laura's eyes, once sparkling with life, have retreated into hollow black caverns. Her lips, once a rosy bloom, have withered into a hard ivory edge, dainty teeth clenched tight.

I tell her of our love, and she laughs again. I promise I will never leave, and she laughs. I reminisce of dancing in the forest.

She laughs, a cruel haunting jag, tormenting my ears. *I'm so sorry*, I cry. I beg her to not leave. She laughs, shrieking, howling echoes that stab my soul like the shards of burst glass from a car wrecked in the forest.

I lay my head upon her ribs and dream the Vancouver fog has lifted.

A Curse
and a Kiss

I WAS INVISIBLE ONCE.

Long ago—though not so long that memories begin to fade like dying rose petals—I was a mere girl, a house servant, under Prince Ruskin d'Auvergnon. Less even than a servant, I was his property, his *chattel*, traded in payment while in infancy to settle an obscure debt my parents languished under. I do not begrudge them. I know what it feels like to be battered by despondency and to wish so desperately to be free of something that you would trade even your own flesh and blood for relief. Now, in my older years, I am trapped in this cursed castle, while the world dies around me. O! The wishes that tremble on my lips!

I wish to be safe. I wish to be somewhere else. I wish I was invisible again and could escape into the forest, walking past the creatures unseen. I wish to still be that mere girl from so long ago, living a simple life and unaware of the horrors the world could unleash. I wish Ruskin had let the old woman into his castle on that fateful rainy night ...

Prince Ruskin d'Auvergnon was a monster—a beast—even before the curse transformed him in physical appearance to match the countenance of his character. Born to a family of privilege, the palace and its staff were gifted to him on his fifteenth birthday. To say he was spoiled and cruel would be an understatement; it would be as if to say a rotting corpse was gray and foul. Of course, that would apply to the Prince as well—a sentiment that even now brings mixed emotions of repulsion and of satisfaction.

The Prince was in a particularly loathsome mood on the night my tale begins. A wild tempest blew outside, and the moans of the trees and beasts of the wood penetrated the stone walls we languished behind. He imbibed many goblets of wine and ale and, as the gale thundered against the castle, he thundered against us, his staff.

"Wretched Gods!" Ruskin shrieked at Pieter, a young valet. "My soup is boiling. Are you trying to scald me?"

He knocked the bowl off his table with a dismissive strike, and it shattered at Pieter's feet. Ruskin continued, "Have the kitchen make it again!"

Pieter nodded and fled to carry the Prince's displeasure.

I stood behind Ruskin with head bowed, waiting for his order. "And you, girl," he said. "You infect me with dejection. Your face droops like a withered sow. Are you that unhappy to stand in my presence?"

"No, my Prince," I replied.

"Good." His hand touched my thigh and slid inward.

I wanted to scream, to flee, but I knew my place. I suffered his grope and understood he would visit my small chamber that night while I lay dreaming of other lives.

Josef, a butler, approached from the main hall, excited and with hands upraised.

"There's a visitor at the door! It is an old woman, and she asks for shelter tonight from the storm."

"Send her away. I'm sure there is a pig sty nearby with vacancy."

Josef nodded and turned back the way he had come. The Prince ran one finger across the hem of my sash.

"The things I will do . . ." he whispered.

I shuddered. Josef returned, appearing uncertain.

"My Prince, the old woman says she has something to barter for your kindness."

Ruskin smirked. "What baubles do beggars have? A knit scarf or perhaps blessed pebbles?"

He stood, and we followed Josef to the main entrance. There were other servants in the grand hall, and they all bowed their heads as Ruskin passed. The front gate was open and under the storm stood a woman who appeared as old as the moon above. She hunched over, and one eye drooped so that it nearly touched the upturned corner of her drawn mouth. The other eye was large and wild, and it tracked Ruskin's steps to her.

"Please," she said. "I ask only for a bit of shelter tonight from the storm."

"I'm told you have something to barter," he coldly replied.

She paused and looked at us who stood helplessly behind the Prince. The old woman wore a cape, brown and tattered from the elements, and from underneath she pulled a single red rose. The flower glistened from drops of rain that speckled each pedal, and its stem curved beneath the corolla, rich green with pointed thorns, like the talons of a great bird.

"I have no money, but I give to you this rose, a token of the beauty found in life."

The Price laughed. "A rose? My gardens are filled with them. I own all the rose gardens in the land." He paused, then contemplated her. "Did you steal this rose from my garden?"

She startled at his accusation. "No, my Lord. I have carried this rose with me from far away."

"If you carried that rose from far away, it would be withered by now."

"It is unlike other roses. It's magical, and I offer it to you."

"The only thing that is magical is the extent of your arrogance. You thieve from me and try to peddle it back for my good graces!"

"My Lord, I swear—"

Ruskin slapped her across the face, and the old woman fell stunned to the ground.

"Please," she softly said.

"I should have my men call the hounds upon you."

She tried to stand, but trembled so that she fell to her hands and knees.

"Can you not even walk upright any longer?" Ruskin asked. "Has age stooped you to trot on four limbs like a beast? Be off, then! Gallop back to the den you crawled from."

And he laughed again. The sound climbed and echoed, as if each snicker reverberated off the drops of turquoise rain that fell. The old woman's face contorted, and I knew not if she was to cry or bellow at her tormentor. Instead, it melted and another face—a younger face—appeared.

A bolt of lightning flashed, and a crack of thunder sounded, and the Price's laugh shattered.

The woman rose, taller than Ruskin by a head. She spoke in voice that was deep in pitch and furious in tone.

"Wicked man. Your heart is dead to the world and your capacity for affection is like a dried husk that was formed hollow and has since withered away. For your punishment, you will be as vile in appearance as that of your character; a man who appears as death—still alive—but rotting as a corpse that is suspended in decay."

More lighting and thunder besieged us, and the sorceress's words wove throughout the fibers of the castle and all its inhabitants.

"You will covet the flesh you no longer possess and will seek to satisfy that craving by ingesting the flesh of others," she said.

As the sorceress decreed, the Prince morphed before our very eyes into living death. His skin turned gray as ash and floated from his once-mighty chest like flakes of bloody snow. Bones pushed through flesh that became thin and translucent as gossamer. And the smell—mercy on us all—caused great retching malaise amongst us, his indentured staff.

Though I bore no affection for my master, I was pained in horror for him. Regardless of his debased manner, he was not meant to suffer as such: touched by death, yet not fully taken.

The sorceress was not completed in the words of her curse.

"Serfs of this wicked man, pay heed. I cannot release you from your oath of servitude. In his undeath, as in his life, you will continue to attend your master. Since he now craves to devour flesh, I must enshroud you from his sight, so he does not consume you one-by-one."

I gasped and raised my hands to my mouth. Then I shrieked, for there were no hands before me. I felt normal as before, prior to her hex, but I was now invisible. I looked down at myself and saw only the cold slate I stood upon. The other servants cried as well in great clamor, so that we sounded as if ghosts haunted the castle foyer.

Ruskin fell to his knees and moaned, his tongue no longer able to articulate words. All that emitted from him were broken bleats, presumably the plea of mercy he surely begged for. Except for the sorceress, he now appeared alone, and they stared into each others' eyes.

"And now, you will take the rose I offered," she said. "For it contains your hope of deliverance. Within these pedals lie the essence of true love. You must find someone who will love you in your current state. Present them with this rose and, if they accept it with their heart and kiss you, the curse will be lifted. Until then, you will rot for your evil."

The sorceress turned and walked away into the forest, her long shadow flickering under bursts of lighting. Ruskin's fingers were stiff and gnarled, and he could barely grasp the rose she had forced into his hands. His jaw dropped open to emit a long moan, and I saw inside his mouth. It appeared as a cavern of horrors, with teeth that skewed like crooked stalagmites and covered with brown sludge such as which forms along the edge of chamber pots. I wondered how anyone could ever feel love enough to kiss that. I felt we were doomed to remain in the perpetuity of her curse for all eternity.

The Prince stumbled to his chambers. His gait slowed so he shuffled when he walked, like an old man, and he wept all the while.

The other servants and I dispersed throughout the castle, occasionally bumping into each other. We each dealt with our grief in different ways. I stared for hours into a mirror that reflected back to me only the opposite side of the room. Some snuck ale and drank away their despair. Some cried until the following morning. One of the kitchen staff leapt to his death from the top of a spired parapet. In death, he remained invisible.

It is the law and life for servants to care for their master regardless of circumstance. The oath is a solemn one and ingrained in our consciousness that we are bound to his duty, to serve and to protect him. Only if our master threatens the life of another, may we cause him harm and only by his word, or his death, may we be released from subjugation.

The next day the storm passed, and the sun dawned over timbered land. Though melancholy haunted my every thought, duty compelled me to engage in daily labor. I swept the halls and gathered flowers from the garden to place in the dining room. While outside, I saw the Prince's rose gardens and shuddered.

The other servants bustled about minding their own obligations. Though not seen, I heard the crash of pans as the cooks baked bread. I saw the Prince's silver lifted in the air and polished with utmost care. I heard the song of the laundrywomen as they cleaned and pressed our linen. Even in difficult circumstances, a semblance of normalcy returns quickly. It is a means of comfort to not dwell on terrible changes, but rather to lose oneself in the mundane activities that make the days pass quickly.

We did not forget, however, what the Price had become. The memory of him transforming to a beast of decay brands my mind with terror still to this day. Even so, the sight of him approaching from his quarters after the bell for breakfast sounded, caused such revulsion that my stomach cramped and I nearly disgorged its contents in heaving. I heard the exclamations and whispers and sounds of retching from others around me.

His chair pulled out for him, and I knew Pieter was there; that was his duty. The Ruskin-beast sat, and beads of amber fluid leaked from his mouth to splatter on the great table. Moments later, gold platters arrived bearing fruit and eggs and cream. The Prince stared at it all, then bellowed. His cry sounded of confusion and of hunger, yet he knocked the trays away without so much as a taste of the food presented.

I suddenly remembered.

"Dear mercy," I whispered. "It's flesh he wants. It's as the sorceress commanded; he craves only flesh."

Gasps filled the room, but they knew I was right.

We called out to the strongest of the servants, the stablemen and groundskeepers, and bade them new responsibilities. They agreed and, two hours later, returned with a wild hog hunted from the forest.

The animal was laid on the dining table, seeping blood from spear wounds. Ruskin squealed in delight. The silverware, carefully polished and laid in arrangement, were brushed aside. He clutched as the hog's carcass and bit down into its flank, so that sinews and muscles tore, snapping like the sound of cracking ice. If you have ever seen a feral dog tear into its kill, that is how Ruskin appeared as he burrowed his head into the creature, rending from side-to-side, while meat and fluids showered the floor.

The Prince's appetite was changed. No longer did the cooks

vex over the temperature of soup or if bread tasted too soft or too hard. All that was needed to feed him was flesh … and well-fed we kept him. When the Prince became hungry, he began to tremble and his eyes dilated, and we knew the lust fell upon him. Being invisible kept us safe from his sight, but we knew not what would happen if he caught hold of someone while in his craving. Each day we brought him pheasants and squirrels and deer and other animals caught from the forest and, in this way, he seemed content.

We lived as such for many years. They were not then—unlike now—truly terrible times. The sorceress's magical rose was placed in the palace vault for safekeeping, waiting for the day when Prince Ruskin might find true love. We became accustomed to him wandering the plush halls, moaning like a lost child, and we tended his affairs as customary. He was fed, and entertained, and his clothes washed daily to scrub off the decay, the rot. We grew accustomed to being unseen, though a numb sense of futility shrouded our thoughts, just as our sight was shrouded from the world. I took Pieter, the valet, to my bed and found a semblance of meaning from his touch. Being invisible is not so terrible while in a lover's embrace.

One stormy night a visitor arrived at the main gate, just as the sorceress had so long before. Josef, the butler, opened the heavy oak door. To the visitor, it must have appeared as if the door opened by itself.

There stood a young girl with frantic eyes and golden hair like spun straw. Her skin shone as porcelain, and I recognized her appearance as that of a debutante, though one who had not been cleaned or attended to in several weeks. She wore a lavender dress and a man's riding coat over that, both which were frayed and soiled from mud and elderberry thistles. Though her face bore fear and pain, I saw too the shadow of avarice when she first spied inside the castle's great hall, filled with crystal and gold.

She began to enter without invitation, when Josef's voice sounded. "Halt!"

"Let her in," I said. The Price, though still master of the palace, had long ago stopped issuing commands. "Haven't we learned enough of the perils of inhospitality?"

The girl gasped at our voices and turned quickly, looking for the source. "Why can't I see you?"

"We are invisible," I said. "Though otherwise, we are just as you."

She slowly stepped inside and gazed in wonder at the interior.

"What is your name, dear?" I added.

"Belle," she replied. "I became lost in the woods, and the storm came. I was so cold but saw the lights of the castle."

A moan from the Prince's chambers echoed through the great palace.

Belle gasped. "What was that?"

"That is our master. But fear not, we will keep him from you."

She looked again around the great hall. Lavish gold-framed paintings of the Prince and his parents adorned the walls, bordered by tapestries of royal silk.

"Is your master a prince?"

"He *is* a prince, though like none you have ever seen."

"I've seen *many* princes," she snapped back, as if I dared questioned her refinement. "They are not so different from the beasts in the woods. They take what they want and then roar and cry when they don't get their way."

If I were visible to Belle, she would have seen me smirk.

"Well then," I said. "A bit to eat perhaps?"

She nodded, and I saw in her manner that she was accustomed to being served. I suddenly imagined her sneering at her own valets and waiting staff, finding flaws in their presentation or even grooming choices. The crook of a nose or style of hair might elicit a cruel derision, and at that moment I felt thankful I was invisible from her sight. Were all the youth of royalty raised in such an arrogant manner? Her character mirrored the Prince's. Though I welcomed her in, I wondered how an aristocratic girl, brushing the edges of womanhood, could end up wandering lost in the forest.

I took her hand and led her to the dining hall, announcing as I went to the others that we hosted a guest.

I saw her admire the furnishings as we walked along: the cheval looking glass rimmed in rubies, the emerald sculptures, the scarlet rugs, the antiques collected from exotic lands.

"Pieter," I called out.

"I'm here."

"Please have the kitchen prepare a meal for our guest, venison if we have any left, stew, peaches, wine."

We arrived at the dining table and Belle startled, squeezing my hand tight. The table had not yet been cleaned since the Prince's last meal. The carcass of a large mongoose lay across, savagely torn apart. Broken ribs stuck out from the chest at all angles, as if an explosion occurred from within. Drops of blood and bits of flesh splattered across the floor.

"The master," I said, "has eaten here last."

She shuddered.

I continued. "Come. We will serve you in another room."

Over the following days, Belle remained, growing comfortable in the palace. The Prince maintained his regular routine of wandering the halls and dining when served. We kept Belle from his presence, for both their sakes. However, I knew the time would arrive that she would see him, and I feared for her sanity. I led her privately into the library to speak.

"My Lady," I said, as that was how she directed we now refer to her. "I'm pleased that we've been able to provide for you during your time of need."

"Yes, I find that it suits me here."

"However, surely, there are others that worry for your well-being. Perhaps the time has come for you to return to your own home."

She frowned and dark clouds seemed to pass across her blue eyes, as if a black tempest formed in the clear sky. "I no longer *have* a home."

"My Lady . . . was I misunderstood to believe that you are well-kept by your own people? I thought you were . . . a princess."

"It is true, I am, *was*, a princess. You wouldn't understand what it's like to be accustomed to only the finest luxuries of life. I was raised in privilege and expected to die in privilege. My parents were nobles and, not so long ago, I was bequeathed to Prince Horace, who was fat and had warts upon his brow like a toad. But his coffers flowed with gold ingots and diamonds the size of cherries. I bought anything I desired, and I was happy. Love, after all, is only an idea, whereas riches are the tangible resources of life, the means to gain anything one desires—power, prestige, adoration."

As she spoke, her convictions perplexed me but, perhaps it was as she prefaced: *I wouldn't understand what it was like to be accustomed to the finest luxuries of life.*

She continued. "Horace was a stupid man with no fortitude. We consummated the marriage on our wedding night and I never let him touch me again. His palace was mine, and I ran it as such. Unbeknownst to me, however, his wealth was a fraud. He had engaged in bad business, *investments*, and squandered our fortunes. In only a year, we lost our rights to the very land that the peasants revolted against us from. Horace owed to other kingdoms and they came and took everything, including him. Horace was sent to debtor's court and hanged. They came for me as well, but I escaped. I fled knowing that providence would aid me, for a true princess is not fated for squalor."

Unwittingly, Ruskin must have passed by the library as we

spoke. He managed to stifle his customary moans and stood in the doorway listening to Belle's tale. We both startled when he suddenly spoke.

He spoke no words, of course, but the Prince's voice rumbled in gargles and growls, and I imagined I comprehended what he tried to say. The intonation of his moans sounded of *welcome* and the excitement that radiated from his yellowed eyes registered the lust of attraction.

Belle, credit to her, did not shriek in horror at seeing the Prince, as I surely would have, should our circumstances been reversed. His blue-gray figure blocked the doorway, and his hands upraised, as if in greeting, to show gnarled, splayed fingers. I believe she suspected something of Ruskin's condition from his daily moans and the raw carcasses left from meals, and she must have steeled herself for the expected meeting. Even so, her eyes gave her away; they betrayed fear and disgust. Quickly, she corrected herself, and bowed to him.

Invisible hands from passing servants quickly took hold of the Prince and moved him along, perhaps thinking he meant to attack her. He was led away, presumably to feed.

"You spoke true," she whispered to me. "Your master *is* like none I have ever seen."

Though she had discovered the castle's secret, Belle remained. We could have removed her by force, but it was comforting to see another person, one who appeared as we once had. Her orders to us became increasingly more complex and arrogant, though there seemed no wish of hers that we had not previously fulfilled under Ruskin's voice. She required to bathe in water that was heated and kept precisely at ninety degrees. She demanded we tailor custom gowns from the most supple of silk and lace. She adored the Prince's roses and bid a fresh one be placed at her bedside each night.

She also ordered us to wear chimes around our necks so that

she was aware of our presence. Though I verbally complied, I wore
my chime only occasionally. I preferred to watch her unknown. I
dreamt I was Belle and I began to emulate the way she dismissed us
with her hand and the way she pursed her lips in the mirror. There
were none who could see my behaviors, but it aided my fancies, to
pretend I was someone else, someone beautiful and entitled. Once,
I spoke to Pieter as if I were her: *What do you know of the ways of
the world? You are but a sad boy locked away in servitude.*
Immediately I felt loathsome, as if a lake of slime formed within
my soul and its ooze overflowed from the weight of those words. I
quickly apologized and thanked the Gods I was not born to
nobility.

The Prince began to follow after Belle, shuffling from room to
room with the bleats of a lamb in pursuit of its mother. If he could
not find her, he bellowed with a ferocious howl and bared his
teeth, so that we feared the outcome of his wrath. They started to
dine together, facing one another across the long table. He would
tear apart the killed animals we brought him and bay with joy as
gore and innards dribbled from his mouth. It took only the sight
of blood or the scent of wound to bring upon the bloodlust that
twisted his face into a mask of uncontrollable frenzy. Belle would
watch, polite though visibly disgusted, as she nibbled at her own
foods, fruits and cream and grains. After seeing Ruskin eat for the
first time, she proclaimed vegetarianism. Belle knew, though she
lived in the castle as if it were her own, she was still only a guest at
Ruskin's whim. Should the mood strike, he could have her
dismissed, and so she treated him with all the distant affection and
courtesy she could muster.

Of course, the more attention she allowed the Prince, the
more he expected from her. I spoke of this with the other invisibles
and we wondered, what if ... *what if* ...

I took it upon myself to tell Belle everything. The sorceress had never indicated rules of confidentiality so, one night wearing my chimes, I sat by the Princess at her bedside bearing her nightly rose. I explained the curse, and I told her that only a kiss of love could return Ruskin to his rightful position as ruler of this land.

"A kiss? That is all?" she asked. "And he will be a man again, as he resembles in the paintings?"

"Yes," I replied. "But the kiss must be from the heart, it must be a kiss of true love."

"Of love," she repeated. "I will think on that."

I bid her goodnight and went to look in on Ruskin.

He was in his room, pacing in shuffle from wall to wall. He never slept . . . apparently rest was of no use to the rotting undead. His body or mind did not need to "refresh" itself or to conserve energy. He always moved, slow and methodically, like the gears of a clock that turn and turn and turn. His instinct seemed driven only to eat.

I watched him from my veil of imperceptibility. Ruskin stopped and sniffed the air once or twice, then continued his mindless pacing. The horror of his visage seemed, if possible, to have grown worse over the years. His features had sunk back into the hollows of his skull. Though we bathed him incessantly, maggots and dark beetles resided in burrows under his flesh where we could not reach. They darted in and out of his orifices and from the open wounds that festered on his body. Black fluids seeped from his ravaged muscles, as sweat might appear on a normal man, though I knew not what that fluid could be.

He paused at his open window and looked down upon the rose gardens that blossomed in the yard. Perhaps he contemplated their significance, reminding him of his arrogance and of his affliction. Perhaps, also, he remembered one rose in particular that held the remedy to his torment. He turned with a wet gurgle, as if crying, and began to pace again.

I knew not how circumstances might settle if left to their own accord and decided to nudge fate in the direction that seemed to favor all involved. I crept to the palace vault and carefully brought out the magical rose. I carried it to my quarters and waited until morning, when the Princess would awake, when a new dawn would rise for us who were cursed.

The morning bell rang for breakfast.

I was up in a flash and carried the rose to the dining hall where Ruskin and Belle would meet again for their morning meal.

Ruskin appeared first and staggered through the entrance as customary, shaking and moaning, trailing drops of slime like the residue of a slug. I held the rose to him which, in his eyes, must have appeared as if it floated. He gasped at its sight.

Belle emerged next, sauntering into the hall with dainty steps. She looked splendid in an azure silk robe and her hair was artfully arranged in wide curls that bounced with every movement. The Princess bore a shine to her face, a glow like sunrise that crests the horizon, and she looked every part of the title she held. I heard a quiet exclamation and elsewhere the sound of a chime, and I knew there were many other servants present.

I placed the rose into Ruskin's hand, and Belle knew from what I told her that the moment of her volition had arrived. She walked across the room to meet him, standing so that their faces were near to each other. He breathed unto her, a smell of wretched decay and wet death, but she did not flinch. We watched the encounter silently and unseen, as if the couple were the only two beings in all the palace.

Ruskin moaned and brought one gray arm to her side. His other arm trembled and, with great effort, he presented Belle the magical red rose. She sighed, for she knew he offered his heart and, with it, his world of privilege.

I knew then that Belle truly had grown to love Ruskin. She loved him not for his appearance or his charm or his kindness, but for his wealth and his land and his title. She so greatly loved those things that were of the Prince, she was able to overlook the abomination of his living death. It is the same as any other quality to love someone by. Appearance, generosity, or wit may all fade away just as easily as wealth, and according to the circumstances of life we can never entirely control. Such is the truest love of all: To cherish what you value in a person that you are able to accept their flaws.

The moment was enchanting. Even now, I do not doubt the wonder and sincerity I felt that two like-souls could find each other in such circumstances.

She took the red rose from Ruskin, and a thorn on its stem pricked the tip of her thumb. Belle grimaced for an instant, then forgot it, and leaned in to kiss the Prince, her lips parted in sweet expectation. But on her thumb a drop of blood welled up, red as the pedals of the flower.

Ruskin's nostrils flared, and he looked at that single drop of red, shining so bright against her porcelain skin. I saw him shudder and watched the change in his expression as one who salivates at the aroma of fine stew. His chest heaved, and Belle thought that to mean he was overcome by passion.

It is true he was overcome by passion, but it was no longer for her love. O! The cruel irony of fate! Had she pricked her finger only afterward, they would have kissed, and the curse lifted. Instead, she wrapped herself around him, and their mouths grew close.

Ruskin bit off her lip, and she screamed.

That sound of Belle will remain with me all my days. It was a cry so terrible, I can only liken it to the heavens being rent from the horizon and raked across with iron spikes. Her shrieks were unearthly and equaled in terror and pain and betrayal.

She tried to push away from him, but it was too late. Their arms were entwined and, as she turned her head to beg for help, he chewed into her cheek.

We shouted in horror, the other servants surely feeling the same sense of rage and defeat as I. We were close—so close—to having the sorceress's curse removed from us all! Perhaps we then acted in loathing of the Prince for causing our invisibility. Perhaps it was years of our pent-up anger and suffering. Perhaps it was a sense of conscience to rescue Belle from his attack. As the rules of vassalage are written, a servant may never harm his master unless that person is jeopardizing the life of another. Whatever the motivation, we acted in unison.

Chimes tinkled, and a fireplace poker rose from the mantel and swung down to smash Ruskin across the back of his head. He grunted and released Belle. A loose brick ascended from the hearth and hurtled into his face. More chimes sounded, as if a choir, and glass jars, chair legs, or anything else that could be used as a weapon were taken by invisible hands and brought to crash down on the Prince. He wailed and flung his arms to fend the blows, understanding our betrayal but unable to see his assailants.

Ruskin caught someone who rushed too close. I did not know who, but saw him bite down and heard a cry of pain. An iron mace was brought forward and it bashed Ruskin's skull repeatedly until his head looked like a wet sponge, twisted and wrung. The Prince collapsed, and someone drove a steel bar through his temple, so that it pierced the other side and impaled into the floor he sprawled upon.

His appearance was no longer deceptive. Prince Ruskin d'Auvergnon was now truly dead.

And then a wonderful thing happened. Our affliction by the curse lifted; we appeared visible again! A great cheer went up, and I fell to my knees in gratitude. I thanked the sorceress—blessed her—for the release of our penance. The servants laughed and ran to embrace each other, remarking how they had not aged one day throughout the many years we lived under the spell. As it was, it seemed our tragedy would bear a happy ending.

Of course, happy endings are only for fairy tales.

I saw that one of us did not cheer for our liberation. It was Pieter, and he suffered from a gaping hole across his neck. It was he whom Ruskin bit, and my excitement turned to despair. Pieter lay next to Belle, and he cried as blood poured between his fingers.

I ran to him and so did several others. There was nothing we could do. His jugular vein was torn, and Pieter—my love—died in my arms. My heart felt crushed, as if mountains of jagged rock collapsed over my spirit.

Belle mumbled some incoherent words and then she also died.

We decided to bury all three of them right away. We would dig two graves: one for Pieter at the edge of the forest, and one for Ruskin and Belle to share beneath the garden of roses. I hoped the dead would find satisfaction in their final arrangements.

Several men dug and the laundrywomen sang hymns while the bodies were brought out and laid on fine cloth. I spoke kind words over them all, and two men bent to lift Belle first into the grave.

Her eyes opened. She made a choking sound, as if trying to speak through a mouth filled with molasses. The shock went through us all. Belle's wounds seemed ghastly, but she was alive! I should have known: As the Princess's will for nobility was indomitable, so was her will for survival.

Josef knelt to her and spoke in reverence. "The Gods have given you new life."

She looked at him from eyes that were pale and speckled with red like the spotted mushrooms that sprout under dead logs. Then she bit deep into his forearm.

Josef cursed and stumbled backward. Belle hissed at him, then grabbed for one of the maids. I screamed, and my screams echoed from behind by others. Turning, I saw Pieter rise from the earth and tear into a stableman. Men rushed to Pieter and Belle and kicked at them with heavy boots. The women fled, and I joined them. We had no weapons outside, where we mourned and buried those we thought dead. I looked back to see Pieter catch one of the men and tear into the flesh above his knee.

We were frantic. Had we known better, we would have fought them then. We would have gathered arms and hunted down each man and woman who was bit. We would have cut off their heads and burned their bodies to ash, and killed any animal or bird that appeared to eat of their remains. But we did not realize then the effect of the sorceress's curse could evolve into such apocalypse. I wonder if she even realized it herself. The consequences of her spell were transmutable through bites, through saliva or blood, to infect others with the living death that plagued Prince Ruskin.

I and the other remaining servants locked the front gate and barricaded ourselves in the castle. From the ramparts, I looked out into the yard that stretched between the rose gardens and the wild forest. I saw Josef and the others who were bit transform into creatures of rot. They shambled around the walls of the castle and, finding no way in, dispersed into the shadows of the woods, driven by hunger for flesh.

Three days later, other undead men appeared at the castle gate. They were hunters, I suspected, and probably the first men that Belle and the rotting servants would have come across in the woods. After them, appeared more cursed men and women, dressed in the faded cloth of villagers from far away. They circled the castle, and roamed senselessly through the gardens, then returned to the mysteries of the forest.

We, the surviving servants, are once again trapped in the castle. We dare not leave for fear of the things that now live in the woods. Our stores run slim, and we ration carefully. How many more weeks or months we may survive here is a mystery, as is wondering how many of the undead now wander the land.

O! Do I pray for the sorceress to return. I call for her nightly when the rain falls, and I promise her such sweet shelter to pass the hours of the moon. I cry out to the world that the Prince is dead and plead for us all to be absolved of her spell. I weep and shout and, when my voice finally grows hoarse, I collapse and whisper for the sorceress to pity me, to at least make me invisible again ... to at least return me to a guise where I am unseen, so I can walk away from this palace of gold and never look back.

But the sorceress does not return. The undead creatures—the beasts—multiply in number. The curse of Prince Ruskin d'Auvergnon is not yet concluded.

Whispers of the Earth

THE DAY WAS MARCH 25, AND IT WAS THE TENTH anniversary of his wife's death.

That day—today—was etched into his mind as permanently as the letters that spelled Hannah's name on the slab of stone in Franklin Cemetery. Her memory would never leave him, but most days he could push it behind him like a signpost he'd driven past and could only faintly make out in the receding distance. Of course, as this day drew nearer, the distance he travelled from that signpost seemed to reverse, and he watched it, like a thing in the rearview mirror, returning closer and closer.

Lyle knew today would be worse than her other death anniversaries, and that knowledge did not deceive. Ten years, after all, was the same amount of time they had been wed. Tomorrow she'd be dead longer than they were together. Married at thirty. Dead at forty. Alone at fifty.

For none of us liveth to himself, and no man dieth to himself.

The words of Pastor Scott, who found it necessary to repeat the passage in simplified terms: *Hannah's love will continue on in the memories of those she touched.*

If Lyle were a vessel for the Lord—as Pastor Scott said—then it was true she would live forever in him, hovering in the back of his thoughts, sharing his intimate struggles, whispering sweet memories of their life together.

Whispering his name.

Lyle, she said. *I miss you so much . . .*

He knew she did miss him, as he missed her. She said as much in his thoughts. Hannah's death was never reconciled, never explained. Pastor Scott spoke of his grief, warned him not to question God's will, to have faith in her absence, to accept that her body was taken back to the earth.

I'm all alone . . . somewhere, lost in the earth . . .

Another reason he could never lay her memory entirely to rest was knowing that stone slab at Franklin Cemetery was a formality, an afterthought. It jutted from a grave filled only with roots and dirt and a lie. Hannah's body had never been found.

The Lord giveth and the Lord taketh away . . .

Her voice sounded stronger today, and he almost spoke out loud in reply. Almost caught himself chatting like a madman to the blue sky above. No one would blame him, of course, but speaking to your dead wife after ten years was a slippery slope. Once you started, it became ordinary, and he knew men that turned odd from lesser cause.

The morning was bright and clear, and Lyle walked the acres of his property recalling good memories. He smelled vanilla in the air, and it was as if her voice became an aroma, filling his nostrils. Every morning she had placed a drop of vanilla oil on the sides of her neck, which he breathed in deep whenever he leaned in to kiss her.

He passed through rows of apple trees and out the other side, and the green pasture land before him shone with sparkles of light as if the world reflected through an emerald. The land was beautiful, and he thought again of Hannah.

The great black hole that lay open in the earth before him was so unexpected he did not immediately register it. Lyle almost walked right in as if that was his plan all along, before yelping and jumping away from the sinking edge.

"God a'mighty," and his face turned pale as ice. He apologized in silence for taking the Lord's name in vain and stared until his mouth nearly fell open as wide as the chasm in the ground.

It was a giant sinkhole, a dozen feet across, and appearing as an elevator shaft that dropped so far down the sun above would never penetrate the darkness of its black depths.

Lyle occasionally read in the newspapers about sinkholes opening up, some so large a city block could fall into them. Most, though, only dropped ten or twenty feet as if that part of the earth's mantle was just the skin of a popped, shallow bubble. He thought he might go mad staring into this hole that, somehow, he discerned as bottomless. The rim of the sinkhole was smooth, too, like a cartoon hole lacking the rough edges that are expected by the ground's occasional movements.

He heard her whisper again, but this time could not be sure if it truly was in his mind, or somehow floated up from the descent of the hole.

I'm here . . .

LYLE CALLED INTO Dunbar City Hall and waited on hold nearly twenty minutes before the clerk finally answered.

"This is Marty Simmons. Sorry for the wait."

"I was startin' to think the city forgot I pay taxes to keep it running."

"Hey, Lyle, it's been a lunatic morning, here. Folks calling in since we opened, until I thought the city woke up with a case of the bat-shit crazies. Anyway, I can guess what you're calling about."

"It's some fright when you're strolling along and nearly fall down a pit that decided to open shop on your land."

"I understand. You're not the only one this happened to."

"There are others?"

"We've been getting calls from all over the city. A sinkhole opened next to Tom Grady's house, and another on Liz Townsend's farm. Got reports from Charles Halloway, John Clark, and a handful of others. One sinkhole opened up on Stephen Brown's land that three of his heifers fell into. He can't hear a cry from any of them, they fell so deep. Hell, one hole even opened up right behind Cornerstone Baptist Church."

"I never heard of the ground turning to Swiss cheese before," Lyle said.

"Nor I. Now you know why it took so long to get your call. Liz Townsend's in hysterics, she even says she heard a voice from the hole on her farm, like maybe someone tumbled in."

"City have any plans about what'll be done to fix this, or should I just build an outhouse over it?"

Marty chuckled, then paused. "I'll make a report for you. Suppose we can hold a meeting tomorrow for everyone affected. Find out who's got it worse and go from there. The news already reached Pittsburg, and some reporters are coming in today."

"And so the vultures found a new scrap to feed on."

"They love to spit on our wounds. Never come around when we're prospering, but if there's an accident, suddenly the news crews appear, calling us superstitious on one hand and cursed on the other."

"Any thoughts as to what may have caused these holes?" Lyle asked.

"Dunno. Maybe an earthquake. Maybe groundwater eating away at the bedrock beneath us. Remember the sinkhole in Allentown last year? Half the city was evacuated for fear the earth was caving in. That's what's going to happen here, mark my words."

"It'll take more than a hole on my property to make me pack it up."

"We'll see. Anyway, pal, I've got the next call waiting on hold. Stop by tomorrow and we'll chat."

After Lyle hung up, the morning didn't seem as bright and clear as earlier, before he nearly walked into the sinkhole. The sky was still blue, as it so often is in southern Pennsylvania, but he discerned a fine veil seeming to drape over his corner of the land. There were murmurs in his thoughts that didn't resemble his own, and a chill touched his skin.

He didn't want to be alone in the house today, amongst the dusty memories and sense of foreboding. As empty as it was, he would pay his respects at Hannah's grave, then fill the day with chores and errands to keep his mind from dwelling on troubles.

And that's what he did.

THE BED SEEMED LARGER than ever that night, a great expanse of stuffing and blankets that, instead of providing comfort, only accentuated the emptiness. Lyle lay with his hands crossed behind his head, resting on the same side he had always lain, him on the right and Hannah on the left. On the far wall, past the void she once filled, a window gaped open, and he heard the late-night critters of the land, the crickets and owls and coyotes.

He heard, too, a woman's voice, like the drifting shreds of a kite, torn and blowing without direction between the tree branches.

. . . no man dieth to himself, she said.

He sat up and cocked his head trying to filter out that voice amongst the other nighttime noises. Hannah's memory had nestled up cozy in the back of his head today, whispering to him louder and louder, and he began to doubt the distinction between what intoned amongst his thoughts and what sounded in reality. A distant dog barked at some unseen foe, and rustling tree limbs pushed against each other. A gust of wind scattered dry leaves against the window, some floating through to land on the floor like discarded broken relics. Lyle found himself wondering what existed in the night, what rose while men slept and moved amongst the mountain's enigmas.

He had lived in Dunbar all his life, the city nestled far into the base of the Allegheny Mountains' green and silver range. There were things in those mountains that the rest of the world never heard about, but Lyle knew since boyhood. There was a man of green light who lived inside Dante's cave, and if you saw him you went blind. A pair of creatures that were half-horse, half-bear lived in the woods on the far end of Hunter's Loop and if you strayed into their lair under a full moon, you'd never stray back out. Goblins and shades and talking beasts all lived within a day's hike of Dunbar, and Lyle knew their exploits. Anything could exist in that territory where Indians once fought using dinosaur bones. Of course, some of those things were mired in superstition, while only one or two were hard-truth, but where myth ended and fact began was like trying to measure the distance of a fart in a whirlwind.

Great are the mysteries of the world, he thought. *But know, too, that God has a place for all things and though we may not understand, it is not for us to question his reasons.*

He closed his eyes, inducing the ritual of memories that preceded sleep.

The woman's voice sounded again, louder this time, more clear. *And to Earth we shall return . . .*

Lyle scrambled to the window and leaned out. "Someone out there?"

The moon cast long shadows pulling each tree into a stick giant. Things pattered and moved in the night, and he smelled the slightest fragrance of vanilla.

Lyle . . .

He got into his trousers and shirt quick as a whistle and dashed outside with his Coleman lantern.

"This is private property," he called out to the stars. "If you need something, you'd best name yourself."

I've been waiting...

This time the voice sounded muffled, as if sinking. It drifted from the apple orchards or, perhaps, what lay on the other side of the orchards. He swung the lantern across the path of trampled grass that led into the trees.

"If you're ribbin' me, I'll knock you into Tuesday," he shouted.

The voice did not reply, and that worried him more than if it continued speaking from the gloom. Was it Hannah's voice in his head, getting louder as if finding a way to break through the aural barrier of his consciousness into the real world?

Something moved in the darkness, a leathery whisk of flight and a shaking branch. Lyle crossed between the apple trees and it flew past with a whoosh. He waved the Coleman and spotted a small bat darting after the glowing tails of fireflies.

The scent of vanilla grew stronger. It was a hypnotic fragrance, an alluring tug that suggested he close his eyes and float along the stream of memories. He kept walking, following it past the apple orchards.

Lyle...

He found himself standing again at the lip of the sinkhole. The lantern shone past its smooth edges into a darkness that somehow was twice as black as the midnight sky above.

Come to me, as we are one...

The misery and loneliness of ten years felt as if it sloughed off like caked dirt under a hot shower. He felt lighter, calmer, as if he had a purpose, a destination.

I've missed you...

The voice was real, was Hannah's, and he wondered at his sanity, if he had, perhaps, even gone crazy long ago, and the sinkhole was really a tunnel dug through his own brain by grief.

He stepped nearer to its edge, so close a tap from behind might propel him forward, and he searched for her face within the ebony nothingness.

How long did it take a body to decompose back into the elements it sprang from? How long for a body crushed and buried to dissolve under the moving earth until its bones became soft as soot and guts the fertilizer for plants.

What did Pastor Scott say? *Earth to earth, ashes to ashes, dust to dust . . .*

She was the earth now, and she called to him.

He leaned forward.

Lyle . . .

The voice seemed to pull him in but, on the brink of surrender, he threw himself backward landing on his ass in the cold grass. The Coleman clattered aside, pointing a beam across the sinkhole.

What am I doing? He thought, and scrambled farther away. *She ain't down there, it's been ten years.*

He looked up to the crescent moon and sprawl of stars, as if searching for a sign.

Lyle retrieved the lantern and rushed back to his house. He thought her voice chased him from behind the apple orchards, like a child's game of tag, but he willed himself to stop listening. Once inside, he locked the doors and closed the windows and opened his Bible for answers, wondering if he fled from the one thing he regularly begged God to return.

LATE THE NEXT MORNING, Lyle drove around the winding mountain roads and into Dunbar. Parking was crowded in front of city hall's red brick facade, most of the spaces filled by out-of-town cars and a couple large news vans decorated with satellite dishes and tall antennas.

He parked and got out and walked to the building's glass front doors. Marty Simmons approached from behind, smoking a Marlboro.

"Don't let those reporters know you've got a hole on your land," he said.

"They makin' a big deal of it?" Lyle asked.

"Bigger than you know." He took a drag and exhaled in a blue-gray cloud. "Walk with me."

They turned away from city hall and strode down the sidewalk toward the gazebo next to Dunbar's library.

"Where's everyone else?" Lyle asked. "Thought we were going to have a meeting."

"Most folks are staying away while the media's sittin' here."

"They sure know how to turn bad into worse."

Marty nodded, and a sprinkle of cigarette ash fell onto his collared shirt. "Remember I told you a sinkhole opened up right behind the church?"

"I do."

"It was a big hole, Lyle, big enough to drive a full-size truck into, and I don't know how deep it went. I was out there yesterday morning after I talked with you. I tossed a rock down and never heard it hit bottom."

"Sounds like what I've got."

"The hole is gone."

"Gone, like filled in?"

"Filled in, closed up, whatever you want to call it. It's gone, and there ain't even a hint there ever was a hole. No depression in the land, no cracks in the earth. The grass is growing green and cut short like a lawnmower just went over it last week."

"That don't make sense."

"Exactly. I went back out there this morning with the sheriff and the news crews. They wanted to film one of our sinkholes, and what better for sensationalism than showing Cornerstone Baptist Church as the backdrop?"

"Of course, so they can remind us of ten years ago."

"Pastor Scott was going to meet us by the hole, too, but never showed. I asked around and nobody's caught a trace of him since yesterday. He was supposed to have dinner last night with the mayor but never arrived. It's like he vanished."

"You think something happened to him?"

"I don't know, but the sheriff sent a few men to look around. The reporters started questioning the sinkhole reports as a hoax, but I'm taking them out to investigate Liz Townsend's farm next. They're talking with some council members right now. Anyway, I'd suggest steering clear of the pack—the media's like a sick dog, and you never know who they're going to crap on."

"Thanks for the advice."

Marty stubbed out the cigarette on the banister rail of the gazebo. He looked around to make sure no one was watching, then flicked the butt into the street.

"Ain't littering if the sweeper's coming by tomorrow," he said.

Lyle shrugged.

Marty went on. "Another thing, and you might think my screw is turning loose, but it hasn't got past me that mudslide disaster was ten years ago to the day."

"Nature's got cruel timing."

"I don't think it's a coincidence."

"The sinkholes?"

"Lyle, it ain't just the hole on *your* land. It's all the sinkholes. Remember, I'm the one logging the reports. I told you some of who were affected ... it's the families of those who were carried away."

"Go on."

Marty lifted a hand and began ticking away fingers. "Tom Grady's got a hole alongside his house. Like you, he lost his wife at that picnic. I catch him crying sometimes, when he's sitting alone at the diner. Then there's Liz Townsend, whose husband, Eddie, was taken. She holds onto the past like a girl clutches her toy doll; they're inseparable. Remember that no trace of Stephen and Ruth Brown's two sons was ever found, 'cept a penny loafer caught on a tree limb. Charles Halloway lost his sister and John Clark lost his parents. Ain't a one of them ever fully recovered. And a dozen others from that day—They've all got sinkholes on their land."

"That's a heavy load. But what does it mean?"

"I don't know. Think about Pastor Scott who put the picnic together. If the Lord was assessing faith that day, Scott was tested the greatest. He lost his wife and all three daughters to that mudslide. A sinkhole appeared alongside his church."

"And now it's gone."

"And so is he," Marty said. "All these years he preached to us, saying those killed were in a better place. But I know it was eating him up inside. It's a Catch-22: He couldn't curse the Lord or question His almighty will for their deaths, otherwise he won't end up in the Heaven he believes his family is waiting at."

Lyle shook his head.

Marty continued. "So Pastor Scott kept preaching at the pulpit, smiling and saying it's all part of a grand plan, everything happens for a reason and it's not our place to question why. If Scott believed that, perhaps he saw the sinkhole as a message, another test of his faith."

"That's a big leap you're suggesting."

"And maybe it brought him back to his family in some way. Or, maybe, I'm just making too much of this, framing crazy assumptions like the reporters."

"Nothing sounds too crazy to me," Lyle said. "That pit on my land isn't natural."

Up the street, people began to exit city hall, milling around cars and talking on cell phones.

"Looks like it's time to get back," Marty said. "I'll see what happens at Liz Townsend's farm."

"Let me know. In the meantime, think I'll check on the Browns' myself."

HE HEARD HER after the mudslide hit, after the crashing thunder of earth silenced and shock passed like a crack of lightning. In that spare second before the others started screaming, he heard her voice from the mud and debris.

"Lyle!"

Then the shrieks sounded, and the pleas, and people scrambling to unbury themselves or their loved ones. It was a dervish of neighbors and fellow parishioners digging through the sludge, shouting for help, ordering commands, moaning, crying.

And he tried to tell everyone to shut up. He nearly wished the panicked and wounded were all dead, so in their silence he could hear Hannah, follow her voice to where the avalanche took her. But the wailing around him increased, and the others thought they heard their own parents and spouses and children crying from under the mud, and everyone then shouted louder, trying to bellow over the others, so that Lyle never heard her voice again.

The morning before the disaster was good, such as days can be when begun with turquoise skies and the whistle of wrens and a plate of pancakes steaming in the cold spring dawn. Her smell of vanilla oil broke through the warm maple syrup and they ate together commenting on what they did yesterday and what they would do today.

That afternoon was to be Cornerstone Baptist Church's annual picnic, set on the shore of McGowan's Lake under the shade of the Allegheny Mountains. Lyle and Hannah almost didn't go, as it was a Saturday afternoon and Lyle wanted to plant and Hannah needed to pick up some camera equipment from Pittsburgh. But the absence from church events is conspicuous in small towns and they knew what sort of comments might be made from behind-the-hand mutters.

So they arrived at the picnic early, in order to stake a location overlooking the cold lake's cyan face. There may have been a hundred people in attendance that bright afternoon. Kites came out and children ran amongst trees. Tables were set with red-and-white gingham and platters shared of fried chicken, coleslaw, baked beans, and cobbler. Lyle and Hannah sat with Stephen and Ruth Brown and laughed at long-running jokes. Pastor Scott spoke to each in attendance, commenting on the chicken's flavor or a mother's pretty dress. Scott's wife picked flowers with a group of children.

Then a rumble sounded and the earth shook, and the world seemed to crack in half. It was early spring and the snow runoff had loosened the slope of Hardy Hill. With a shattering detonation, the slope slid down in a great wave of mud and rock and swept away the picnickers.

In that spare second after the earth settled and before the survivors started screaming, he heard her voice from the sludge and debris.

"Lyle!"

LYLE STOOD WITH Stephen and Ruth Brown and looked deep into the sinkhole on their pastureland. The hole was identical to his own, as if the chasms were born as twins, each about twelve feet across and cut perfectly into the earth like someone drilled cylinders straight into the ground.

"Can you hear them?" Stephen Brown asked in a voice so tiny, mice could have roared louder.

Lyle shook his head. The hole may have led to another universe for the depth it appeared to fall.

"They're our sons," Ruth said. "They're callin' to us from down there."

He looked at each of the Browns, then back into the hole. Lyle didn't know if coming here was a mistake or a vindication of his sanity. At least he knew he wasn't the only one listening to voices that weren't there. He shook his head again. "I don't hear anything."

Ruth sobbed and Stephen almost did too. "We've still got his shoe, Jeremy's little shoe. He's down there with a bare foot."

"What do your boys say?"

"They're looking for us. They miss us. They say, 'Where are you, Mommy and Daddy?'"

Stephen reached around his wife's shoulders, and she turned her head against his chest and held him tight.

"I can't say whether you're imagining it or not," Lyle said. "I hear Hannah on my own land."

Ruth spoke into her husband's chest. "Pastor Scott said the same about his own family."

Stephen nodded. "I was at the church yesterday afternoon. I saw the sinkhole, and Pastor Scott stood so close on its edge his toes hung over. He told me they were down there, all of them, his wife and three daughters. He said, 'The Lord was giving them back. The earth would make them a family again.'"

"Pastor Scott's disappeared," Lyle said.

"I know. A deputy came by a bit ago, asking when I saw him last. He tried to tell me there wasn't any hole on the church grounds at all. But it was there. I saw it."

"I believe you. Marty Simmons saw it too."

"Maybe they weren't supposed to have been taken from us that day. Or maybe we were supposed to have joined them. Maybe whoever plans these things made a mistake. But that hole is speaking to us. It's telling us our boys are down there," Lyle said. "I'm going in. I'm going to find our sons, no matter how far down they've fallen."

Lyle thought obligation should compel him to convince Stephen otherwise, tell him it was madness to climb into that pit looking for people who were missing—surely dead—for ten years. It was duty to talk a friend out of doing something that would likely lead to injury or worse.

But, at the same time, he believed them to be right. And what he wanted most that moment was to return home, because he then believed Hannah really was there, calling for him from the darkness of *his* sinkhole. He decided such, because she didn't call for him on the Browns' land—here, her voice was silent. Here, it was the sinkhole only for the Browns' sons. This was no trick of his brain, no phenomena of his surroundings. She called for him from one place only, that place she was taken, as she had called for him the day of the picnic . . .

NIGHT FELL AS IT DOES at every day's end, and Lyle sat on his porch listening. She was out there, whispering to him.

Come to me, Lyle.

He had a decision to make, but he let it stretch out before him, allowing the moment to simmer, listening to Hannah's words as if she sat on the porch alongside him.

I've been waiting such a long time . . .

If he decided her return was a transgression against natural order, he could simply leave and didn't think she would follow. Lyle considered that whatever caused the earth to open up its secrets for him was a one-time offer. Whether it was the Lord's choice or a trick, she was here and here only. If he left, he would never hear her voice again.

Or he could find her. She *was* down there, like all the other people killed that afternoon by McGowan's Lake, returned to collect their loved ones. Without Hannah, there wasn't much in the world that kept him going, no other family or opportunities, just gray age and loneliness. Was it different for any of the others from that church picnic? Had they ever stopped grieving, or did it matter? Maybe it wasn't just the survivors who grieved all these years, maybe it was the dead, too, stolen from the sunshine and arms of their loved ones, buried under the mud and never found.

Until now.

Lyle...

The Lord giveth and the Lord taketh away, he thought.

He thought also of the message saved on his phone. Lyle had arrived home from the Browns' farm and saw the blinking green light on his answering machine. It was Marty Simmons.

Stay away from the sinkhole, Lyle. Whatever it is you think you hear, stay away. Liz Townsend is missing, the hole behind her farm is gone. I saw her earlier today with the reporters, and she swore her dead husband was calling. Now John Clark is missing and Charles Halloway. The holes on their grounds are closed up, too, like they never existed. Something took them away. It ain't natural, Lyle, not to hear someone who's been buried ten years. Listen to me, call me, come back to town. Just stay away from that hole.

But Marty was only another voice now, like Hannah, a murmur without physical form, a ventriloquism speaking from the chasm of his mind.

We're all just earth, after all...

He found it took less time than ever to make his way across the yard, through the apple trees, and out the other side into the pasture. He brought the Coleman to light his way, though he didn't need it. He could close his eyes and she would lead him to the brink of reunion. Vanilla curled around his limbs and the moon split in two.

When Lyle again looked upon the black sinkhole, he realized it wasn't a sinkhole at all, and he wondered how he ever thought different. It was a mouth, and her lips began to rise from the edges of its opening, parting slightly to show the curve of a coral-pink tongue.

The contours of the ground flexed and eddied as if made of soft mud, and Hannah's mouth moved, opening wider. Her lips pursed, bulging from the land in prodigious mass, and she spoke.

Come to me.

The night critters were silent. He no longer heard their chirps or howls or croaks.

Earth to earth, ashes to ashes, dust to dust.

He saw a vision of himself sitting on the porch, contemplating the years since Hannah's death, when a crash sounded and a mudslide roared from the night stars to carry him away. He was wrong to think he would be allowed to leave; he could never escape the earth.

So he leaned in to kiss her lips the way he did every morning after she placed a drop of vanilla oil on the sides of her neck.

I've missed you . . .

Lyle knelt, and vanilla-scented mud gathered at his feet.

He was sucked into the hole before he could say goodbye. He fell through memories and dreams and thought he heard Stephen Brown calling for his sons.

Whether he was dead or insane, touched by God or called by Hannah, he couldn't say. He wondered why the voice in his head turned silent.

The faraway sky vanished and the sinkhole closed its lips and Lyle was swallowed into the earth.

A Serving of Nomu Sashimi

TERRY SIGHED, CURSED. HE RAN HIS SALES REPORT for the fifth time that night.

His numbers were low. Too low. The amount of business he brought in should have surpassed every other sales representative on the floor, but instead he was down. *Again.*

It was 7:00 on a Friday night, and he knew he should go home, relax, watch a movie with Shannon. But then he reconsidered the sales report . . .

Low-performing reps didn't last long in commission-driven careers. He'd been working at Global Bank for a year and had never busted his hump so hard, but he could not catch up with the others. Compared to his co-workers, he was a flop.

The door to Dean Kleggman's office opened and the others poured out, laughing and high-fiving each other: Dean, Brett Cohen, and Marc Buchs, the top three sales reps at Global Bank.

"—so then I told Bitzy Carole that if the players were reversed, he'd be driving a *hatchback*!" Dean bellowed laughter, and Marc fist-pumped into the air.

"And wait until you see the swing!" Brett added. They doubled over in hysterics.

Dean, Brett, and Marc had ridden the top three sales spots since Terry started working at Global. He couldn't come close to producing the volume of any one of them, and it drove him half-insane with frustration.

"Yo, T-Man," Brett called across the floor to him. "What're you still doing here this late? Working hard or hardly working?"

They guffawed with a sound like belching turkeys.

Terry made a face that he hoped looked like good-natured sincerity. "Gotta put in the extra hours to catch you boys."

His remark made them laugh even harder.

"It'll never happen, buddy." Marc said.

Terry's fake-smile faltered. "I'll find my way into your ranks. I don't give up."

Dean winked at Marc. "Sure. You'll get real far with tenacity and low numbers."

Brett shook his head. "I don't know, maybe it's time Terry came out with us. Learn how to close some *big* biz."

"What're you saying?" Dean asked. He punched Brett in the shoulder. "I thought we agreed not to tell anyone else."

"It's okay. I think Terry's a good guy, and we could use another top earner around here to pump up the investors' confidence." He paused. "You can keep a secret, can't you T-man?"

Terry nearly leapt from his cubicle chair. He knew sales reps kept to a hierarchy within the company, and the elite associated with each other after hours; success mingled with success. Shannon might be a little upset that he was going out—probably to drink—but this might be the opportunity he'd been waiting for, a chance to bump up his numbers.

"Of course I can keep a secret."

"Then c'mon," Brett said. "We're going out for sushi."

TWENTY MINUTES LATER, Terry sat in Marc's Mercedes with the others. They sped through a labyrinth of darkening city streets.

Dean chattered from the front as they drove. "You think you've had sushi before, but this isn't like anything you've ever eaten."

"It's not *really* sushi 'cause it's not from the sea," Marc said.

"True. But sushi's the closest comparison." Dean turned back in the seat to look directly at Terry. "It's exclusive."

"Really exclusive," Brett added. "If not for us, you wouldn't get in."

"And if there are any problems, you won't be coming back."

Terry nodded. He felt a pang of nerves and wondered if he should have stayed back at the office. He wanted to improve his presence on the sales floor, though personally couldn't stand any of these blowhards. "You're talking to me like a kid," he said. "I can handle anything you bring."

"Sure, just like the Constance deal, right?"

Terry grimaced. Last month his biggest project collapsed, and his commission went into arrears.

"Don't worry," Brett said. "After tonight, those things won't happen to you anymore. Just stick with us."

"*If* he can handle it," Marc said. "Remember Lance Thompson?"

"If he turns into another Lance, I'm finding a new restaurant."

The name sounded familiar to Terry. He thought back to when he first started working at Global Bank and realized with a sense of dread that he was hired as Lance Thompson's replacement.

The car slowed, and for the first time Terry studied where they were driving. Neon marquee bulbs flashed pink and white as they passed recessed shop doorways and covered windows, each with placards offering specialties in languages he couldn't understand, though the pictures left no doubt as to what unsavory pleasures lay within. They were deep in neighborhoods he normally tried to avoid, and the dread that coiled in his gut grew stronger.

Marc parked in the shadows of an alley, and the four of them made their way to a plain metal door embedded in a brick wall.

Dean pounded on the door and an eye slot opened. "We're here for Yuki," he said and stuffed a pile of bills through the slot.

The door opened and they entered. Terry thought the building's interior appeared as another world, all red.

He saw gold trimming on the bar and frames of menu boards, and there were hints of black and white, but otherwise it was red everywhere. The walls, floor, even the furniture and glowing fluorescent bulbs—*Red as Hell*, Terry thought. The red lights were dim, and the room was filled with clouds of haze circling red tables, so everything appeared distant and lost in shadows.

The doorman led them to a private booth. Across the floor, other tables were filled with boisterous men in business suits, smoking and playing cards or eating slices of razor-thin meat between chopsticks. In the distance, Terry saw a great glass aquarium stretching along one end of the bar. Trapped inside were little creatures with humanoid appearance, each no taller than half-a-foot. Some banged on the glass and seemed to shout, while others darted from side-to-side in their confines. Most just sat, forlorn, with head in hands.

The other sales reps chatted excitedly though Terry didn't pay attention to their conversation until Marc slapped him on the back. "You ever eat *Fugu Sashimi*?"

"If I have, nobody's told me," Terry replied. This brought laughter from the others.

"You'd know if you ate it," Brett said. "Fugu is pufferfish. The Japanese consume it to gain fortitude and sexual virility. Real masculine food, y'know? Shows how brave you are."

"I remember now," Terry said. "The news runs stories sometimes about businessmen dying when it's not prepared right."

"Fugu's for pussies," Dean interrupted.

They laughed again, and Terry felt further out of place, glancing at each of their braying faces in turn, tinted red by the lighting.

"We're eating gnome," Dean said.

"Say again?"

"*Nomu Sashimi*," Brett explained. "Right here's the only place in the city you can get it."

An elderly Asian man garbed in perfect tuxedo jacket approached their table, smiling wide. "Welcome, gentlemen."

"Yuki, my man," Marc greeted him. He slipped some bills into Yuki's pudgy hands then nodded to Terry. "We brought a newbie."

Yuki narrowed his eyes, seeming to appraise Terry, contemplating his privilege to dine in the restaurant. He rubbed sparse gray hairs sprouting off his chin, then carefully bowed. "Very good. Nomu for four?"

"Only your best," Dean said.

"*Always* the best," Yuki replied. He began to depart, then turned to face them. "In the matter of disclosure, we do have a new chef this evening, although he comes highly recommended for his skills of preparation."

"If he's good enough for you, then he's good enough for us," Marc said. Yuki walked away, disappearing through red shadows.

Terry frowned. "We're eating *gnome*? I don't even know what that means."

"Gnomes, buddy," Brett said. "You know, little people who live in the forest. They have white beards and pointy red hats and talk to the animals."

"What's the punch line?" Terry asked.

In the smoky distance, he saw a man in a white chef's hat open the top of the long aquarium and reach inside with metal tongs. The little people ran in disarray, and Terry thought he heard their faint screams echo across the room. He felt a queasy sensation in his guts like the beginning of seasickness as he watched the creatures flail against the glass. They clearly moved like people, but only in diminutive scale, and he thought of small infants fed to villainous ogres in the dark fairy tales of his youth. These were no fairy tales though; they were little men and women and children, naked but for scraps of bright blue cloth hanging from their pale bodies.

"No joke," Marc said. "They're mythical creatures for a reason: Gnomes have magic. It's part of their flesh the way DNA is part of us. Every gnome is different, but their magic—that *power*—is absorbed by anyone who eats them."

"You *absorb* magic?" Terry blanched.

"Not too much, or you'll get poisoned," Dean said. "But just a little goes a long way. Your wishes come true, Terry. Why do you think we close the big accounts, month after month? I used to sell newspapers before eating the gnome. Now I make twenty thousand a month at Global and bang every chick I want. You can't make wishes that you couldn't normally do in life—I can't say I want to be the king of Spain or anything. But the magic makes happen what otherwise might have been offset by the potential for failure."

"Nomu Sashimi has to be served just right," Brett added. "The preparation takes a very steady hand. The meat must be sliced in the right direction, thin, and not tainted by the gnome's toxins. They're boiled in hot water, like lobster, seasoned and served. *Voila!*"

A tuxedoed waiter approached through the haze bearing a tray of drinks. He appeared as a wraith, shifting soundlessly, until he spoke as he set a collection of bottles in front of them. "Shots."

The waiter flashed a smile when he spoke, and Terry saw his teeth were plated in silver. A dragon tattoo climbed the side of his neck. *Yakuza, the Japanese mafia.*

"Sake bombs!" Marc shouted.

They drank and pounded the table. Terry noticed there were no women in the room. Marc must have read the expression on his face.

"This is a men-only club. Very old traditions here."

The others fell silent, watching Terry's reaction.

"So, you in on this, T-Man?" Brett asked.

Terry's mind fired through a dozen different scenarios, each ending with his co-workers laughing at him. If this were some sort of twisted orientation or hazing, he would do it. He was ready to try anything to get into their good graces, though he was loathe at the notion of being dubbed a sucker.

"Sure, I can do anything you boys can," he said.

"My man!" Marc exclaimed. "More shots!"

They drank. Several rounds later, Terry started to laugh like the others, fist-pumping and mirroring their animalistic cackles with jokes and business tales of his own.

Brett reached over and punched Terry in the arm. "By the way, don't ever accept gnome prepared by a one-handed chef."

This caused another round of raucous laughter. Terry joined in, nodding his head in agreement, though he had no idea what that meant.

"Nomu Sashimi's not for everybody, but it's worth the risks. Men die from eating gnome much more often than the pufferfish, but their deaths don't ever reach the news. However, Yuki's a legend—his chefs are immaculate in their preparation."

"Except in Lance's case," Dean said.

They nodded and drank. Terry wanted someone to explain that remark, but thought asking outright would be an admission of his ignorance, a reminder that he wasn't *really* one of them yet . . .

Again, Marc seemed to read his mind. "You hear what happened to Lance Thompson, right?"

"He got drunk and rolled his car off a cliff last year," Terry replied.

"And you heard they never found his body?"

"Guess it was incinerated or something."

"There *was* no body 'cause Lance didn't roll his car," Dean said. "He ate the gnome and got Nomu Sashimi poisoning."

"But he survived," Brett added. "Though he wasn't Lance anymore."

"What do you mean?" Terry asked.

"The toxins changed him," Marc said. "The chef didn't prepare it right and instead of enhancing, the gnome-magic *infected* him. Yuki cut off the chef's hand as punishment."

"That's why you never accept gnome prepared by a one-handed chef. It means he's a flop."

Laughter again. Terry grit his teeth, thinking that Hell couldn't be any worse than listening to these three laugh at each other's jokes. Marc was short and the other two tall, but each of them had the same gel-spiked hair, wore the same gold-and-diamond watches, slapped each other on the back the same way, and pointed at themselves when they wanted attention.

Terry knew, too, he was going out to buy his own matching gold-and-diamond watch this weekend. He joined in their laughter as he stood up.

"I'll be back boys. Gotta take a leak."

"Knock yourself out," Mark replied.

Terry walked across the tile floor toward the restrooms, following an aisle that curved past the aquarium. He told himself not to, but he couldn't resist peering in close to the condemned inhabitants. Up-close, their expressions were unmistakable: Wretched sorrow and the hopeless fear that goes along with being fitted to a short noose. The gnomes were less tall than the length of his forearm, though pudgy for their size, with round bellies poking over squat thighs. Their faces were rosy and, under happier circumstances, would surely be filled with mirth in song and laughter. Here, however, they only wept. The gnomes clumped in families, men and women clutching each other, and trembling elders holding tightly to small infants. It was gnome holocaust. Terry envisioned himself gripping the glass enclosure and overturning it with a mighty bellow. *Run, little people, run for your lives . . .*

But to what purpose? Terry didn't know how gnomes could exist in the modern world, or how they were brought here in the first place. They would probably just be quickly gathered up again. And, if this was a Yakuza joint, he would be killed, no questions. Just taken out back and executed.

No, best to just play along and ride easy-street with the top sales reps.

When Terry returned, the waiter was back at their table, hunched over a serving tray. The alcohol was beginning to make everything fuzzy and slow for Terry, and the room looked surreal and tinted, like a sepia-toned photograph of a thirties speak-easy.

He sat, and a plate was placed before each of them. Thin ribbons of pink meat lay delicately atop a bed of rice and mint leaves. The meat looked like shavings of tissue paper. One tapered off at an angle as if sliced from a bent leg.

"Enjoy," the waiter said and flashed his silver smile.

"May the devil look past us another night!" Marc exclaimed. He pinched his chopsticks together around a slice of the Nomu and popped it in his mouth. "*Mm-mm!*"

Brett and Dean ate their portions in quick gulps, making slurping sounds like sucking up wet noodles.

"Good stuff, tender cut," Brett said.

Terry lifted up the first slice to his mouth and hesitated, looking at it.

"What's the matter," asked Brett. "Is there still some white beard on it?"

He and Marc laughed.

Dean suddenly gripped the table with both hands. He groaned, his eyes bulged, and he leaned forward, shaking. He threw his head back as if trying to escape something clawing at his face.

Terry jerked away. "He's sick!"

Dean sat up quickly with a shriek of laughter. Food flicked from his mouth, and he punched Terry in the shoulder. "I got you, dude! You thought I was poisoned."

The sales reps all laughed again, an ear-splitting peal that sounded in unison. Terry wondered if they practiced together at home, like a garage band. He was ready to slug the next one in the face who punched his shoulder. He popped the Nomu Sashimi in his mouth.

Actually tastes pretty good, he thought. *Sweet, not like the salty sapidity of regular sushi. Doesn't taste like chicken, as most exotic meats do. More like cooked peaches in a cobbler . . .*

"Not bad," Terry said, nodding.

"Not bad," Marc mimicked. "Wait until you *feel* it. Takes a few moments for the magic to absorb into you, but you'll know when it does. It's like an orgasm while doing a line of coke. We've got a lot to teach you, buddy."

"More shots!" Brett shouted.

Terry raised his glass, then something curled inside his guts, like a white-hot snake. He groaned and gripped the edges of the table, and black dots flickered in his vision. He wondered for a moment if the alcohol had caught up to him, then his body bloated.

Brett waved at Terry in dismissal. "Dude, Dean already played that gag."

Terry felt as if his skin caught fire. He jumped from the table and tried to pull off his jacket, but his hands didn't work as they should. They swelled, fat bubbles pulsing at the knuckles.

"I don't think he's faking," Marc whispered.

The sensation of the curling snake bit through his stomach, and Terry screamed.

"He's got the gnome poison!" Dean shouted.

Terry doubled over from the splitting, tearing pain that seared his guts. He screamed again, then belched, and black vomit spewed out like a geyser of oil.

The other sales reps screamed, too. Yuki and several waiters rushed toward him through the smoke and dim red light.

Terry puked more across the table, the oily expulsion filled with pulsating shapes, like bulging worms. He collapsed to the floor, convulsing, while things moved under his clothes as if parts of his body broke free and scurried to join different parts of his body. He felt himself lifted through the air by Yuki, and the world turned dark. The last thing he saw were the gnomes watching him, upside-down, as he was carried past.

TERRY WOKE INSIDE a cell within a larger room that echoed as if underground. Every part of him ached, and he gasped for breath, but it felt that when he breathed there was a weight on his chest, so he could only inhale shallow pants. He sat up and his neck twisted and sagged . . . it took a moment of mounting dread to realize he looked *backward* across his confines.

The back of the cell was iron-gray bars, like an animal's cage. Terry turned his head around so that it faced forward—a motion that should have been physically impossible—and saw that the front of the cell was the same, framed in iron bars, though a locked door was mounted on that side. His body felt much too heavy and sticky, coated in secretion like the residue of strange jelly. He turned his head in a complete circle and saw with increasing visibility that there were other cells in that underground room and other motionless *things* contained within.

Outside the cell, Yuki stared at him, holding a silver platter.

His white tuxedo jacket gleamed. Behind him stood men with guns.

Terry wondered how long they'd watched him, how much time passed since he became ill.

"I'm sorry for your unfortunate dining experience last week," Yuki said. "I hope you will find comfort in knowing the chef will never make that mistake again."

He lifted the lid of the silver tray and presented it to Terry. A severed hand lay on top, its fingers loose and curled inward, like a great bug that died upside down. "Satisfaction has been made on your behalf. I wish I could do more."

Terry tried to shout, wanting to curse Yuki with threats of what his lawyers would do on behalf of gaining *real* satisfaction. His mouth opened, but no words came out, only garbled clicks and gasps as if his throat filled with marbles.

"I *wish*," Yuki said, "this could be undone. However, the magic of Nomu Sashimi does not work like that. I can only wish for something to happen quicker and more definitely than it otherwise would."

Terry lurched at them. Air seeped from his lungs, and it became more difficult to replace exhaled breaths with fresh inhalations. He brought his hands to his face and saw in horror there were more than two; the fingers were dark and gnarled with green buds, like baby leaves that sprout from branch tips.

"The magic turned you. Your body absorbed it, but not like the others. You are changing, and you are dying. I can only wish for you to die quicker."

The men behind him brought up their guns.

"Do you ever wonder where gnomes come from?" Yuki asked.

Terry's stomach grew, and things were inside, pushing out.

"*Hahaoya Nomu*. Mother Gnome."

Terry shook his head, and it simply flopped from side-to-side.

"That is you, Hahaoya Nomu. My supply of gnomes was running low, so I wished for more. You were transformed, and I cannot let your magic go to waste. Some men die immediately, while others are *fertilized*. It is a slow death, but also one of great blessing. I will not let you suffer any more than you must."

Terry's stomach split, and the first baby gnome erupted, cartwheeling to the floor like a tumbling dandelion. One of the men grabbed it up with a pair of tongs and placed it into a pail.

"Hahaoya Nomu, we honor you!" Yuki said, and his men repeated in solemn chant.

Terry convulsed, and more black oil spilled from his mouth. A wave of baby gnomes poured from the tearing fissure in his belly.

Yuki motioned for the men to fire. "Hahaoya Nomu, we honor you!"

CERTAIN SIGHTS
OF AN AFFLICTED
WOMAN

A DARK SUN CLIMBED THAT MORNING OVER THE crust of scorched earth known as Post Rock, but only one pair of eyes remained to watch its ascent.

Half that pair was infected, which caused Margie great torment. Her left eye swelled and leaked, and certain things she saw became slightly distorted, the constant tears overlaying a watery effect across her vision. In this way the land sometimes appeared like a mirage that wavers and blurs. It was a chronic eye infection, and Margie blamed its latest resurgence on the unnatural winds that began buffeting Post Rock three days ago. The infection always had that same effect on her when it reoccurred, being the discomfort and distortion. But although her eye was wretched, it was the reason she remained alive.

Margie was the last of the living after her sister, Pearl, succumbed during the night to the plague, enduring longer than any of the others, all the while hacking blood, gasping for air, drowning in mucus, but breathing and surviving, until she didn't. Margie prayed for Pearl, shielded her, nursed her, begged for her perseverance, but had known, even while both of them were healthy, even while the rest of the town sickened and died where they stood, that it'd be too much to hope that whatever powers brought down such pestilence would allow the survival of two sisters together.

And she'd been right. Margie had the benefit in her bad eye while Pearl ended up taking that terrible trip alongside all five hundred others.

And maybe Margie was next anyway, maybe she wouldn't be able to 'see' the germs any longer, wouldn't be able to evade them. Maybe she'd start coughing tomorrow the way the rest of Post Rock had. The year was 1918, and maybe this would be the last year of her life.

She remembered Pearl saying once that she'd always protect Margie.

I will save you in ways you cannot even imagine . . .

Margie never made that assurance in return. It wasn't because of it that Pearl was dead, but neither did it make Margie feel any better. She bore the heartache of her sister's loss as she did the pain in her eye: a recurrent suffering that would remain forever unhealed.

On her deathbed, Pearl murmured her final words as her own vision wore down. "I see 'em, sis . . . You were right all along . . . about the clouds."

That didn't make Margie feel any better either. The clouds had been haunting her since she was a girl. She thought back to her childhood, and she shuddered at the premonitions that came true, and tried instead to concentrate on the present, which was equally dismaying.

MARGIE RUBBED HER infected eye, then cursed, then made peace for having profaned. She needed the telephone at the sheriff's office. It was the only one for twenty miles around, and she set her mind to return there for the dozenth time in recent days.

Though she knew what awaited along the way . . .

From outlying farms straddling Route Four to the clustered shops anchoring Main Street, corpses covered the land like strange leaves blown along by a horrible wind. Sometimes those leaves piled in heaps, ten, twelve high, and sometimes they were sparse scatterings but, excepting Margie, they'd all taken their fall, and they all rotted now, moldering in the trappings of their lives. It was a mortifying shame that their bodies lay as such, unburied, mounding flies and ravenous worms and other things not affected by the sickness. They were neighbors and friends of Margie's, laid waste while they shopped for sundries, toiled in the field, or groused at Tilmon's Cafe about the rest of the nation seeming intent to foxtrot its way to Hades. Each was dropped swiftly by a malady thought no more insidious than a summer complaint.

And she survived because of her infirmity.

Margie's bad eye—that sick eye—caused her to see things she couldn't observe while healthy. It wasn't a magic, not like Pearl who had imagination, nor was it a hex, but rather the watery, quivering upshot of looking through the very lens of infection. Her vision would become maladjusted (that's what Doc Stevens called it) when the world twisted before her to reveal strange carrying-ons. Of course Doc Stevens didn't believe the things she claimed to witness, but said instead that the mind played funny tricks on a person when illness got involved.

There was plenty illness now, but the tricks weren't too funny. Horrible plague floated through the air, carried along by resolute gusts that hadn't let up for three days, and Margie could see it all.

The germs were little creatures, beasts with thorny heads and wicked intent. She heard Doc Stevens call them 'bacteria,' and that sounded fine enough. She also heard Doc Stevens declare that Post Rock had caught a bug, some affliction not unlike the medieval Black Plague, but worse in terms of an accelerated incubation period. But he also said he wasn't sure of anything since it wasn't easy to tell between viral or bacterial infection, with the symptoms being so similar. Besides the plague-like traits, he'd have claimed it as some strain of influenza, a far-flung product of the Great War that still carried on in the trenches of Germany and France.

He said all that right before he died.

The bacteria were tubular, like tiny wriggling hairs crawling on the wind, softly glowing with some green luminescence of evil. Walls didn't stop 'em much, just slowed some a little until they found cracks to sneak through. When she'd first seen the things blowing into town, she hadn't known what they were, but had the good mind not to touch them.

She saw where the germs clung to people or objects, spoiling them, and she kept her distance. She saw where the germs floated in the air, great swarms like hordes of locusts, and she turned the other way. Margie even tried warning people, but they didn't listen. And those that did, it didn't matter. The plague germs came at them from all directions. Margie kept healthy by evading the germs she saw but knew there'd not be relief forever; it was impossible to remain alert at all hours, when one single bacterium could be crawling under her dress that very moment. Even Pearl, who Margie tried so hard to safeguard, grew infected.

Unavoidably the question came to mind, though it still caught her unawares: *What to do now?*

And the answer came as it had before: The phone, the phone, someone would call, someone must know what she should do. And so it was to the sheriff's office to try again.

Though the germs were the harbinger of Post Rock's death, it wasn't they she was most concerned with, but rather the vehicle of their deliverance.

The damnable clouds . . . or, rather, what took their form . . .

WHEN THEY WERE GIRLS, Margie and Pearl loved to lie outdoors and talk of schooling and books and ponies and even boys, when then their voices fell to muffled giggles behind cupped hands. Pearl's favorite place was beside a large twisty oak tree that extended a thousand fingers as if trying to touch everything at once, and they'd lie there on their backs, holding hands. After awhile, Pearl would begin to devise stories about the clouds that languished very high above, yet entirely close, as if one could only jump just a little higher, their fingers would run through the downy wisps of dandelion fuzz. They'd lie there on the grass, and Pearl would point to the strange, morphing compositions.

"That one's a tortoise," she'd say, "and it's swimming in a sky of topaz. It's a mommy tortoise and it has eggs to lay, and it's looking for a place here on Earth to put her babies to bed."

The tortoise would soon dissipate or blow over the horizon, and Pearl would point to the next. "That one's a prancing horse and it's been trained in a circus to do wonderful leaps and to hold its head very high."

Margie would nod and smile, though never able to visualize the whimsical things of her sister's imagination. As much as she tried, as much as she squinted her eyes one way, then the other, turned her head, blinked, or concentrated, all she made out were smeared blobs that could've been an ugly bird or a deformed foot. Margie didn't care much for the cloud game, but indulged it, as Pearl enjoyed so much to daydream of things that didn't exist.

One afternoon, lying in the shade of the twisty oak, beneath the great, great sky, Pearl asked her sister, "Margie, what do you see in the clouds?"

Nothing but daubs of whitewash, Margie thought, *but I'll try again for you.*

That day Margie was sick. Infection rose in her eye and she should not have been outdoors, but instead lying in bed covered by a warm handcloth soaked in herbs and tonic. Their parents, however, were away, and she suffered the same itch and pain of the infection's resurgence whether she lay beneath a cloth or not. So now she looked upon the clouds, comfortable with her sister, and saw through septicity what she'd never seen before.

She cried out and wished she'd stayed in bed.

"What is it?" Pearl asked.

Margie scrunched up her face and closed her eyes. "I don't want to see them."

"Why not, what's wrong?"

She shook her head and whispered in Pearl's ear, so that the clouds could not hear, "They hate us."

"Margie, that's horrible!"

"I know," she replied, quite plainly.

Above, she'd seen faces concealed within clouds, entirely unlike the jolly elves of her sister's claim. These were wretched masks of pestilence and woe, and they were alive.

The miserable visages glared upon the girls, and now Margie's imagination, previously a mouse slumbering in some dark crevice of her brain, began to wake and scurry about, gnawing on common sense, and she thought the clouds were gathering strength, accumulating in the heavens, waiting for their moment to strike. The faces were as alike, yet as dissimilar, as peering at any group of men dying a long death from starvation or consumption. Margie had an old, old uncle who'd fought in the Civil War, and when she looked upon these clouds, she was reminded of him: withered from dysentery, slack-jawed from a saber slash, limping from a bullet wound, angry and weary at life.

Margie had been raised on the belief that evil was all around and she must mind her tongue and her manners to deter it. The truth of such parental assertions never before manifested so apparently; the cloud faces glared not just at her, but at all the town of Post Rock, all the world. Some hung with wretchedness, burdened by icicle eyelashes, giant gray eyes twisted and weeping, cheeks hollowed and storming. Others burst with fury, curlicue lines for eyes that widened with hideous schemes. The sky was a rage, a horrible, judging sentinel, and it found fault with what it beheld.

When Margie confessed all this to her sister, Pearl said, "I don't see what you do, but I will always protect you. I will save you in ways you cannot even imagine."

And Margie was satisfied with that.

She witnessed the masked clouds thereafter, infrequently over the years, and only when her eye was sick, only when she suffered infection, and people around her spoke of fever dreams. The clouds, regardless of how alarming their demeanor appeared, proved harmless. After all, what malevolence could billows sow? And Margie wondered why she alone saw them, and she wondered why her bad eye showed so much more, shadows that walked of their own accord, ghosts of people she'd never met, reflections *inside* reflections that hinted at other things, the same as trying to make sense of shifting cloud shapes. But whether she thought them physical aberrations or madness, when Margie felt afraid, she remembered what Pearl had said.

I will save you in ways you cannot even imagine . . .

And if that were so, Margie would always remain safe. Pearl was the most inventive person she'd ever known. Pearl could image anything to save Margie . . .

But now Pearl was dead.

MARGIE MADE HER WAY up Main Street, as she had oft before, in carriage or buckboard, on horse, or even a big-wheeled bicycle. The dead watched her pass, sightless eyes staring. Gusting winds seemed to carry whispers from silent lips: "Nice enough day, ain't it, Marge?"

There, Earl Thompson's slat-side truck—the first motorized vehicle in town—slumbered on wood blocks, its front hood popped open in display, some lever or gear in mid-repair. That repair would never be completed, at least not by Earl. He draped over the front seat, dressed in coveralls, crimson dried in rivulets across a face gone blue. Down the road sprawled Greta Chandler, crumpled as a discarded rag, dung running down the backs of her legs. Maybe she'd been on her way to find her husband, Jack, watching the dreadful occurrences all around and not wanting to face such ruin alone.

She'd not made it to him.

Margie passed Jack Chandler farther up Main where he lay on the front steps of a granary, one bloated hand clutching his mouth, as if trying to keep that final breath from escaping. In between Greta and Jack lay fifty others. Around Margie hovered the green plague bugs, like floating, twitching fireflies. They seemed to be increasing in number, but still could not ensnare her.

Her mind was tired at guessing what to do next. Pearl would've known, or at least had an opinion on the subject. Pearl had said they should get out of town, but then Pearl had gotten sick, so they'd remained while she died.

There wasn't any easy means to escape. Post Rock was a prairie town, built of tarpaper lean-tos and starshine hope for the future. A railroad track was once laid down, then, realizing it didn't have anywhere worthwhile to go, slipped into dereliction. But the town had already founded and there was plenty of land for homesteading, and crops were bounteous, so people stayed. The next nearest town was Norton, forty miles away, and by then you were half way to Kearney. A good horse and a long day might make Norton, but all the horses died alongside the people, as did the mules, donkeys, oxen, and other pack animals; the saddles, carriages, wagons, and carts were all useless.

A forty-mile journey on foot, half along Route Four, then half across brush and rock wasn't an impossibility, but it begged the question of futility: *Would Norton even be safe or was it just as decimated as here?*

Margie felt more fearful of what the rest of Kansas was like, the nation, the world. 'Course, Margie was always the more fearful of the sisters. But if Post Rock could collapse so suddenly, what was to stop everywhere else? There were other towns to try at other points of the compass, farther distances that, in lieu of a wagon or horse or her feet, she'd need a car, though there weren't any useable ones left in town. Post Rock was home to just three motorized vehicles: Earl Thompson's slat-side truck that was under repair, and two Model-T Fords that had absconded away as soon as the sickness began, their drivers shootin' up dust and debris from the back wheels in a rush to cut across the prairie.

She arrived at the sheriff's office, its door held open by Deputy Morgan's bowed corpse. The metal star on his shirt was covered with a sticky substance that also covered his mouth and chin. She wondered if he'd been coming or going from the office when he dropped.

Margie entered, stepping carefully over him. On a back desk was the town's singular telephone, installed only months prior. It was a strange wood box with corded cylinders for the mouth and earpiece, and brass bells that supposedly knocked against each other if someone called.

How many times had she tried to figure it out? The contraption was infuriating. All she wanted was to hear another voice, to know if outside Post Rock the world went on, or if everyone else had fallen to the plague.

There was a crank on one side that spun, though she had no idea if that was part of the telephone. A receiver hook held the earpiece, and when she removed that cylinder and pushed the hook up and down, again and again, nothing occurred. There was a button on the stand and a latch on the box, but when she began fiddling with it, a wire fell off.

Margie hurled the telephone off the desk.

"Useless devil-trick—" She covered her mouth so the germs wouldn't attract to her cry.

Her head ached from fever, and she was wary from guarding at all hours against the disease, and she chastised herself for cursing aloud. Pearl had understood mechanical devices, but Margie found them baffling. She half-believed that If Pearl wanted the phone to ring, she could have thought it, imagined it, and it would have happened. Margie wondered at what she expected now, the ghost of Pearl to call and tell her what to do?

She left the office, stepping carefully again over Deputy Morgan, and trudged back down Main Street and three miles south to her parents' house. She still called it that, though her folks passed a long time ago, and only she and Pearl had remained living there, spinsters to the end.

Overhead the sun lifted high, and she guessed it to be noon. So too overhead were the vicious clouds; their haunted gusts growing stronger, as if to blow Post Rock back to the open prairie land it once had been.

She wasn't brainless and she wasn't deranged. Margie had only schooled through the third grade, but she knew that clouds didn't cause wind, didn't have nothing to do with spreading hematic death to the land. She knew clouds were just so much water vapor rising and falling in the sky, knew they didn't give two hoots about what folks did far below, knew they certainly weren't mechanisms of genocide . . .

And yet now they were.

One time when her eye turned sick, she'd seen a creature bounding from behind Yeddi Jameson's barn, keeping within a dusking sun's long shadow. The creature was small and slight and quick, sized like a goat standing on forelegs, with a head that was much too big for its form, as if a man wore a giant wheel around his skull, looking ready to topple over any moment from the imbalanced burden. But the creature did not topple; it instead leapt easily into the air and sailed upward. Its head that she thought so large and cumbersome was but a weightless orb, glowing like a great star. It was vaporous, and its rays of light shifted many ways. The creature travelled higher until entering a cloud, and then the cloud opened its eyes and stared back at her.

Perhaps the clouds were just as tainted as herself by some affliction . . .

The wind picked up, and a wild shrub uprooted and blew past. Margie quickened her pace, fighting through the gale until she arrived at her parents' house. Sod buffeted away, and a fence post leaned into the ground, and the shingle and tar roof danced a ragtime against the building's frame.

Margie froze, suddenly sensing a change in her surroundings, sensing that while she thought of other things, the swirling air lost its edge. The yard around her parents' house was mysteriously free of the bugs.

The scrabbling, floating germs hadn't relented yet in three days, and her first thought was that her infected eye simply healed so she couldn't discern the horrible things any longer. At this, an unexpected relief arrived that at least it would all be over soon, one way or the other. Looking upward though, she saw the cloud faces, and the sight remained terrible. Their images were those of cruel children finding new joy in ripping the legs off spiders. Whorling cheeks billowed and they blew the wind around her in tantrum, picking up dry earth and crops and a chicken coop, hurling them in loose twisters.

But the bacteria were not around . . .

She went inside her parents' house with its shades and shutters kept perpetually closed. A faint glow came through the wallpapered-halls, and there Margie did see a few stray germs pulled along, like being sucked down a slow riptide, to the furthest room where Pearl lay. The house wasn't big, and she could see across it to her sister's shut door. The glow seemed brightest there as it slipped out the cracks of the doorframe, a throbbing cloud in its own right, green as pond scum and radiating wisps like uncombed hair.

Pearl's in there, she thought.

Of course Margie knew Pearl was in there, as that's where she'd left the body. But it was a different sense; something *else* about Pearl was in there.

The flooring was made of slat wood boards, and they squeaked as she stepped on each, moving slowly, pulled toward that shut door as inexplicably as the germs. She passed portraits of mother and father and Pearl and herself, all smiling, all outdated. The door glowed brighter, the luminescence behind it pushing to escape. When she reached it, her hand felt the knob to be cool and she wondered briefly if it were an illusion. But then she opened it, and Pearl lay in bed, mottled hands crossed upon her breast, head angled to look out the window, just as deceased as when Margie left her. Only now, she glowed ablaze. The germs covered her, piled atop each other rows and rows high, countless even if she tried.

The dead of Post Rock—when they first died—all held this faint glow, a color like the pulp of a ripe lime, the color of the plague bugs. But the glow diminished as the body cooled and grayed. Pearl was the opposite, her radiance was increasing until it became hard to look at her. Her corpse attracted the germs in the area; the plague bugs were amassing on her. But what did it mean?

I will save you in ways you cannot even imagine . . .

Pearl was drawing in all the sickness to herself so that Margie would be less endangered. Like fluttering gnats caught on flypaper, the bacteria stuck to Pearl in mounds, and Margie thanked her sibling for so much, so much for this relief!

But the more she looked at this miracle, the more she saw, too, that the germs did not perish, nor were they purposeless. They clung to Pearl, and they seemed to be eating her, to be *rotting* her. Pearl's weathered frame was already decomposing much too fast for normal putrefaction. And more germs floated into the room, joining upon her with greater and greater weight. The corpse shifted, and it was like a mushroom shriveling in the sun; Pearl was breaking down, slowly imploding within herself.

No, no, no, Margie thought; it was a lure, not for the bugs, but for herself. Once the body decayed into bone fragments and dust, she'd be next sought. Margie turned and fled Pearl's room, fled her parents' house, fled the property, not knowing if her sister had tried and failed to save her, or if something else conspired against them.

Now there was nothing holding her in Post Rock, surely no fears lessened by the unknown; the unknown still confronted her even where she lived. For Margie, it was back up the three miles of road, back up Main Street, and she'd be out the other side where crossed Route Four toward the long footpath of chance. The wind blew at her, and she tripped, and she ran, then coughed and rested, and she heard a distant 'poof' and looking back, her parents' house, far in the distance, fell in on itself, just as Pearl must have, and a sky-high wall of plague rose from the remains of all she loved.

She wished now more than anything for a vehicle. *Someday,* she and Pearl had mused, *they'd get a car and drive away from Post Rock.*

The world seemed to spin faster now, the sun bolting in getaway. The ghosts of Doc Stevens and Earl Thompson and Jack and Greta Chandler and all the others lined the road, shaking their heads in silence, as if disappointed in her, as if she'd done them wrong. Maybe 'cause she resolved to leave, maybe 'cause she was the last one standing and didn't deserve to be. Maybe a lot of things. Her infection was getting stronger though, that was sure. What Margie saw appeared more vivid, more substantial. She felt déjà vu as she passed Earl's slat-side truck and the granary, and then appeared the open door to the sheriff's office.

From there, she heard the telephone ring.

Margie's heart leapt almost as much as she herself at that sound. It rang a second time, a jangling blare cutting through the whoops of wind. She ran into the office, this time leaping over Deputy Morgan.

There was the back desk, but the phone wasn't on it. Margie's eyes widened and she made a noise like stepping on a thorn. It rang a third time, there, on the floor in the corner where she'd earlier hurled it. She shot to it and picked up a brass cylinder in each hand, placing one to her ear, one to her mouth.

"Hello! Hello!"

Silence.

She flipped the box around and switched the cylinders. "Hello?"

Nothing but silence. The cord to the mouthpiece hung loose, and Margie stared at it. The telephone wasn't connected to anything, and she remembered before that a wire fell off. *It was broke.*

Outside, the biggest gust yet tore through town, and she heard glass shattering in the distance, and buildings squealed as their attics stretched from basements, like grabbing someone's hair and twisting upward 'til that person stands on their tippy-toes. A mighty roar thundered along Main Street and she saw through the Sheriff's window, a tidal wave of germs breaking along where she'd just walked.

She would have been contaminated for sure. 'Crushed' might be the more appropriate term. It was the wall of plague following from her parents' house.

The germs flooded the street, then rose up from the ground and dispersed through the air, searching for her. They could seep through buildings, sure, and they'd soon enough make their way into here, but Margie was safe for a moment.

She looked again at the busted phone, the mystery ring that called her inside.

I will save you in ways you cannot even imagine . . .

Was it Pearl all along, leading her, protecting her? Margie knew she had to get out now, before the multiplying germs reamassed.

She stepped over the deputy and went through the door and hugged the walls outside, making her way north up Main, from building to building, trying to stay beneath overhangs, in alleys, wherever it was dark, wherever she was sheltered from the sky. The town's clustered shops petered out quickly to a few lean-tos. The wind caught her and pushed her out into the open, and it roared, and the plague bugs sallied forth.

Away in the distance she saw a sparkle that was sunlight striking metal. From its location, it appeared to be on Route Four, snaking around the bend that broke away from the road to Norton. But with the wind whipping debris and grit across the sky, it was hard to tell.

She squinted her eyes. Her left eye immediately hurt and teared up, but she focused through her right and, *yes, it was a car!* It really was on Route Four and it was coming toward town. It was difficult to make out, but there were great billows behind the vehicle; it must've been shooting up dust from its wheels as it sped along. She thought she'd be rescued, and she thought she had to warn the driver not to get any closer, because surely he'd catch the death that swirled amongst Post Rock.

And the winds blew greater now, the clouds moving in, the things that they were, the faces of goblins, blowing and blowing with spewing mouths. The bacteria spread and bred, disease marching across every gust, every building, every corpse.

They were swarming and turning frenzied, and Margie thought: *Was it because their sole captive might finally have found means to liberation?*

In an instant, she was running.

Where before the germs lingered and wafted, they now hurtled toward her. The clouds huffed and exclaimed and blew billions of the things around in maddening squalls, trying to infect her, but they worked against themselves in that regard, too. The germs were blown so rapidly and irregularly about, they could not latch onto the escaping woman. Those tubular forms of pestilence brushed against her and then slipped past, swirling in wild loop-de-loops.

Margie was never a fast runner, such is the life in small prairie towns that excitable actions were discounted, and folks grew accustomed to meandering when they needed to get from one point to the next. But she strained every muscle in her legs, charging with untested velocity out and along the road, sliding on loose gravel, dodging around the worst of the spinning germs, climbing up the paved incline and stumbling down the decline, gasping and waving her arms wildly above her head.

If only she could get to the car, and the driver would turn tail and ferry her away. But still, she realized, she knew not how far the plague had spread. The winds of woe may blow across all the world.

I'll take the chance, she thought.

Weaving and bobbing, Margie continued, clawing into the storm, occasionally looking up, and if the flying rubbish happened to part at just the right moment, to see the car ahead. It seemed impossible, but the distance between her and it had hardly lessened. Whatever minor piddling advancement she made, surely the vehicle should have travelled ten times that amount in half the time. She should be near, but the car was still so far, dust continuing to billow out from behind its back wheels!

Blasts of hot summer air assaulted her, exhalations from the clouds trying to check her flight. Their shriveled, hateful faces realigned and, instead of gusting in wild maelstroms, they blew together now, against her, so that Margie had to lean forward, like the slope of a roof to the ground. But she progressed, one foot after the other, shouting over the storm's vehemence for the car's aid.

And the germs sought her still, but they now numbered less, by chance blown backward as the clouds railed against her. This angered the shapeshifters further, for they had thwarted themselves again, and still Margie advanced, one foot after the other.

She was gaining ground, drawing closer, closer.

The sky began to darken unreasonably for a summer 'noon. As if realizing their quarry might chance away, more cloud people blew across the heavens, coming in from far behind the car, where rose another wave of heaven-high wriggling, flying, heralds of disease.

Margie reached the car.

It was a Model T, once gleaming black as polished ebony, but now scuffed and dented from wind damage. The driver's door hung askew, sometimes swinging closed, sometimes swinging open. A dead man lay on his side in the fetal position about ten feet away on the ground, his long tongue like a pink snake, extruding from behind desiccated lips. The car was cold and lifeless and appeared not to have been driven for some time.

The billows of dust she'd seen from behind its wheels were merely the work of the wind; little dust devils spurted up, giving the illusion of it speeding along.

Margie's spirits collapsed, and her body nearly followed suit. The goblin clouds roared in laughter at their trickery; she'd be going nowhere. The germs circled all around, a rising flood, on which her island was receding. They'd saved her last, she who had dared espy them, she who knew their true form.

If she closed her sick eye and gazed out through her right, she was only caught in the midst of a nasty little squall. If she looked out only through her infected eye, however, she saw masses of glowing microbes converging on all sides. Weariness surged, and Margie remembered it'd been a long time since last she slept. She took a step, then another, climbed the car's running board and swung into the driver's seat, closing the door after her, though the effort was negligible. It was an open-air vehicle and there were no side windows. She'd never been inside one before and hadn't that been a dream of hers and Pearl's, to someday drive away?

The winds blew crossways, and the car shook. The nearing disease landed where it wanted and advanced upon the metal hood, then reached over the lip of each door. She was entirely surrounded. If the germs were a cyclone, she was in its eye, protected in a convulsing, spinning pocket of safety that gradually narrowed and faltered. Either by momentum or their own volition, the plague bugs lurched over the frame and that safety was no more. They fell onto her legs, and they tickled as any stray hairs would, then she felt their clawing under the bodice of her dress. She threw her hands out by instinct to brush the wriggling things away, but wherever she touched them in flailing, sweeping motions, the germs stuck to her fingers like so many parasites caught upon flypaper. They scuttled under the beds of her fingernails and soaked into the knuckled folds of her skin.

The winds screamed, the clouds howled, the sky broke apart in millions of cracks that spread from horizon to horizon.

Margie coughed. She coughed again. The fever throbbed between her temples and she wondered how long it'd been rising, wondered if it was her eye infection all along. She leaned back and the leather seat made a sound like crinkling paper. The bacteria—

or was it a virus? Even Doc Stevens hadn't been sure—washed over her in silence. The clouds had won.

It wasn't as bad as she expected, though she wished her breaths weren't so difficult to take. Margie wished a lot of things, not least of which involved seeing her sister again. Her eyes drooped, closing slowly on that wish.

"You tried, sis, as I tried," Margie whispered, "but there ain't no saving either of us." She hoped for, but didn't expect, any reply.

And then a new wind—gentler than the plague winds—took hold of the car's front grille and began to push the vehicle in reverse. The Ford rolled effortlessly back up the road, back past fields of wheat and hay, past dead horses laying in their pastures, past other Model T's, motionless and forgotten like children's lost toys, back past Route Four that led to Norton and Kearney, past the Oak tree with a thousand fingers, past the dreams of hers and Pearl's childhood, and then the car began to rise up into the air, still in reverse, sailing, sailing high amongst the clouds, and these were regular clouds, scoops of ice cream and twists of vanilla taffy, not the cruel shapeshifters filled with hate and disease. Margie looked through the windshield and out onto the land far below and thought nothing about being turned loose upon the skies, carried away on Pearl's promise.

But what she did see, so very far down, were pale faces of two pale little girls, so like clouds themselves, looking back up at her as they talked of schooling and books and ponies and boys, and she wondered why they showed such different expressions, one of amazement and one of joy.

A JOURNEY OF
GREAT WAVES

THE AMARANTHINE PULL OF THE OCEAN IS A
marvelously ominous sensation, thinks Kei, the tugging from the
surf like little tendrils dragging back what it can from piebald sand
into the maw of the briny void. The pulling, too, gives her thought
of some urgent love a mother must have has for its newborn; the
instinct is deep-set as any lightless fathom below, of a maker
reaching desperately to its lost child. Such is the ocean as our own
progenitor that we are drawn to her from birth, screaming and
obtuse at the sea's allure until it snatches us back finally into the
same great womb from which we were born.

So here the tide creeps forth, surge by surge, reaching for Kei
with those very same tendrils. She lets them caress her feet, her bare
calves, tasting, tempting, and a shiver comes with it. She moves
through spume, searching the wreckage, but with no great interest.

*It is not flesh and blood but the heart which makes us mothers
and daughters.* This proverb comes to her suddenly, and Kei
remembers her grandmother, *Sobo* Youko, repeating it often. Last
week in English class, Kei's teacher, Ms. Onuma, claimed the
quote to have derived from an old German poet.

*Baka bah oom, Ms. Onuma, those will always be Grandmother's
words, not some rich lord's from two centuries ago.* Of course, if she
answers that on next Monday's exam, she'll fail... such is
American high school.

A seagull squawks. A dolphin leaps. The air is warm and drowsy. Kei feels old and young at the same time, already grown weary in the yearning body of a teen. She does not understand how her classmates can be so *kuso* happy all the time; there is only one thing left that brings her joy, one person, and that person languishes in illness...

Today, more wreckage than ever clogs the shore, leavings from the ruinous tsunami far away, and questions fill her if it is of the maternal bond that she searches these castaway things, the sea offering gifts and baubles as to a child... Or is it all but taunts? Kei escaped the ocean once before and now, perhaps, the ocean sends her reminders of whence she came, where she'll return, for what else has an islander to expect?

The beach is filled by flattened soccer balls and scuffed plastic bowls and gasoline cans riddled with rust. Unmated sneakers weep strands of seaweed. There are shattered planks, blobs of hemp and sodden foam, a clammy metal drum, waterlogged books, fishing buoys, a dog's carrier filled with muck, tires encrusted with mussels and barnacles and sea stars; the enormous steel hull of some lost vessel stabs up from the tide, broken at mid-ship, though even halved it seems to tower upward a hundred feet, while millions of empty water bottles with the Japanese writing of her homeland clutter the sand like worshippers at the great altar of ruin. A couch cushion that is cross-hatched black and delicate gold molders... the pattern reminds her of home, of her 'old' home, her 'real' home. There is much more, and part of her aches to discover anything in the brine of that life she lost.

But the sun is waning, and she has a new home, on a new island, and knows she'll be missed, will be worried over if she does not soon return, though before she puts her back to mother ocean to retrace steps over the pigweed-lined banks, up three carved stone steps, and through a screen of satin leaf trees, she spots one more sea-swept gift languishing on the beach: a small porcelain doll with black cloth hair and the bright kimono dress of an imperial *ojou* or a haughty *no kimi*.

Kei pauses, bends to look closer at the doll. Its face has a slight knowing smile, one corner of tight red lips pulled higher than the other corner. Its eyes are . . . red, painted red as its lips, red as bright pooling drops of blood. The doll is beautiful and strange at the same time, cast off as she feels of herself, and she touches it. The doll feels somehow warm, fleshy. But isn't that so of any waterlogged thing, beach-landed and cooking days under a long sun? There's a familiarity to the doll also, although it's any toy that could have been replicated a thousand times over.

Without warning a voice cries in her head, and it sounds as she imagines her own mother's voice once to have sounded: *Throw it back! Throw it as far as you can, Kei-Kei, and run away, run, run!*

But that's silly . . . And Kei has long grown weary of others telling her what to do, even if such a demand were coming from an instinct within herself, some ghost of a memory, as irrational and hysterical as that instinct or memory may be. Another voice—this one emotionless and sensible—argues immediately that such a throw would be pointless. She'd have to hurl the doll a hundred yards beyond the pull of the tide . . . otherwise the surf would just return it back to shore, and then what would be the point?

Kei brushes sand off it, the doll's silver and scarlet kimono still damp on one side, but so are islanders as herself used to dampness; the ocean has a way of pervading the broadest of walls, the thickest of blankets. Damp is in the air, it is all around, it is life. Otherwise, the doll is unmarred from its oceanic voyage.

She brings it home.

"THANK YOU," LEOLANI SAYS as she takes the porcelain doll. Her smile seems too big to fit any child's face, less so one waning under the illness she suffers.

"A gift from the sea," Kei replies. "My grandmother used to collect these. She was your great-aunt."

"Of course I know that! Because we're second cousins."

"How'd you get so smart? I did not understand great-aunts and distant cousins when I was your age."

Although that is not true; heritage has always been important in her family, and Sobo Youko drilled her frequently with relationships and ancestral names. But Kei will say anything to see the smile return to Lani's face.

"I was born in the year of the rat, so Mom says that makes me extra clever."

"It must be true." Kei nods to the doll. "What will you name her?"

"Hmm . . . I think she wants to be called *Obaasan*."

"Old grandmother?"

"Yes, like the oldest of all the other dolls."

"That's funny. Have you been learning Japanese?"

Lani shrugs. "I just thought it, like somebody said the name in my mind."

Kei furrows her brow, and that haunting voice of her mother comes again: *Throw it back into the sea! You were wrong to take it . . .*

"I guess she doesn't look very old, but you don't look old either, and you're almost an adult." Lani giggles. "You are Obaasan Kei!"

Kei can't help it, she giggles too. Lani's joy is infectious.

Oba Hana's call for dinner sounds from the dining room.

"Walk or be carried?" Kei asks.

"It's only the house. I can walk."

"And you'll be running again in no time. Should Obaasan stay with the others?"

"Of course it's where she belongs if she's their old grandmother."

"Of course."

Kei sets the new doll above Lani's bamboo-and-velvet bed, into an alcove made from the shelves of rich koa slabs, between a pink panda, long-stained from spit and apple juice, and a baby-blue child in pajamas, praying with Zen expression on its face. There are others. Lani is old enough to no longer play with the dolls, but not so old as to forget the comfort they provide late at night.

The girls make their way across the small house to a dining nook, where Kei's aunt and uncle await. Oba Hana is really her mother's cousin, which makes her 'once removed,' but Kei thinks of her as an aunt, feels closer as an aunt is a maternal figure, not a cousin. Oji Tommy's a California poster-boy who served in the navy and now charters diving excursions around Honolulu.

"Who's ready for boiled asparagus and steamed peas?" Oba Hana asks.

"Yuck, no," Lani cries.

"Okay, double servings then for Leolani?"

"Are we really having that?"

"Just kidding, Dad grilled burgers."

"Yay!" The relief on Lani's face is palpable.

They eat in a room that is snug and warm, adorned with Oba Hana's water color art and the surfboard of Oji Tommy's youth, facing to a picture widow that is aptly named, as what Kei sees through it is no less fantastic than any picture ever made.

Oranges and browns and mauves tangle in leaves, and the sky is a jungle of overgrown clouds as much as the island is overgrown by shifting bracken. The sun sets low behind a purple ocean, the waters seeming to devour it like a piece of great red fruit, its own weight the very thing that pulls it farther and farther down into the maw of the waves. Tall palm trees silhouette the glass like fingers of an extraordinary animal trying to reach inside, dreaming, perhaps, of life as their own. Hoary bats dart by, chittering love songs, and lazy drops of rain begin to fall.

And if Kei squints very hard, she can still see the beach, filling by each crashing wave with more of the tsunami's debris: soggy wicker baskets and sun-stripped row boats; crushed sandals and tires marred by shark bites; dolls and bloated bodies, sometimes difficult to tell apart. It's overwhelming at times.

What will be done with all that rubbish, that wreckage, those memories? Eventually it must be taken away, disposed of, *abandoned.*

They feel sorry for her, everyone does. It is something that cannot be helped. It is nature that she was cast adrift… *It is Obaasan come to claim her family…*

Kei winces at the strange thought.

"How was the beach?" Oba Hana sounds slightly hesitant to ask, but it's a thing that cannot be unsaid. "Anything interesting, or just rubbish?"

"Mostly scraps and trash, the hull of a freighter. I'll never use a plastic water bottle again. The beach is drowning in them."

Oba Hana's eyes soften. The laugh lines at her mouth pull taut. "Does seeing the wreckage hurt?"

Kei bites her lip. "Yeah… I keep expecting to find a photograph or one of Sobo Youko's oil-paper umbrellas."

"But you're drawn to it anyway, you have to sort through it all?"

The word barely comes out. "Yeah … "

"It's so hard, dear. No one wants their grief to return years later, and yours has come to literally surround you. But still, I worry when you're down there—"

"Kei found me a doll!" Lani interrupts.

"I did," Kei grabs onto Lani's excitement, happy to change the subject. She hates when Oba Hana talks about her being a worry, like a guilt she's responsible for. "It reminded me of Sobo Youko's dolls."

Oba Hana snorts. "What doll would not remind you of her collection? She had near ten thousand."

"This one wore a kimono."

"Ah, her favorite."

Kei loses herself in recollection for a moment, the rows upon rows of her grandmother's dolls: porcelain, cloth, china, corn husk, leather, bone. Sobo Youko kept so many, and each with its own story, like their ancestors. Already her memory grows hazy as to keeping them separate. *But Obaasan, Obaasan, why did it seem familiar?*

Oji Tommy breaks the silence. "I sailed off the coast of Haleiwa today, and there was a house floating in the distant waves. No kidding, an entire house, its windows and tile roof perfectly intact."

"Some homes float because they have walls made of foam instead of wood," Lani says importantly, "to save money."

"I never heard that before."

"I saw it on Discovery channel."

"Wow, you teach us new things every day, baby."

Lani smiles, and so Kei smiles. It fills her with joy.

She thinks again of Sobo Youko's words: *It is not flesh and blood but the heart which makes us mothers and daughters.*

If that is true, Leolani is truly Kei's heart, for it is not relations that define us, but the love we bear those relations. How often had Sobo Youko drilled such words into her, rapping her knuckles to pay attention? How often does she see herself in Lani? How long can she bear the pain?

"How long?"

The question startles her, as if Oji Tommy has read her mind, parroting her thought. But when she looks up, he's speaking to her aunt.

Oba Hana replies, "Four years since March . . . I still can't believe it."

"There are websites tracking the disaster, the Tōhoku

Tsunami's debris," Oji Tommy adds. "It took that long to reach us, four years, after running the coast of Alaska and Oregon. All that wreckage is swirling in a big pool; what doesn't wash up on Hawaii's coast will head back home to Japan and then circle around the Pacific again. The currents, you know, it'll spin around us forever."

Her clothes, her memories, floating in the ocean until the end of days . . .

Oba Hana had proved Sobo Youko's words true about the heart which makes us mothers and daughters; she'd taken in Kei four years ago, when no one else was left. And before that, it'd been Sobo Youko who'd fostered infant Kei, when Kei's parents drowned in a sinking ferry.

Sobo Youko had been full of love and the most regal of poise, but so too had she been filled with bitterness and small-minded judgment.

It is because Hana married a *gaijin*—a foreigner—*that their daughter fell frail.* So once said Sobo Youko in her crisp, emotionless voice.

Sour old bitch. So once replied Oba Hana in her fury.

Cruel words on both sides, though the dispute was long ago. There is no grudge any longer; the tsunami took care of that. The tsunami took care of everything Kei knew, everything she'd worried about, everything she'd disliked, everything that had not fit into her life then of twelve years old; as it was useless, so was it taken, but at cost too of all she loved, all she desired, all she cherished, all of it crushed by the sea, sent to swirl forever in that great sink.

Yet she wonders: *Would Sobo Youko have ever recanted, given time changed her ways? Found the joy that Lani gives?* Would her heart have ever swelled to know that family goes on, regardless of circumstance? Or would she have ticked off her fingers the number dead, the number remaining, until all her brood joined under the waves?

"Want to play a board game?" Oji Tommy asks Lani as they finish eating.

"Yay, which one?"

"Whatever you want, baby."

"How about Clue, but only if Kei can play."

"Set it up," Kei replies. "While I help your mom clean up."

They leave, and Oba Hana clears dishes to the sink, where Kei wipes away crumbs and mustard blobs.

The rain begins to hasten, rattling upon the roof like tapping at a door to come inside. A moan of thunder sounds from far away.

"Are you feeling okay?" Oba Hana asks Kei. "You seem so—"

"I'm happy, of course," Kei lies. It's not bad on Honolulu, but neither is it where she belongs.

"You say 'of course' like Lani says it, not dismissively, but like it's something that should be assumed and not discussed further."

Though she bristles, Kei forces a smile. "I *am* happy, it's just different than before. You and Oji Tommy have done so much."

"Lani loves you being with us, she's always wanted a sister."

"And a pony, and a unicorn."

"Don't make fun, every girl wants one of each, not to mention the prince to whisk us away."

And all I wanted was a mother . . .

"You know my childhood was also in Japan, in the Setagaya Ward," Oba Hana says, "Before I came here with my parents, uprooted from all I loved so my father could earn an extra nickel in the seafood markets."

"Sobo Youko complained often about your dad. Said he splintered our family by leaving the homeland."

"Yes, she'd say such things. I remember your grandmother too well—she was *Oba* Youko to me, spoiled and stuck in her ways. I remember her doll collections, filling up shelves on walls and old display cabinets that were inlaid with ivory slabs and memories, as old as Grandmother's Grandmother's Grandmother, she said."

That brings a cheerless smile to Kei's face, wistful in truth. "Sobo Youko loved her dolls more than anything."

"More than anything but her family. Family was always foremost, venerate one's ancestors, foster your heirs, and such."

"Except those who leave for new countries."

"That is true," Oba Hana says with a laugh. "When I was a bit younger than you now, fifteen or fourteen, I stayed at Oba Youko's house for two weeks. I'll never forget how she dressed every day in those *tsukesage* kimonos. They're very . . . modest."

"Because, heritage," Kei and her aunt say together and giggle. Leolani inherited that giggle from her mother. It's endearing.

"Did your grandmother take you to the *Ningyo Kanshasai* festival?" Oba Hana asks. "The doll appreciation ceremonies?"

"I'd go alone to watch the dolls burn."

"I'm surprised your grandmother let you attend alone. It's not a place for children."

"Yet it's filled with children giving funerals to their dolls. I watched them paying last respects to their toys and then setting them to fire."

"Still, that she let you . . . "

"Sobo Youko did not know everything I did," Kei says with a wry smile. "She took her naps."

Oba Hana elbows Kei gently. "Hey, I take naps too. Should I worry?"

"There's nothing here to sneak off to, only the beach. At the festivals, I just found it . . . *comforting* to know one's doll could surpass fabricated flesh. Weird, I know."

"The great dollhouse in the sky," her aunt quips. "I remember Oba Youko believed dolls hold memories and are filled with souls.

You cannot just throw one away, that would be like discarding a child. There are great spiritual repercussions for not disposing of them honorably, of course."

"Of course," Kei says with a mock. It strikes her, not for the first time, that her aunt has lost all hint of homeland accent.

A gust of wind howls outside, soft and sad, pushing through curtains of rain. Through the picture window the sea has blackened but for moonlit crests of froth, slobbering like the spit of fleeting mad dogs.

"The festival is Shintō tradition," Oba Hana says. "It provides homage to used dolls. Families share thanks for the joy brought by their toys, and priests give rituals to release the dolls' spirits before cremating them."

"Sobo Youko never gave funeral for any of her dolls."

"She'd never burn her own dolls, because they always had a place in her heart, in her house. Your grandmother wanted to save them all forever, as she wanted to save all her family forever, to keep everyone together under one roof, locked in old traditions, ancient customs. The world moves forward, but not for her."

"I'd bring her gifts of dolls sometimes, when I'd find them. That'd make her happy. Sobo Youko was not often happy."

"Oh, I know." Oba Hana sighs. "She loved her kimono dolls most, like herself, the ones of heritage."

Yes, Kei thinks. *Like the doll I found today . . .*

And a memory is triggered, a day in Japan, at the last *Ningyo Kanshasai* festival, when the priests had called forth those spirits from the dolls, ready to cast them into the furnace, to release them, and how silly it all seemed. Kei walked by the alter, looking at each, dreaming of their doll lives, the way she dreamed of her grandmother's dolls; she spoke to them, played with them, watched them slumber, while alone in the large *shoin-zukuri*-style mansion as her grandmother napped or wrote letters to distant cousins.

The kimono-clad figure with black hair and red eyes had *whispered* to her of a girl needing a doll, a doll needing rescue from the flames... Kei had taken it from the pile, while mourners bowed their head in prayer. Once she'd got home, an uneasy misgiving began tingling in her thoughts at having swiped the strange porcelain doll with red eyes. But she'd presented it to her grandmother so as to curry favor; that was before the night of the tsunami... before the night that all she'd loved was taken by the sea.

That doll was Obaasan...

But Kei's sensible voice, emotionless and rational, argues immediately that of course many dolls would appear the same: *What is a doll but a replica of something real? And what is real, but has a million duplicates, a million ilk?*

What are we, but a replica of our own forebears?

And the voice returns of her mother: *Throw it back, Kei-Kei!*

And she wonders in reply: *Do the dead mourn the living?*

The rain is falling harder now, battering their tin roof like *taiko* drummers pounding *chū-daikos* in epic song, all booms and peels. The waves crash in and out, adding to the cacophony, the rhapsody. The wind moans, echoes of ancient gods at eternal war.

She almost does it, almost flees to Lani's room to take the doll and hurl it back into the waves, but Oba Hana breaks the moment.

"Hot weather storms are the worst," she says absentmindedly, toweling plates with painted rose vines snaking along each lip. "Would you mind checking the windows? We don't need water getting in tonight."

Kei does, and afterward the dread has passed, and she joins Lani and her uncle playing board games in the den, where any one of six friends again plot to murder the unfortunate Mr. Boddy.

THAT NIGHT KEI DREAMS of the dead, the drowned worlds of the spirits that dwell far beneath the waves, farther even beneath the muck of the seafloor, the worlds of darkness that the tides orbit, cold and soundless. They climb from their clamshell sepulchers, wearing funeral garb of the abyss, long white fingers like flitting tendrils reaching for her, surge by surge as the current pulls them along, and her, by equal measure, sucked down to meet their spectral grasp, down to depths without end. She knows it's where she belongs.

Obaasan is amongst them in all her ageless splendor, wearing the kimono robe of her realm, hued by wisps of plankton and swirling gyres. Each upward stroke of thin arms illuminates the darkness from which she rises with glittering brine like a universe of flashing stars. She is beautiful, she is magnificent. She is dreadful.

The distance between Kei and the drowned grows less. There is no sound, her vision dims as she descends. A chill takes hold, a sense of arctic ice that has never known light. She is weightless, yet she sinks, while Obaasan rises, rises without form, like a bottle of myrtle-green ink dropped into water; the fluids do not mix, yet neither can they entirely separate.

The distance grows less still. Grandmother Youko is behind, and there are her brothers, Oji Toshio, and Oji Bunta, and Oji Nori, all drowned, all taken by the sea. Grandmother's mother is there, and her mother before, and their husbands and sons and their wives and cousins.

We are all cousins, Kei thinks. *We are all family to Obaasan, born from her womb, and she has come to collect us home, to our true home at the bottom of the ocean . . .*

Goddess, demoness, mother, it does not matter. A vision overlaps the dream, or perhaps it is the dream itself, of a drowned girl's doll sunk long ago upon the silt. Obaasan clothes herself in that doll much as a hermit crab puts on new shells, for without form she cannot leave the sea to reclaim her family.

A sound like crying comes to Kei, and she cannot understand, so deep are they beneath the waves that all is dead, even noise, but then she suddenly rises from the depths, faster and faster, and the cry is louder, a shriek now, and Kei wakes, damp.

Lani's late-night cries are something Kei's grown accustomed, but this is a different sound, a wail of terror, not of pain from illness.

The house is rocking gently, like a ship on waves.

She leaps from her bed, thinking only of the girl, and runs to Lani's room, followed by her aunt and uncle.

"Earthquake?" Oba Hana asks, out of breath, but no one responds.

Water pours from under Lani's closed door. The house rocks harder.

Kei takes the knob. It is wet. She turns it, hearing the click of tumblers, then the squeal of hinges, then a monstrous whoosh as the door is forced open from behind, and seawater pours forth in an impossibly rushing, swirling green torrent.

Oba Hana screams. Oji Tommy buckles from the flood, falling, dragged down the hall. Kei feels the pull too, but she holds onto the door knob, grips it tight with both hands, and her feet are yanked out so that she glides atop the water, like a ribbon dragged skimming over a pond.

Lani cries again, gurgling, while the depth of water falls away, the bottled surge dispersing through the house like the crest of a wave that has overturned itself and diffuses rapidly. Kei can find footing again. She stumbles in, splashing. Water pours down into Lani's bamboo-and-velvet bed, filling it; the water falls from above, from the koa-shelved alcove. Lani's caught under this deluge, unable to escape the bed, imprisoned by the frailty of her body, cornered by fear, ambushed by Obaasan.

Obaasan...

Oba Hana pushes past, seizing Lani from her bed and they stumble away, as Kei stares at the doll.

The pink panda, the Zen child, the others are gone, swept away, there is only the porcelain doll she found washed up on the beach, its eyes twinkling red like jewels lost from a sunken galley, its hair black and long, snaking out like tentacles rising up from the depths, its kimono pulled open to release the jet of water, pouring out where a mothers' breasts would be.

A roar comes from the doll, while outside the house there is a roar too. Obaasan's slight, knowing smile is grotesque, somehow turned upward to reveal hints of shark's teeth. It is no less strange a thing than the torrents gushing from behind its robes, the doll calling to the sea, and calling too for its children to come home.

The house shakes more, Lani stumbles. The storm has worsened. The wind shrieks, the rain smashes their roof.

"Kei!" A voice yells for her. Dimly she recognizes it as Oji Tommy. "Where are you?"

She reaches to seize the doll and is almost buffeted away by the force of ocean. Obaasan feels still fleshy, how Kei first found it, but no longer warm. The doll's chill stiffens her fingers.

She holds the doll outstretched in front of her like she would a yowling, pissing cat.

Her aunt and uncle's voices run over each other.

"We must go—"

"We'll flood!"

"—up the mountain!"

The floor seems to fall from under her as water rises, the walls of Lani's room pull apart. The salt of the ocean splashes in her face, stinging her eyes, mixing with tears, or perhaps it is also seawater she cries, cries for her loss. Regret and sorrow and fear are all sharp sensations, and the sting of each is the same. The pull of each is the same, tugging us down into its dismal riptides...

She breaks free, escaping the room.

The voice of her dead mother joins the others, prompting her escape: *Keep running, Kei-Kei, you must flee!*

She ignores them all. Kei has long grown weary of others telling her what to do, even if such a demand were coming from some instinct within herself to get away, to gain safety. It is her fault she took Obaasan from the sea, her fault Obaasan is pulling the sea back to it. There might be time, if she hurries.

Yes, run, that sensible voice says. *Run to me . . .*

She races down the hall through water that rises to her knees, across the house, the roar louder and louder in her ears, and she reaches the front door and wrenches it open, and she makes it outside where rain strikes her face so hard it is like a hundred hands trying to slap her into submission.

She sprints through the screen of satin leaf trees and expects the ocean will come into view, and then she'll go down three carved stone steps and across the pigweed-lined banks to the shore, and it will be over . . .

But she is stopped, for the ocean in all its might is already running to her. A tsunami wave grows, rising a hundred feet into the air, or perhaps higher, reaching for the stars as if to drown even them. And there upon the water's crest is Obaasan, in all her beauty, her great kimono robes twining through the foam and swirls of green and black waves.

Kei has time to wonder—to hope—that her aunt and uncle and Lani may reach higher ground, but she doubts it . . . She doubts it very much, and for what does it matter?

It matters not at all, whispers that emotionless and sensible voice in her head, the voice of Sobo Youko and the voice of Obaasan; they are very calm, very curt in such a matter. *It is not flesh and blood but the heart which makes us mothers and daughters . . .*

And no greater heart is there than Obaasan's.

The doll opens its arms to the sea, to accept its return, and so the sea takes it and its children, and Kei wonders at the leavings of her own existence that will someday be cast back to land, fragmented and mysterious as tsunami wreckage, while she churns downward, swirling and spinning amongst the currents forever to the home she has always known.

A Quaint Ol' Bigfoot Tale

"GRANDPA, WHAT REALLY HAPPENED TO YOUR hand?" Freddy asked.

"Eh, what's on my hand?"

"No, Grandpa, what happened to it? Why don't you have it anymore?"

"Oh, this here? I thought you knew already. It was bit off by a Sasquatch. That was back in . . . say, early spring of 1899."

Freddy paused, waiting for Grandpa to elaborate with some colorful yarn. Grandpa didn't. He went back to reading a Jack London novel, the cover crumpled and pinched from imprints of the metal split-hook that stuck out from his left forearm. Freddy and Grandpa sat on opposite ends of a sagging old linen couch.

"Dad said you had a hunting accident."

"Well, I guess that's one way of puttin' it. I was out hunting a Sasquatch."

"What's a Sasquatch anyway?"

"Your generation calls him the Bigfoot, but that's just a nickname some dimwit yellow-paper journalist called him. It'd be like callin' a raven a 'Black Feather,' on account the bird's feathers are black. Not very inventive, you ask me."

Freddy wrinkled his nose and rolled his eyes. "A Bigfoot, Grandpa? There's no such thing. That's a fairy tale."

Grandpa tensed like he'd been electrocuted. He shot a look of pure outrage over the top of his thick reading glasses and laid the book on one knee, all tales of Yukon adventure forgot. "Fairy tale? Boy, fairy tales are for little girls where knights ride in on horseback and save some broad from an evil witch. Fairy tales ain't true, but the Sasquatch sure is. He's as real as the stink from a summer outhouse."

"You pulling my leg?"

"*Your* leg? Shoot, I was about to ask you the same question. Sweet mother of Abraham, what do they teach you in school these days?"

"Math and reading, I guess."

"Well then, you need to get readin' about Sasquatch. There's plenty writ about him. Sasquatch is a wily beast. He ain't big on socializing, but there's enough folks all over the world that can attest to his living out there in the woods."

"How come I've never seen one?" Freddy asked.

"Have you ever looked for a Sasquatch?"

"Well, no, not really."

"Sasquatch ain't gonna come out to you and declare, *boy-howdy*. Besides, you don't ever want to see him anyway."

"So how did *you* see him?"

Grandpa let loose a long sigh. His own son, Fred, would be back in an hour to pick up the kid. He knew he shouldn't, but he figured it was time to tell his grandson about Sasquatch, to educate him a little on what lay out there lurking in the shadows of the world. He supposed if Fred the senior and the school system had their way, Fred junior would never hear otherwise. Grandpa peered out a dusty window. The sun was starting to go down, and the night bugs were flying up. It was just about this time of dusk when the whole thing had first started.

"Well, I must have been only about twenty-one or twenty-two years old back then and was courtin' your grandmother. I wanted some extra money to buy her pretty things, so I went out trapping with some other fellas up in the mountains. Times sure were different when I was a young man," Grandpa began, scratching the side of his whiskered cheek with the tip of his metal hook.

Freddy moved closer to him, turning sideways to sit cross-legged on the stained old cushion.

Grandpa went on, "Like I was sayin', it was the early spring of '99..."

... THE SUN WAS STARTING to go down and the night bugs were flying up. Mosquitoes, gnats, and moths were all hovering in the air, flitting in and out of mesquite smoke and darkening sky. Curtis had just kindled a fire outside their small log cabin, and the men sat down around its growing flames. A tin of beans mixed with rabbit meat simmered, and they passed around a bota bag canteen half-full of whiskey. The three hunters, Fritz, Curtis, and Willie sat on one side, and their Indian guides, Joseph Redpaw and Tyee, sat on the other.

"Well, boys, it's gettin' to be slim pickings out here. We've either killed everything off or scared it away. I'm saying it again. After tomorrow, I think it's time to pull in the traps and head home."

The Indian guides looked at Curtis, then at each other and shrugged their shoulders.

Willie spat into the fire. "I ain't ready to go back yet. We've hardly got anything. A few furs and some elk meat."

"Shoot, I'm agreeable with Curtis," Fritz said. "I've got a little lady waitin' for me back in town that I'm fixing on makin' an honest woman out of. The longer I'm up here, the more I get to thinking some other fella's gonna make his move first on Ruth."

Willie flicked a hunk of meat at him. "Why'd you want to do

something dumb like that? I can sell you an ass that'll kick just as hard, but at least you can put her out in the barn each night."

The men chuckled. Even with the marginal stores, they were in good spirits. The recent rain had let up, and worries floated away like tobacco smoke on the wind.

Suddenly, the night's peace was shattered by a monstrous roar of pain, nearby, up the mountain slope. Birds shot out of trees like arrows darting through the air, and the men froze, struck by the sheer power of that sound. Joseph Redpaw and Tyee spoke Klickitat in swift hushed tones and started to creep away real fast.

Fritz gathered himself first and grabbed his rifle. "Sounds like we caught a bear! I'll check it out."

Willie stood with him. "I'll go too, though that don't sound like any bear I ever heard."

They loaded up their rifles, older model Winchesters, and went quickly up a dirt path that broke through pacific silver fir and mountain hemlock. The sun had nearly fallen from sight and the sky turned a murky swirl of indigo and maroon. Dark shadows crawled through the underbrush, and twigs snapped. Ahead, a strained commotion was heard, grunting and thrashing.

Fritz reached the edge of the clearing first. He stopped abruptly, under cover of a growth of conifers, then knelt slowly and motioned for Willie to do the same. Before them struggled an image that would surely plague the rest of their lives with nightmares.

They *had* caught something in their steely bear trap, a monster that Fritz could never have imagined, twice the size of a grizzly bear, but black as a fresh-tarred road. The bear trap's metal jaws were locked tight, slicing through the monster's lower leg, like a skewered kabob. Those metal jaws, though, were nothing compared to the oversized fanged jaws of the monster itself. It sat on its ass in the dirt, great clawed hands each the size of a cooked chicken, trying to figure out how to pull the bear trap apart. The monster grunted and muttered, its mouth opening and closing revealing glistening sabers of teeth that together looked like some twisted iron rake.

"Holy Hannah," Willie said. "What is that?"

Fritz sighted down his rifle. "I don't know, but I ain't aimin' on finding out too closely."

The beast jerked its head when it heard the rifle's bolt sliding back. It stood, fast, posturing like a man and bellowed a mammoth's roar. Bushes flattened and Fritz, who was over thirty feet away, felt it strike his face like a balmy slap. He fired the Winchester at the monster and a spiral of the creature's blood and black ooze flung into the cascading night air.

The thing wasn't fazed. It leapt at them, and Willie screamed like a Yankee tart. The hunter dropped his rifle to the dirt, spun a wild half-circle, and fled back down the trail. Fritz tried to load his rifle and fire again, but he started shaking as Willie's panic spread to him like a sickness. The monster was halted by its first charge from the length of five-foot chain, bolting the trap into the ground. It grasped the chain with both hands and with another shrieking bellow, snapped it apart into flying fragmented shards.

Fritz turned and followed Willie in a race back to the cabin.

"Get your guns! Get your guns!" he shouted down the trail to the others.

He felt the monster's presence behind him, a lurching, clawed hand swiping at the air behind his head. Then the monster stumbled in the brush, buckled by the skewered leg, the clattering of the bear trap remnants and broken chain trailing behind. Another echoing roar followed.

Fritz burst onto the campsite yelping and sweating.

Curtis was there holding a hammerless shotgun, his eyes wide as saucer pans. "Is it behind you?"

"I didn't stop to look!" Fritz gasped for breath, trying to calm himself. He took up position next to Curtis, aiming his rifle at the direction he'd run from.

Willie slunk up behind them holding a six-shot revolver in each hand. "I'm sorry I ran, Fritzy. I'm gonna have to live with that, I reckon."

"*Yellow* Willie's your name now."

"That was a Sasquatch monster back there, Fritz."

"That's what the Injuns said too," Curtis added softly, still aiming his shotgun up the dirt path.

"Where's the Injuns at?" Fritz asked.

"After that second roar sounded, them two lit out of here like their rears was on fire. They called it the Sésquac, and they said it was angered."

"A Sasquatch, just like the Injuns told us earlier. I thought they were trying to spook us with their ghost stories," Willie said.

They waited, but nothing came out of the bushes, and they waited more, standing stock still by the cabin door. The campfire started to dim, casting an ominous red glow. The pack mules were tied up nearby, and they pushed against each other in a huddle, sensing something lingering in the forest.

"We saw a Sasquatch," Willie started again, "and you shot it. It wasn't even hurt. It just got madder."

"I hit that thing dead center."

"The Injuns said those monsters live farther up the mountain. They said don't ever bother them, and they'll just leave you alone."

"Well, you set the trap that it stepped in. I think it was bothered already by the time it saw us."

"You shot him, Fritzy. The Injuns say Sasquatch can't be killed. We gotta get outta here before that thing comes back looking to get even."

"Hells bells," Curtis interrupted. "I only heard one gun shot between the two of you. If that thing's as fearsome and big as y'all say, then you just need to shoot it to Dutch. I mean, you don't shoot a grizzly just once do you? You open up with everything you've got. Anything living can be killed."

"You didn't see it, Curtis, it wasn't natural. It was a demon incarnate."

"Listen you two," Curtis said. "Have you ever heard about Sasquatch before?"

Fritz pondered and nodded his head. "Yeah, a couple times out in the saloons. Just from prospectors and lumberjacks, but no one believes the stories those old coots tell."

"How 'bout you, Willie?"

"I heard it once from a couple railroad men, but their story just didn't seem truthful, like they was talking about dragons or something."

"Exactly. No one believes this thing is real, 'less they see it with their own two eyes. You boys say you saw the Sasquatch monster up there and I'm inclined to believe you. I'm saying that if we haul a Sasquatch carcass back into town, we're gonna be national known men, like Andrew Jackson or John Colter."

Willie and Fritz muttered at each other and shook their heads. Willie's moody eyes were downcast in shame, and Fritz was still shaking from his hasty retreat.

Curtis continued, "I even heard Barnum & Bailey Circus will pay ten thousand dollars for any creature never before seen. We wouldn't have to work another day in our lives!"

Willie's shaking head halted and he raised his eyes. "Nobody has that kind of money to toss around."

"Believe it. I heard that P.T. Barnum has more money than every man in France put together."

Fritz contemplated Curtis's words and kicked around the glowing edges of the campfire embers. "I don't care how much money Barnum's worth. You'd need an army to take that Sasquatch thing down, not just the three of us. Yellow Willie here was scared off with one look."

"I was just surprised, is all!" Willie countered. "I wasn't expecting no Sasquatch to be sittin' in our back yard. Tell you what, I'm with Curtis now. I'm gonna redeem myself. I ain't letting you call me 'Yellow Willie' no more."

"Fritzy, don't let us down, or your name's gonna be 'Yellow Fritz'." Curtis eyeballed him hard.

"Sister of mercy, all right, I'll go. But if Willie runs again, I'm hightailin' it back to town with or without the rest of you."

Curtis beamed and bounced on the edge of his faded leather boots. Curtis was the oldest of the three young men, but Fritz thought he was also the most impetuous. His judgment didn't extend farther than a silver coin on a stick. Fritz felt a portentous foreboding, the way the sky stills before a twister hurtles down.

Each man took stock of his weapons. Curtis gave Willie his shotgun and went into the cabin to load up his hunting rifle, a long Trapdoor Springfield. Fritz scanned the murky woodland surrounding them, then followed Curtis into the cabin to get his buck knife and extra shot for his gun. Willie holstered his revolvers and paused by the fire pit, cradling the shotgun, looking to imagine himself standing under a waterfall of currency pouring down, paper bills with the profile of P.T. Barnum on each face.

Willie struck up a little humming whistle, an army melody which he could not place a name to. He spat into the fire. An owl hooted nearby and then halted in mid-call. The forest went silent but for a rustling through the boughs. Willie sniffed in the air, seeming to catch the downward draft of a pungent odor. He raised the shotgun and searched quickly in all directions, waving his head from right to left like a flag unfurling in the wind.

"Fritz, Curtis," he hissed faintly. "Something's out here."

The two other men came to attention from the shelter of the doorway.

A whistling windy sound grew from the darkness, and a granite boulder the size of a Conestoga wagon wheel rocketed through the air, striking and decapitating poor old Willie. The boulder slammed into him so hard his head crumpled up like an uncooked flapjack and popped clean off its scrawny unshaven neck. The shorn body flipped a cartwheel under the stars and fell in a limp pile of splayed limbs, half in the fire pit. Immediately, his flannel shirt and greasy skin started to smolder and burn.

Fritz and Curtis shrieked in duet. They fired their guns into the forest where the boulder had departed, but the black forest shadows were many and those shadows were all ominous and great . . .

"GRANDPA, I HAVE TO tinkle," Freddy said.

"Tinkle?"

"Yeah."

"You gotta piss?"

"Yes, Grandpa."

"Why didn't you say so?"

"I did."

Grandpa shook his head exasperated, and the two looked at each other expectantly, each waiting for the other to say something else.

Grandpa gave in first. "Are you asking for my permission?"

"No, I just didn't want to interrupt your story."

"Well go, boy. When you gotta relieve yourself, there's no use debatin' the issue."

Freddy hopped off the couch and went to the small paneled bathroom to the left of the living room.

Grandpa sighed. Freddy was his only grandchild and he often despaired to think the boy didn't have the sense of two toddlers. He loved the kid, but just wished he wasn't coddled so much by his parents. He decided spontaneously that he was going to show Freddy *The Box*. A peculiar excitement—something akin to happiness—rolled across his chest at the thought. He stood up, old bones creaking, and walked over to an incense cedar hope chest, sitting in the corner under an old quilt.

Grandpa's wedding picture was on top, a sepia-toned portrait of him and Ruth. She had loved him despite the loss of his hand. Hell, maybe she loved him more because of it. She was the kind of woman to love a bird with a broken wing because of its frailty. He got along fine one-handed; there was nothing Grandpa Fritz couldn't accomplish that two-handed folks could. But he felt his disability most when he had embraced his wife. He lamented that he could only wrap one good arm around her and caress the small of her back, while he tucked his hooked hand neatly and coldly against his own side.

Under albums of photographs and newspaper clippings lay a warped wood box, the size of a Sears catalogue, with a split running through the grain on one side. It was musty and locked under tarnished brass fittings. He brought it out along with a small key on a chain.

Freddy was back on the couch waiting for him when he returned. "What's that, Grandpa?"

"It's something very special, Freddy, and I reckon it's your birthright."

"What's a birthright?"

The old man grit his teeth and sighed, but took a moment to tamp the feeling of annoyance down. He didn't want to get cross with the boy at a time like this. "It's like your inheritance. It's the heart of a Sasquatch."

Freddy scrunched up his face, one eye going wide, one eye closed tight, his mouth big enough to shoehorn a size 13 boot. He hadn't the slightest how to respond.

Grandpa continued, "You said there's no such thing as Sasquatch, and I said there is. This here's the proof. Sasquatch may have taken my hand, but I got his heart. I cut it out myself. It was still beating two days later."

Real astonishment spread across Freddy's face and Fritz could see the imagination at work, considering the still, strange content slumbering inside that box. Freddy asked, "Can I see it?"

"Yes, but you can't tell your father. Him and I ain't friendly about this matter. Honor?"

"Honor." Freddy's eyes grew even wider. Grandpa could not determine if those eyes were shimmering with fright or with excitement.

"Okay, where was I? Ah, so me and Curtis started shootin' into the forest, but it was dark and everything was a great shadow that looked like it could be a Sasquatch monster and—"

"Grandpa, what about Bigfoot's heart?"

"Eh, what about it?"

"Aren't you going to show me?"

"Yeah, yeah, Freddy, I said I would. I've got to finish my story first so you'll have an appreciation of it."

"Oh, sorry."

"It's all right. I reckon I'd be restless to see it, too. I'll hasten up my words to get to the good part."

Freddy resumed his position, sitting cross-legged sideways, facing Grandpa. His eyes bounced between the old man's face and the wooden box reverently held in hand.

"So me and Curtis started shootin' into the forest . . . "

. . . BUT THE BLACK FOREST shadows were many and those shadows were all ominous and great. A monstrous bellow rose from the woods and another slab of granite came hurling through the air. It crashed against the wall of the log cabin buckling in the cross members with a splintering din.

One shadow from the forest rose above the others and stepped nearer, issuing some sort of triumphant howl, and the three mules brayed in fear, bucking at their tethers and kicking each other.

The campfire—and the fire from Willie's headless burning body—lit up the creature as it came. Waves of flickering light spread across the Sasquatch's massive face and chest. The beast stood with a limp, favoring one leg over the other, which was bloody and swollen above the ankle where the bear trap had earlier skewered it. Its eyes glowed a yellow so evil, the devil himself might have cried in fright at its sight. Those eyes turned upon the two men in the cabin's doorway.

Curtis gasped and fired his Springfield. A new spiral of the creature's blood and black ooze flung into the night air. The beast grunted and grabbed at its chest, lurching backward. Fritz fired his Winchester next, but could not tell if his shot was successful. They popped open the rifle breeches and loaded new shells, but the Sasquatch disappeared back into the shadows where all manner of rodents fled the other way.

"I got that bastard good," Curtis shouted triumphantly. "We gotta finish it off!"

"I dunno," Fritz said. "Willie's dead ... I'm thinking we outta just sit here 'til the sun's up."

"Sit here? Fritzy, it's hurt. All we gotta do is pour some more buckshot into its hide and it's done for. We're gonna be the first ones that ever brought down a Sasquatch!"

"You saw how easy Willie was taken out! It's a fool's mission, chasin' a demon in his own backyard."

"We owe it to Willie to get vengeance for him. Hell, you outta think of that gal you're pining for. You and Ruth'll be sitting pretty after this is done."

Fritz paused and considered, his heart pounding like a bullfrog in heat. "All right, but I ain't gonna venture out there far."

Curtis hopped out the door with some catcall of glee. He wore a bandolier of rifle cartridges slung loose across his chest. Next to Willie's corpse, he picked up a wood bough, burning at one end from the fire pit, and held it high in the air as a torch. "Let's go get us a Sasquatch!"

Fritz sheathed a large buck knife into his rawhide belt and

followed Curtis out into the nighttime. He carried his rifle tightly like an amulet, and picked out a burning stick from the campfire as well to light their path. The new moon was waxing crescent, a thin lemon rind in the sky. Little moonlight filtered down through the trees upon the murky ground below.

The two men dodged quickly into the forest. Fritz saw that even without their torchlight, it wouldn't have taken any effort to follow the destructive path of uprooted brushes and snapped tree limbs left by the retreating creature.

He recognized the familiar upward slope of the path. "He's headin' back to where I first saw him in the clearing."

"He's headin' home to Hell, and we're gonna hasten that journey," Curtis replied.

They reached the clearing. The dirt path Fritz had earlier travelled ran parallel to the trail they were on now, moving through the undergrowth. Across the clearing where the trees and shrubs grew thick again, the men saw a branch swing back, a dark movement in the gloomy woods. A quick snuffling growl sounded, rough and laced with assurances of their nearing oblivion.

Fritz realized it, and he said it. "Monster's waitin' for us."

A flash of yellow eyes moved through the leaves, a glowering glimpse, and then branches rustled back into place. Curtis fired his rifle into those shadowy woods. The branches did not move again. They did not hear anything.

"Did I get him?"

"I can't see a thing over there."

"All right, I'm going in. Cover me."

Curtis hunched down and crept into the clearing, moving through wisps of gunpowder smoke and mist.

Almost as soon as he'd gone out, a metal snapping clatter shattered the silence, and Curtis screamed in agony.

"Oh God! Oh God!" he shrieked, falling. "I stepped on a trap!"

Curtis's lower leg was crushed in a bloody pulp of trouser and bone. He bawled in pain, rolling on the muddy dirt, clawing at the shut bear trap. "Help me!"

Fritz stepped forward holding the dim torch and saw that the bear trap was connected to a length of chain that'd been snapped apart after only a couple feet in length, the last link simply twisted asunder. It was the same bear trap the Sasquatch had stepped into, and he realized the creature had pulled off the trap and figured out how to reset it…. The horror set in, that the damned beast had actually set a bear trap in the middle of the clearing and lured them to it.

The Sasquatch rose from the dense woods, yellow eyes gleaming large and bright like two flaming cannon balls fast approaching.

Fritz dropped the torch. He fired his rifle at the monster while Curtis screamed anew. The Sasquatch took the bullet as he had taken the others. Then it reached down and grabbed the broken length of chain, yanking Curtis to him.

Curtis's screams went two tones higher. His shrieks and pleas turned so incoherent that for a moment Fritz thought he was babbling in another language. Fritz loaded a new cartridge into his Winchester, and Sasquatch and Curtis disappeared behind the trees.

The open clearing was about forty feet wide and Fritz charged across it in several leaping strides.

He passed through the first line of trees and, unexpected at reaching them so fast, almost collided directly into Sasquatch and Curtis, who was being held upside down by his mangled leg.

The beast took one look at Fritz, gave him a smile that could fry an onion, and opened Curtis's chest with a single swipe of his clawed hand. Curtis, at least, didn't scream no more.

Fritz cursed, knowing he'd only get one shot at this near range, before the creature would be on him, so he made it count. He fired his rifle point blank into Sasquatch's face. The monster bellowed and one of those horrible yellow eyes rolled up deadened.

But it wasn't enough.

The creature swung Curtis's body at Fritz like some medieval mace. Curtis's head cracked into Fritz's own and Fritz bowled over backward, nose snapped askew, and ringing flashes circling all the world. His senses blinked out, and only by sheer will did he not give in to merciful unconsciousness.

When he regained his thoughts, Fritz found himself in the most vulnerable position of laying sprawled on the ground, without weapon, and with his head pounding so hard he couldn't hear anything else.

Sasquatch took his time limping over until he stood above Fritz, straddling him with black-haired bowed legs thick as a pair of stone chimneys. It reached down and lifted him up by the throat, one massive clawed fist encircling and crushing Fritz's neck. Fritz's breaths stopped. His body danced. He looked the monster directly into its one good eye, and they stared at each other for some time while the world seemed to slow around them.

Fritz wrapped his right arm around Sasquatch's own and tried to lift himself up, to relieve the pressure on his suffocating, collapsing throat. He kicked at the monster, futile strikes into Sasquatch's side and legs. Sasquatch held him still and managed an all-too human grin of conquest on its gory face. The bullet Fritz had shot in the creature's face had gone in at an upward angle, entering through the lower cheek; it was a big bloody cavity, charcoaled and ragged and showing white flashes of skull underneath. Fritz didn't know how the Sasquatch could still be standing, but he'd have only one chance to break the creature's hold, to hurt him, before he suffocated or the bones in his neck crumbled to dust.

Fritz reached out with his left hand to dig two fingers deep into the bullet hole that smoked in the beast's face. He almost had it, when Sasquatch dodged its head at the last second, then jutted forward and, with a mighty snap, bit off Fritz's hand just above the wrist.

Fritz would have screamed had he the breath to allow it. The only fortune he felt was that the pain was not as severe had it occurred with all his senses in full capacity. So instead, he just grew faint, numb, and the amputation of his hand struck almost as a delayed afterthought. His vision dimmed, he heard nothing but a sharp ringing. His legs stopped kicking. He saw the monster chew, its jaws working up and down twice and then a hearty swallow.

Fritz's life faded, and his last thought was of Ruth, and of some other man waiting in line to put a ring on her finger . . .

No! he tried to scream.

An anger—a bubble of rage and spite—welled up like a vestige of air rising through a pit of tar, and when it popped he felt something shift inside and got the strength to fight one more time . . .

He let go of the creature's arm. The pressure on his windpipe ratcheted up as the weight of his body dropped again, pulling him down like dangling from a hangman's noose. He felt around his rawhide belt with his last hand and found what he was lookin' for: His knife.

He yanked it out, and in one wild, twisting lurch brought up the knife and plunged it deep into Sasquatch's good eye. Sasquatch roared so loud, one of Fritz's eardrums burst, but the monster dropped him, and Fritz could breathe again.

The beast fell back onto its knees and brought both arms up to its eyes, both now blinded. Fritz collapsed to the mud, tears and snot flowing down his face, but gasping air that felt nothing but divine. He didn't savor too long, but leapt at the monster. He still held the large buck knife and now thrust it between the beast's upraised arms into its exposed leathery throat.

The Sasquatch let out a wheeze and swung its arms feebly;

even half-hearted, the blow from the back of its hand sent Fritz airborne into the unwelcoming trunk of a hard pine. Fritz righted himself and leapt again and stabbed the monster in the chest, burying the blade up to its hilt. The Sasquatch batted its arms again, but this time the motion was more like trying to wave away the nuisance of a hovering gnat, until it fell onto its back, spewing inky blood.

Fritz sat next to the creature, watching it convulse and then turn still. The pain and shock from his broken nose and severed arm and all other injuries began to magnify, and he felt dizzy as his own blood poured rapidly from those wounds. He stripped off his cotton shirt and wrapped it tightly around his arm, using his teeth and feet, stemming the blood flow. Then he just stared at the creature's corpse for a long time.

Things began to creep and rustle in the thick undergrowth around him, and Fritz grew wary. He went to the Sasquatch and pulled his knife from its chest. He started to walk away then paused and turned again to the fallen monster. He thought he could see more glowing eyes begin to appear in the distant woods, waiting, probing, coming nearer . . . His half-stunned mind dreamt feral things. He found it difficult to think rationally, but knew that he must flee.

Before doing so, he went back to the beast and, with his buck knife, carved out the Sasquatch's heart . . .

"Wow!" Freddy said. "Wow."

"Then I stumbled back to the cabin and took one of the mules and rode it down to town. Next morning I returned to that mountain with a posse of soldiers and ranchers, walkin' uphill in the rain, limping and freshly one-handed. I was told to bed rest, but I wouldn't hear of it. I swallowed the pain and did what needed doin'. Our Injun guides, Joseph Redpaw and Tyee, came with us back to the cabin, and we followed the trail to where I'd killed Sasquatch. They couldn't look me in the eyes, they was so shamed. I showed them the heart I had cut out and they fell to their knees in awe. They knew what I'd done. Folks call them 'braves,' but they weren't so brave that night." Grandpa chuckled.

"What then? Did you find Bigfoot, *er*, I mean Sasquatch again? What'd you do with him?"

"Nothin'. Sasquatch's body was gone. Vanished like a banshee. Plenty of blood and mud where we struggled. We buried the bodies of my two friends up there. Nobody doubted me back then. They called me a conqueror; I was what a man was supposed to be. These days though . . . " Grandpa trailed off. "At least I still have this."

He raised the cracked wooden box. It rested evenly upon one hand of warm flesh and one of cold steel. The brass key lay on top of the box's lid. Grandpa offered it to Freddy. "Would you like the honors?"

"Yes, Grandpa." Freddy's hand trembled. He grasped the small key, and almost dropped it. "It's cold."

"There's nothin' mystical about it, just been under the vents. Go ahead and open it."

"Okay."

A gasp came from behind them. "Jesus, Dad! What are you doing?"

Fritz and Freddy both startled, almost knocking the box to the floor. Fred had come into the room unnoticed by either.

"We didn't hear you pull up," Fritz said cautiously, like a guilty child with cookie crumbs smeared across his lips.

"I guess not. Put that box away."

"Dad, Grandpa has a Sasquatch heart!"

Fred glared at his father. "No he doesn't, Freddy. It's a Grandpa story. There's no such thing as monsters in the woods."

Fritz locked glares with his son. "It's true, and you damn well know it."

"There's nothing inside that old box. It's just a cruel joke."

Freddy gulped, the bystander in a crossfire. "But Grandpa said Sasquatch is out there . . ."

"And I say he's not. Freddy, go wait out in the car."

"But Dad—"

"Now!"

Freddy sulked out, deflated. He turned back and glumly waved. "Bye, Grandpa."

"See you around, kiddo."

"Not likely," Fred muttered to his father. "How many times have I told you to lay off the Bigfoot stories? It's getting really old."

"I've always told you the truth. Sasquatch lives in those mountains and I fought him and I survived. It changed my life in more ways than you'll ever know. I think that's something worth passin' down to my kin."

"Don't you remember how much you terrified me of Bigfoot as a kid? For years, I had reoccurring nightmares of monsters chasing me. I was afraid to ever step foot outside, much less into a forest."

"You don't need to live a life of fear, son, in order to know what's around you. It's called appreciation and respect for your surroundings. Sasquatch don't bother folks unless they bother him. I know because I was the one that attacked him first."

Fred lowered his voice, pleading. "Dad, I know you lost your hand, and I know whatever occurred to you was unimaginably horrific. You survived a terrible ordeal. But Bigfoot doesn't exist. It was just a bear."

Fritz's eyes glinted sparks of rage. "I know what I saw, boy. I have the proof right here." He held up the locked wood box.

"What proof? There's nothing inside that old box. I've seen it. It's just a moldy stain."

"It was in here."

"How long ago was it when you fought your monster?"

"Say, early spring of 1899."

"So it happened over half a century ago. Things die, Dad, and they decay and rot away unless they're properly cared for. If you had something that was remarkable, you should have taken it to the museum or to a scientist back then."

"The bastard took my hand! Sasquatch's heart was mine. I earned it. I wasn't gonna hand it over to some stuffy antiquarian. It belonged to me!"

Fred shook his head. "Dad, I've told you before and I mean it. No more Bigfoot stories, especially around my son. I forbid it. He gets teased enough at school as it is, without repeating your fables." Fred didn't say anything else, but turned and walked away, out the door.

Fritz stood and watched him go, just quietly holding the box. He didn't move for a long time. He listed to the car outside turn over its engine and then accelerate with a growl that sounded only haunting. Then the sound dimmed as the last of his family line drove off into the distance. He felt an inward collapse, a fainting of his spirit, but he stood there still.

He stood for a long time more, just thinking. Then he went to the hope chest in the corner. He placed the wooden box back beneath the photographs and newspaper clippings and his wedding portrait, and closed the lid, burying the legend of Sasquatch under the sentimental trappings of an old man.

DREAMS OF A
LITTLE SUICIDE

WHAT IS A HEART?

By any definition it's the mechanism of our body that keeps us alive, pumping blood to all the other organs we require to live. If we were a movie, it would be the producer, pushing, pushing, pushing the blood to move, to circulate, to oxygenate. We don't see it, working behind the scenes, toiling without respite, and often we don't even think about it. The heart is a workhorse, and without it we would die.

But cannot the same be said about Love?

After all, are not the heart and the sentiment of love wound so inextricably as to be inseparable? I would declare that it's not only one heart that keeps us alive but two, for we must have the physical heart beating within our chest, but we must also have the heart of another, the love which motivates our cardiac producer to continue laboring with gusto. Otherwise what would life be, but a series of futile motions, a strip of test screen shots that are cut and quickly discarded?

And what would *we* be, but a race of tin men shambling down the brick road of life, mourning the emptiness within our chests? I wonder how long Baum's Tin Man would have lived, had the Wizard not granted him the heart he desired? I wonder how long until the rust that eroded his exterior would have eaten through the mechanisms of his insides as well? Or, I wonder, how long until he took his own axe and cleaved his metal chest in two or severed his head off its bolted neck? You see, the Tin Man *had* a heart once, when he was a mortal woodsman, and in love. But he became a man of tin, without a heart, and his capacity for love was gone . . .

I say this as barely three months had passed after I met June Haley. In three months, how a life changes! How it grows large and brightens, then dissolves like a shimmering rainbow that fills the air with brilliance, only to vanish once looked upon for too long. Poetic flair aside, life really is a wicked bitch sometimes.

I hail from Milwaukee, and before my recent arrival on the Pacific Coast I'd never before left that 'Great Place on a Great Lake.' But I'm special. Some call it a deformity and some call it a *difference*, as if it were an amiable conflict of opinion. Whatever you call it, it got the attention of a Metro-Goldwyn-Mayer scout, who invited me to be part of a movie. A movie!

I hopped on a train for California faster than Fatty Arbuckle chasing a fifteen-year-old with a sandwich. I may never have been in a film before, but I sure watched 'em. Every week at the Emerald Theatre, I dressed to the nines and escaped my miserable Wisconsin life to sweep Greta Garbo off her feet, or blast James Cagney in a quick-draw, or dance alongside Fred Astaire and Ginger Rogers.

I was twenty-six years old and still lived at home with my folks. Where else could I go? People daily whispered I was a freak, a half-man. I couldn't land a job, especially during the Depression. Businessmen were hurling themselves out of windows, they lost all their money during the stock crash. It didn't bother me as I never had money to begin with. You never realize what you can't live without, until you experience it first . . .

Anyway, before I left home I told my folks. Of course they didn't want me to go.

"The studios are just going to exploit you," mother said.

"What am I doing here? Making sure the couch still works?" I replied. "I'd rather be exploited by the likes of Errol Flynn and John Barrymore than stared at by the neighbors."

"But you're not Jewish. You'll never survive the movie business," father said.

"That's just ignorant. Buster Keaton isn't Jewish. Neither is Katharine Hepburn or Jean Harlow. Look at them," I said. "Los Angeles is the city where dreams come true. I'm going to be a star!"

So I arrived in Los Angeles in early December, 1939, and from there took a bus to its heart in Culver City. Filming had already begun, but there were problems with recasting actors, and the executives said the script's pace was too slow, and most of it was being scrapped in order to start over again under a new director, Victor Fleming.

I'd not read the book by L. Frank Baum, but I was familiar enough with the story and I knew exactly who I'd be playing. Me and a hundred other midgets were gathered from the distant corners of America to populate the land of the Munchkins.

For that, I was paid $125 a week and given board at the Culver Hotel with most of the other actors and actresses. My father, who'd worked the assembly line all his life, never made $125 a week, *and* he had to pay rent.

It was winter in California, and residents wearing short-sleeve shirts said it was cold outside. Meanwhile, back home in Milwaukee, there was a blizzard. In California, people smiled and waved at each other, even to strangers. In Milwaukee, people were born grimacing. In California, I was celebrated. In Milwaukee, I was mocked. Here, I dreamed of things I'd never thought possible. There, I stared at floral print on the walls.

Then, on top of everything else, I met Juniper Haley. If my life in Hollywood came any closer to Heaven, I would have sprouted wings and a halo.

June was a seamstress in the Costume and Wardrobe

Department, and I saw her scurrying about on the set, threading a needle here and stitching a scarecrow patch there, ordered around by the head designer, Adrian Adolph Greenberg, or his busybody staff.

She was not a little person like myself, but neither was she tall as most other women. One day on set she fitted me for costume, and as she stood over me the bottom of her bosom touched the top of my head.

"If my chest ever needs to rest I can use you as a shelf," she said.

I thought I should be infuriated by that remark, but it was *funny*. The intent wasn't malicious, as it would have been back home. Plus her fingers ran across my arms and legs and chest as she measured, and I liked that. I replied, "Everyone needs the experience at least once."

She laughed. The sound was musical, like something the orchestral department would have composed for a Judy Garland solo. She said, "I always knew there was something missing from my life. Now I can die fulfilled."

She told me her name. I told her mine.

"So where'd they find you?" she asked.

"Milwaukee, the envy of America."

"I've done some work out there. I remember watching *A Star is Born* at the Emerald Theatre."

"That theatre is right down the street from where I lived!"

"Small world," she said, then placed her open hand against my cheek. "No offense!"

I flushed. "I might be offended if you weren't so fetching."

She flushed in return. "I guess you can make fun, too. I deserve it."

"I'm serious."

"You've got bad eyes then."

I stuttered, and my flush brightened. I always thought myself adroit with words. I wrote poetry back home, expressions—like my emotions—that I never showed to anyone. I wrote about love and lust in my diary, then hid it all under the mattress where other men might keep saucy photo cards. But now I had to voice something which I normally imagined only while lying in the dark: "Maybe I can take you out for dinner tonight... if you don't already have other plans ... "

"Me with someone like you?" she asked.

I don't know what was more mortifying—the expression on June's face or the tone of her voice.

"I'm sorry," I blurted. "I shouldn't have said that. I mean, I just meant, well, I don't know anyone else out here—"

"No, no," she said. "It's not that. I just meant you wouldn't want anything to do with me. You're too nice, and I'm dumped from a string of bad relationships. My heart is frozen hard... You'd probably hate me."

"What halfwit would dump someone like you?"

She turned her face from me, and I didn't know if she was going to sob or sigh or walk away. I placed my hand on her forearm.

She turned back, and she looked hopeful. "I'd love to have dinner with you."

So we went out. I had an advance on my first week's wages and took her to a club that served porterhouse steak and souffléed sweet potatoes while the *Artie Shaw Band* played on stage. It was a hit.

The next night we went out again. Then again after that. She opened up to me, and I fell for her hard.

June Haley had travelled all over following the movie industry's shooting stars. She'd worked on *Captains Courageous* in Massachusetts, and *City Lights* in San Francisco, and even *The 39 Steps* in Scotland. Though she was a Hollywood hand, she dreamed of making leading lady. But she could never get onto the big screen, no matter how many filmmakers she took under the sheets and let direct between her legs. Her body was too thin, her limbs too stumpy, her face too round.

But her eyes were flecked by the quiet dreams of magnolia blossoms, and the depth of sweet seawaters, and the eager longing for approval, as if she were a hitchhiker waving her arms along the side of the road, watching all the cars pass by without acknowledgement. You could not see that in her eyes, unless you looked deep. I don't think anyone had, before me.

A week later, Christmas skies rained winter chill outside her apartment though, inside, her bed smoldered hot as a steamer, its covers pushed to the floor in waded lumps. We sighed and lay tangled in each other, our arms and legs loose and caressing. My eyelids were weighted by great comfort, and it seemed the world had at last emerged from the womb of the cosmos.

She whispered to me, "I think you've melted my heart."

"I'll never let it freeze again."

"Of all the men I've met in California, it took one from Wisconsin to renew my faith in romance... Wisconsin, of all places."

"No one should ever treat you less than the best."

"I wish. No one treats you like a lady out here; all you are is a conquest, a statistic. It's like a bartering system: I'll give up a piece of me if you can do me an industry favor. Get me a part, introduce me to someone, bring me to an event."

I understood.

She told me about her last relationship with the film's costume designer, Adrian Adolph Greenberg. He promised to get her an audition with Louis B. Mayer, and so she did whatever Greenberg asked. Then she caught Greenberg diddling with a make-up girl. He blamed June for his own indiscretion, then dumped her, screaming he would ruin her career. A few months later they made up, and he promised things would be different. Things were, only that the next time she caught him fooling around, it was with a lighting boy. He blamed her again, and she crawled away, sobbing.

"I'm not like that," I said.

"I know."

"Dreams really do come true," I added, though I don't know if I spoke to her benefit, or to my own. "But never in the way you expect."

She kissed my forehead, just where Glenda kisses Dorothy. And, like the Land of Oz, the next ten weeks were enchanted.

The ten weeks of June.

WHAT IS COURAGE?

It is said that courage is the strength to confront difficulty. It's an intangible faculty, and a part of us that has the potential to uplift humanity. If we were a movie, courage would be our cast, the actors who brave formidable roles like ferocious lions that rule as kings of the screens. Sadly, as we all know, not every lion can be a king, and not every lion is courageous, and many actors simply lack the fortitude to persevere in the face of a challenge.

Some, you might say, are even cowardly, and I count myself amongst their number.

By mid-January, filming had picked up on *The Wizard of Oz*, and scheduling rushed forward at a frantic, breakneck speed. We worked like shackled convicts, six days a week, on set from four in the morning until eight at night, always in costume, always in makeup. I got so used to grooming an orange wig and wearing buckled shoes and green newsboy pants, that I nearly forgot what my normal appearance should be.

Victor Fleming said we would be done shooting by March, but I doubted it. Like any great undertaking, there were set-backs that put us behind schedule: the Hays Commission was all over the

Studios' backs about moral censorship, causing constant script changes; Margaret Hamilton, as the Wicked Witch of the West, was burned during a scene in which she made her fiery exit; and the Technicolor process to colorize sepia film was such a cumbersome burden that it required sequences to be refilmed over-and-over.

And I didn't mind—I wished to stay part of that production forever. For at nights, June and I managed to steal away to one of our apartments for a few hours of fervor, those passions that flare greatest at midnight.

One evening in February, June ran her fingers over my chest, each tip tingling against my hot skin. "If you could meet the Wizard and ask him for something—anything—what would you wish?"

"Nothing," I said. "There's nothing I need to make me any more content than I am right now."

"Oh c'mon, don't be a stick-in-the-mud. Everyone wants something more."

I thought about it. I knew it would sound hokey when I said it, but I was feeling lighthearted, a warmth that was half passion and half maudlin, although what I said was also true as the bliss I felt in her bed.

"I'd want to make someone happy. Genuinely happy, like a happiness that's life-changing. Not even my folks have ever been happy with me, as if they felt my deformity was their penance for some grave sin. I've never brought any real happiness to anyone, and I want to know what that feels like."

"Well, that'd be a wasted wish," June said. "You make me happier than a warbler on Broadway."

I smiled big and believed her. "Then the Wizard has granted my wish already."

I imagined a great rainbow arching over our bed and knew I'd made it to *the other side*. We were so different, June and I, but I realized that must be what love is: the fulfillment of that which you're lacking. Whereas I was a realist, June was a dreamer. I imagined lying in that bed with her forever, growing old and speaking of wishes, and then I caught myself and wondered if it was not I who was the dreamer after all. I felt giddy. What else could joy be, if not for this moment?

I sensed her waiting, trying to read my thoughts.

"Okay, your turn," I said. "What would you ask of the Wizard?"

Her green eyes glistened like wet emeralds, and a frown sank her ruby lips. She rolled away from me and looked up to the ceiling.

"I'd ask him for second chances."

"A second chance for what?"

"Everything," she said. "I screw everything up."

The rainbow seemed to dim. I placed a hand reassuringly over hers.

She continued. "Whenever something good happens to me, I somehow poison it. If someone offers me their hand, I bite it. I'm self-destructive and I don't know why, as if I don't believe I deserve anything good in my life, so I turn from it. I'm like Dorothy, given the keys to the magical world of Oz, but all she wants to do is run away, back to her little gray Kansas farm. If I were Dorothy, and taken away to Oz, I'd never want to return home."

"But we're already in Oz," I said. "Look around. What could be more wonderful than what we have now? You'll never have to leave this and return where you came from . . . I know I never will."

She smiled and nestled her head against my shoulder.

But it turned out to be true, what June said, and the rainbow over our bed soon vanished as if a dark twister had come along and sucked it away.

She *did* screw everything up that was good in her life. *Me.* The one thing that brought her happiness, and she left it. She ruined our perfect future! We were meant to be together, like a movie romance set in real life. I gave her my love, my heart, and she reciprocated. I'd never felt like that before—the passion! The ecstasy!—and I knew I never would again . . .

It was only two weeks after the night we shared our wishes that she wrote me a *Dear John* letter. I'd been floating through the days amidst visions of marriage and children when I found it stuffed inside my wardrobe locker.

Darling, I'm sorry, but we can no longer see each other. I thought I had feelings for you, but my emotions were so topsy-turvy. My heart is with another. Please don't let this note get you glum—You're the biggest man I've ever met, and I had a swell time while it lasted.

XOXO Juniper

I wept, and the tears washed away my make-up, so that my old face reappeared, my miserable and forlorn Milwaukee face. Time muddled after that and shot by, a reel of film that spins too fast on its projector, until suddenly slowing and sticking at all the wrong moments.

It was the beginning of March and production had somehow caught up to schedule. Filming would end soon, as Fleming predicted. There wasn't much time left to win June back . . . Letter be damned, I sought her every chance I could.

She'd been promoted from working with the Munchkins to become the personal assistant for Ray Bolger, the Scarecrow. Apparently, part of her job duties were to hide whenever I was around. One afternoon while the cast went to lunch, I hid in Bolger's dressing room and waited.

She entered, alone.

"Who is he?" I asked from the shadows.

She startled, then replied, "Please, darling, it doesn't matter. Our lives move forward."

"But why, June? You owe me an explanation."

"Don't torture yourself. There are plenty of other women better suited for you."

No, I thought, *there aren't*. Instead I asked, "It's not Greenberg, is it?"

If June could have slumped at that remark any more, she would have been a puddle.

"I'm sorry," she whispered.

"Don't you see what you're doing, what *he's* doing? He's toxic, he doesn't care about making you happy, not like me."

"Adrian's really a sweet guy, he just slips up sometimes, like we all do. But he makes up for it."

"Did he promise to get you a role again?"

She couldn't look at me.

I kicked at a sitting table, and a glass with a single daffodil crashed to the floor. "Damn it, June! I've seen Greenberg with three other women this past week alone, not to mention the men. Does he offer everyone the same carrot?"

I stomped on the flower.

Bolger flung open the door. Greenberg stood right behind him.

"What're you doing in my room?" Bolger said, then followed with a cry. "My daffodil!"

He was still in costume and sank to patchwork knees, shaking his head in dismay. Pieces of straw that clung to his hair bounced back-and-forth like crazy pigtails. I didn't wonder why he was cast for the brainless role.

"You *little* monkey," Greenberg said, emphasizing the reference to stature just for me. "Time for you to scurry away." He made a series of chittering sounds, which I can only assume were meant to sound like a slow-witted primate.

Bolger stood, then took hold of my shoulders and nearly lifted me off the ground as he shoved me out the room. "You killed my flower!"

"June!" I shouted.

"Stay away from her, munchkin," Greenberg said, his voice cheery as a ringleader. The dressing room door slammed shut.

I was twenty-six, and I was a man, regardless of my height. But I retreated to the washing room and cried like a child. It was *me* who brought her happiness, *me*! That was my wish of the Wizard, and June said it was so. *It wasn't fair!* The Wizard couldn't take wishes back... that wasn't part of the story. So was it my fault? Had I done something wrong or shown myself unworthy?

Or was this just a challenge, a test, like Dorothy tasked to defeat the Wicked Witch before the promise of her wish could be granted? Perhaps hardships must first be endured before a gift can be fully realized? It was as if the great voice of Oz boomed in my ear, commanding me to conquer Greenberg.

I wanted to look at my reflection and scold myself for having been such a sissy, but the mirror was too high. I left the washing room, storming back up the hallway.

Ahead, Bolger was walking away, still clutching the crumpled flower. Greenberg and June stood in front of his dressing room, arguing.

"I don't want you around that deformity," he told her.

"I didn't ask for him to stalk me," she replied.

"It didn't sound like you were telling him to leave, either."

"And who are you, the prince of fidelity?"

Greenberg scowled and raised a warning finger. Before he could speak, I stepped in front of him, hands clenched to fists.

"I told you to stay away," he said to me.

I fired a straight punch at the first target in my range: his crotch.

Greenberg made a sound like a deflating balloon and doubled over, his face turning crimson. Now we were eye-to-eye.

"She's mine," I said. I swung a jab that knocked his nose sideways.

Then I punched him in the eye, the jaw, the temple. I'm not that strong, nor do I claim any skills in boxing, but Greenberg shattered like a man made of china. He dropped to the ground, pouring tears and shouting for help.

June pulled me off. "Let him be!"

I heard voices down the hall, running footsteps.

"Come away with me, June. Leave this place. I'll make you happy. Leave Greenberg and the deceit, and we can be together forever."

"No, I'm not leaving anything except *you*. We're through. Get over it, it was just a fling."

"But you belong to me!"

"I'm not a poodle, I'm not your pet. I don't *belong* to anyone. I'm sorry I ever wasted my time on someone like you."

"You're ruining everything!" I shouted.

June's face seemed to morph with meanness, like a piece of celluloid that catches fire, then crinkles and shrivels black. "What exactly am I ruining? After me, your life will still be the same as it was before. I didn't make anything worse. You'll return home to Wisconsin and still be jobless, still live with your parents, *still be a midget.*"

Two security guards dressed like runway showmen arrived and picked me up, one at each of my arms.

Bolger stood behind them. "That's him! That's the dwarf who killed my flower!"

Greenberg sobbed on the floor, and June knelt to him, comforting.

"No, June!" I shrieked. "Don't go back to Kansas. I have to

give you happiness! Me! You'll never be happy without me, the Wizard said so . . . "

The guards dragged me away.

June yelled, her final words echoing down the MGM halls like gongs in my mind. "You're delusional, little man. I thought you were fun, but you're crazy, you know that? Crazy as a loon!"

My feet were dead weights, and the guards dragged me like a broken prop across the lot. Bolger followed, babbling nonsensical threats. I thought I would cry, scream, but instead all the waterworks stayed inside of me and turned cold and hard.

I was hauled to MGM's gates, then heaved to the sidewalk on Culver Blvd. One of the guards kicked me in the ass while I fell on my knees. "And don't come back, runt," he said. "Consider yourself blacklisted."

I curled into a ball and laid there on the concrete. Tourists stepped around me, pointing and snapping pictures. They smiled and waved and pretended life was a fine jamboree. Nobody asked if I was all right, nobody cared. I was just another sight to see: *Look! The Egyptian Theatre! Pershing Square! A jilted Munchkin!*

There was nowhere to go but return home to Milwaukee, beaten, broken, alone. June was right about that, and I knew what awaited me there.

Only she was also partly wrong. Although circumstances might return to how they were, life could never be the same. I remembered thinking about the rich businessmen throwing themselves out of windows after they lost all their money during the stock crash. You never heard of poor people killing themselves because their pockets were empty . . . it was only those people who tasted the riches and decided they could never continue living again without it.

And that was me.

Granted, I was emotional, furious. I knew, even then, I should have thought the decision through, knew it was the passion of the moment. But I wanted her to see the pain she caused me, the inconsolable agony . . .

I wanted to die, and I wanted her to be part of my death. I wanted June to know it was her fault.

I snuck back into the studios and returned to set. Creeping backstage, I found a piece of heavy rope used to hoist lighting reflectors. I took it and moved to the back of the lot amongst the constructed forest glen. A set hand had left a wood ladder propped behind the green-roofed shack that was used as the Tin Woodsman's house. I took that too.

The assistant director announced the call to take places, and cast and crew assembled at their positions along the front of the set. I leaned the ladder behind a gnarled, dark oak and crouched beneath. *Seven years bad luck*, mother used to say, but what use was luck now? I looped one end of the rope over the other, again and again and again, until a noose hung completed from my fingers.

Truth be told, it was not the first time I'd contemplated suicide . . . I'd tied this noose a dozen times before.

"Action!"

They were refilming the scene where Dorothy and the Scarecrow discover the Tin Man. He sang his solo, "If I Only Had a Heart," and I quietly accompanied the lyrics as I climbed the ladder, up the tree. I moved in shadows, away from the spotlight. But across from me, beyond the actors, I saw the crew's faces outlined by the soft glow of arc lamps, watching each movement of the characters intently. June was amongst them. Though she also watched, her eyes appeared lost, as if she thought of faraway places.

Judy Garland and the others began skipping away from me, singing merrily how they were off to see the wonderful Wizard of Oz . . .

The noose fit snug. I looped the other end over a thick branch and swung my legs out, so that I sat on one side.

The actors suddenly turned direction and skipped toward me,

then past, where I crouched high above. The yellow brick road looked longer than ever, as if there was no end to it. The Scarecrow tripped, and Toto barked. I jumped.

I fell from the tree and felt the rope immediately squeeze around my neck. By reflex I gasped for breath, but it was all wrong... nothing came in, like a door had been slammed shut. My mouth gaped wide and air dried against the roof of my mouth, so I knew it was there... but instead of flowing down to my lungs it all just swirled back out to the world, rejected.

I had an audience, but nobody saw. They were transfixed on Dorothy and company singing gaily away. My final sight was of their backlit faces, and one in particular. June was framed by a glow arching over her head like a sparkling tiara—no, like a *rainbow*—and her lost eyes were crumbling emerald cities.

Suddenly I regretted what I had done. For I realized that she loved me still, no matter what her letter said, no matter what she told me, for Oz can never be taken away. Oz is within us all, and she loved me still, and I gave up on her and everything else, choosing the coward's way out.

June only needed a second chance... That was *her* wish of the Wizard.

My legs kicked higher than a Rockette. Instead of trying to suck in air, I struggled to scream but, like breathing, that too no longer worked. No sounds were made from me, unless someone was near enough to hear the rustling of my fingers clawing at the rope, or my buckled shoes clacking against each other, until I grew still.

Fleming yelled, "Cut!"

And my body slowly turned, suspended from the branch. They had filmed my death and no one even saw. The last thing to go through my mind was Margaret Hamilton's voice: *I'm dying! Dying! Oh, what a world! What a world!*

WHAT IS A BRAIN?

By all accounts, it is the control center of our body, the cerebral organ that oversees our other mental and physical capacities. Its size is small, but its command is great. If we were a movie, the brain would be our director, issuing actions, ordering us when to move, when to stop, when to cry, when to laugh.

And, occasionally, it storms off set, leaving you to wonder: *What am I supposed to do next?*

You see, though it *is* our brain—our director—it is not always right. Sometimes, we don't realize the brain has its own flaws, as does everything else. Or, sometimes, we *do* realize the flaws, recognize that the command it's giving is not right for the scene, yet we follow its directions anyway. How else do you explain screaming in anger at the ones you love most? You know it's wrong, it's irrational, yet you do it nonetheless, as if someone else controlled your emotions.

The brain tells us what is real and what is not. But again, I declare that the brain is not always right! So how do we know when it's mistaken? How do we realize something is not true, if we *think* it to be? The brain says that when we die, our body decomposes. Our mortal remains should lie motionless, unfeeling, the spirit released, the brain *dead*.

But I am moving still, thinking still, loving still.

My brain did not believe in magic, but perhaps the Wizard does not *need* to be believed in, in order to bestow wishes. Perhaps he is not the huckster that Baum made him out to be. Or, perhaps, the real magic was created on set, forged by the thousands of people who believed in a fantasy. After all, what conjures wonder more than a movie to be made in color? And the witches and talking animals and hopes and dreams! It was romance and adventure, and a charm to escape the dull grays of life to start over somewhere new, somewhere enchanting.

My brain was still alive, as was I then, as am I now. I'd been returned to life, and brought back *different*. I was made *powerful*.

I know what a ghost is. I know what a zombie is. I know what a ghoul is, a vampire, a warlock, specter, spook, and kelpie. I am none of those. I thought at first I was simply the result of a wish, like Lazarus rising from his tomb . . . but I had it all wrong. I am not the wish of a wizard . . .

I *am* the Wizard.

When I woke for the last time, it was in Hillside Mortuary on Centinela Avenue. I was shocked to rise in unfamiliar surroundings, as if waking from one dream, only to find myself in another. Once that passed, I discovered I'd been slated for burial in the Jewish cemetery. Of course I'm not Jewish, but it didn't matter to Louis B. Mayer and the rest of them at MGM, did it? They thought I was a nobody. A *little* nobody. The studio heads were Jewish, and I suppose they had contracts with Hillside. MGM didn't want bad press so I was an affair that was hushed and rushed nine miles away from the lots and out to the cold metal slab in Hillside's vault.

My folks ended up being right on both accounts. The studios only wanted to exploit me, *and* I didn't survive the movie business, although not being Jewish had nothing to do with it. I doubt MGM even sent notice of my death to them; better for no one to know. Of course, Mother and Father will still think I'm out here drinking champagne from glass slippers, livin' the ritzy life of a glam celebrity like Clark Gable or Tyrone Power. I'd only written home once since I left, and I wondered when anyone would begin to miss me.

And part of me felt saddened by all that befell me, and part of me felt angry.

I was the Wizard of Oz, but I could not undo my past. So Milwaukee no longer mattered. Nor did my folks matter, or

Metro-Goldwyn-Mayer, or religion, or movies, or cemeteries. None of that was for me.

Death was not for me.

Only June. Only Love. What else was it that brought me back, but for the last thing I felt? The one thing I feel still? The desire to grant June her second chance.

And yet I still seethed that Greenberg had stolen June from me like a highwayman who carries more riches in his pocket than his victim. It still stuck in my caw that the studios couldn't bother to return my body home to Milwaukee, where my family's burial ground covers one side of Rose Meadows Cemetery. It still agonized me to look upon my life and consider it had been meaningless... even my death—a statement that went unheeded—was meaningless.

I was the Wizard of Oz, and I could change this world into anything I wanted! I wondered briefly what compelled half the witches to become good and the other half evil, and that perhaps each of us has a defining moment to make such a choice. And then the thought vanished in a fiery poof of black smoke. Nothing mattered, but that June belonged to me.

And my insides were still cold and hard, and I remembered them freezing when MGM security threw me onto the sidewalk.

I returned up that same sidewalk, leaving Hillside Mortuary in flames far behind. I was tired of everyone looking down on me ...

I was a giant and all the people of Los Angeles the munchkins. They saw me and fled, or fell to their knees in reverence, as they should. I kicked at sleek automobiles that drove across my path, and they flipped over like dried poppies blowing in the wind. The earth shook at my steps, and a great storm followed in my wake, trumpeting thunder and waving lightning's banners.

I took the city and folded it, and stepped across to June's apartment. Crouching down, I spied into her room. She and Greenberg lay in bed, tangled in each other, their arms and legs loose and caressing, as ours once were. I flushed, and steam rose from my skin. Greenberg got up, and put on a robe, and came outside to smoke beneath the bright full moon.

He did not see me at first.

He gazed up to that pale moon, perhaps contemplating his conquests and wondering if the twinkling stars were not next for him to step upon. But things began to fly across the moon, so that it vanished, and the sky turned black and filled with shrieks and the flapping of immense wings.

"Who's a little monkey now?" I said, and my voice cracked the streetlamps.

Greenberg turned to me and screamed, and an army of winged monkeys fell upon him. I commanded them to tear him to pieces, and they raked silver claws across his face. His screams died, as did he, and the street outside June's apartment littered with his scraps.

And my happiness was boundless. It was life-changing, as I wished, and I had so much to share with June.

I looked back into the room, prepared to take her in hand and fly away forever to enchantment. But Greenberg returned from smoking outside. He commented that next week he would try again to get June a role through Mayer, then lay in bed beside her.

I shrieked! The monkeys sat on the street staring at me with ebony eyes, awaiting my next command.

I flew into a rage and ushered a fierce tornado to tear into her apartment. The walls lifted, bursting outward with a roar, and her bed rose through the debris in wild circles. June and Greenberg clung to each other and cried out, until the centrifugal force sent them spinning in opposite directions. Greenberg landed on the ground upside down, his legs stuck comically above him like the stem of an upended flower. I stomped on him as I did Bolger's daffodil. June landed in my arms, and when she saw me her smile flashed brighter than every theatre marquee in the country.

Then she was gone from my arms, back to her bed, in her apartment, with Greenberg, making love.

I wailed and gnashed my teeth and kicked at the monkeys. I tore the roof off June's apartment and plucked her from bed.

"No, June, come with me! You're mine, you're mine forever!"

But I spoke only to my empty hand.

I took June again and again, but she seeped through my fingers like trying to clutch water.

It's not fair, it's not fair, it's not fair! What use were my powers if I could not control the world? I raised mighty walls around June's apartment, but people passed through. I rained fire upon Los Angeles, but it immediately extinguished. I amassed armies of tin soldiers, but there was no one to conquer. Life became nothing but a mirage, a cruel and fleeting glimpse of what once eluded me . . .

What *still* eludes me now.

In resignation, I built a great emerald tower that climbed high above the MGM studios and confined myself to contemplate amidst dreaming clouds. I remained there, alone, and wondered as to my purpose. What good was I as the Wizard if I didn't have power to grant wishes—or was I truly delusional as June said? Was I just a small, timid man hiding behind the curtain of reality?

I conjured a small crystal ball and gazed through it, watching June Haley far below. I held the ball to my chest and imagined it as her, the words she repeated to Greenberg instead meant for me.

But perhaps there was more magic in my capabilities than I yet understood. Wasn't it true that the Wizard did not actually grant the Scarecrow the physical brain he wanted? The Wizard bestowed upon him a doctoral degree instead, a simple piece of paper with fancy words, which impressed upon the Scarecrow the belief he was turned smart, when he truly had been genius all along. To the Lion went a medal, and to the Tin Man, a ticking clock. Those also were not the literal realizations of their wishes, but the impetus to achieve the wishes' intent, which in all cases was simply acknowledgment of something the recipients already enjoyed.

So I contemplated the nature of desire: *What we think we want may not be as it seems, and fulfillment may not be in the way we expect, but it often brings to us realization that what we crave most, we already possess.*

And because of that, I knew it was true that my love for June would somehow bring her home. I had only to figure out the faculties I possessed, and how they would assist in getting through to her.

Soon, my pretty . . .

WHAT IS HOME?

Ask a dozen people this, and you may get a dozen answers, but I would claim it as simply that place where we *belong*. Dorothy knew it, and she did everything possible to return there. If we were a movie, home would be the world we create, the dream of Hollywood that is imagined and then brought to life, just as a pile of straw transforms into a talking scarecrow. It's not just the background set, that wood and canvas façade we pretend to be as something else, but it's the mythos we commit our lives to exist within. For some, that world is a transient phase, and for others it's a shifting labyrinth. For me, it's a final destination, the palace at the end of a winding brick road.

A palace with thrones for two.

I had resigned myself that I could not have an effect on the world, outside of Oz. I could not free June from her bleak existence, by my own physical efforts, and carry her home. The throne next to me remains empty.

But I am a resolute wizard, and I did discover a way to her, much like pushing from one bubble against another; the film walls may not break to let you through, but their elasticity does not halt your arm either. The walls merely stretch along with your reach and retract as you draw back.

It's an obvious egress, but I did not consider it immediately.

I discovered it the night Greenberg dumped June to marry a wealthy widower. June sobbed in grief and stared at her reflection in the mirror for what could have been years. I looked at her, from the other side of the mirror, and whispered: *It is time.*

I know not if I had her attention, but I whispered of my happiness, here in Oz, and that I waited for her to join. I whispered from the water that ran hot from the faucet, and I whispered through the steam that filled the air. I whispered that she could never be happy without me. I whispered for her to take a razor and pull it across her wrists, and that all the pain, all the loneliness, would melt away when she took her place on the throne next to me. I whispered I could make her wishes come true.

And she did it. June picked up a razor and began to slice through one thin wrist as easy as cutting an apple. But as the blood welled up like blossoming ruby flowers, she shrieked and collapsed, and threw the razor into the corner.

I cursed. She *still* screwed things up... June couldn't even bring herself to leave that dirty, gray world for a wonderful new land with me.

But as I said, it led to discovery, and I realized a way to help her, a way as I had helped myself.

I visit in June's dreams, night after night after night. She may live without me in her physical world but, like bubbles, death and dreams have a permeation to them, and my reach extends to her slumber. We face each other, standing on a yellow brick road. The road runs in every direction, though it leads to only one thing: a gnarled, dark oak with a ladder leading against it.

It's time, June, time to leave Kansas.

I hold a noose, composed of heavy rope that was once used to hoist lighting reflectors, and I offer it to her.

It's time, June, time to take the noose.

Sometimes she tries to flee and sometimes she tries to hide, but there is nothing around us in which to abscond. The world is a brick road, and it anchors a blue sky filled with a thousand rainbows.

Take your second chance, and let me bring you the happiness I promised.

She does not speak, she never speaks. But if only she would use the noose!

Do it, June, and return to Oz . . .

I don't know if I affect her in dreams, but I want to believe. Like magic, it requires a certain amount of faith, and I must trust that I'm connecting with June. I must trust that my perseverance has its due effect, night after night after night.

And perhaps it does.

For as I look through my crystal ball and watch the days go by, she grows gaunt and harried. Her eyes begin to twitch, as if she's constantly looking for something from her peripheral vision that isn't there. When she talks, there's a sense of desperation in her voice. Men come and go from her life, though their stays are increasingly shorter and crueler.

The seasons pass, like peoples' fancies, and each one takes a piece of June as it departs. I continue to whisper in her dreams, night after night after night, and I tell her to take the noose.

Dark circles form under her eyes, and hard lines pull at the corners of her mouth. Her hair grows brittle and breaks, and she takes to cutting it short.

She's given up on her Hollywood dream long ago, though she hasn't left the city. She grows old, and stars come and go, and she talks to herself, and she talks to them, when she is alone. But she doesn't speak to an unheeding void, for I am there, and I listen to her, and sometimes she laughs while facing the back of an old alley, and the singsong quality of her voice still reminds me of something the orchestral department would have composed for a Judy Garland solo.

I tell her to take the noose, take the noose, it's time to take the noose.

And sometimes she cries when she sees pretty girls on the arms of older men, and sometimes she smiles when she sees flashes of a movie shimmering from a storefront television set. And one time she saw a little person, as I once was, walking along the street, and she attacked him so viciously that police sent her for a year to the women's prison at Tehachapi.

And I follow her always, holding the noose. I watch her always, holding the noose. I whisper to her night after night after night.

Her body grows weak as a scarecrow, her jaundiced skin yellow as a lion, her movements rusty as a tin man. Had I not followed alongside her over the years, and watched the changes myself, I would never believe the person she has become once travelled the world for movies and flitted with the royalty of cinema. No one else does.

She lays in a hospice bed now, afraid to close her eyes, afraid of the thoughts of suicide that take hold when she sleeps. Winter has come again, and perhaps she thinks back to long ago, to the nights we kept each other warm and made promises that could never be broken. Or perhaps she remembers the time she watched *The Wizard of Oz* in Grauman's Theatre, so proud to have been part of that production. Then, during the scene where Dorothy and the Scarecrow discover the Tin Man, she saw the shadow of a hanging munchkin fall behind the trees, and she screamed so loud that people stampeded out, thinking there was a fire.

But as June once said, 'Our lives move forward,' and her final credits will be rolling soon. She slumbers more frequently, and my visits grow longer. She gazes upon the noose and begins to lift her fingers to it, so close, oh, so close.

I believe that movies should always have a happy ending, and I hope only that the magic still holds, the magic of Hollywood and the magic of love, enough magic to bring us back together. She's waited so long, but I have too.

And I'm waiting still, to give June her second chance to return to this wonderful Land of Oz. Our home is here, for us together, and everyone knows . . .

There's no place like home.

Publication Acknowledgements

With great thanks to the following publishers who first printed each of the stories included within this book.

"A Case Study in Natural Selection and How It Applies to Love" © 2015 by Eric J. Guignard. First published in *Black Static #47*, July: TTA Press.

"Last Days of the Gunslinger, John Amos" © 2014 by Eric J. Guignard. First published in *buzzymag.com*, July: Buzzy Magazine.

"Momma" © 2015 by Eric J. Guignard. First published in *Nightscript I*, edited by C.M. Muller: Chthonic Matter.

"Footprints Fading in the Desert" © 2013 by Eric J. Guignard. First published in *+Horror Library+ Vol 5*, edited by R.J. Cavender: Cutting Block Press.

"The House of the Rising Sun, Forever" © 2016 by Eric J. Guignard. First published in *Out of Tune II*, edited by Jonathan Maberry: JournalStone Publishing.

"The Inveterate Establishment of Daddano & Co." © 2016 by Eric J. Guignard. First published in *Nightscript II*, edited by C.M. Muller: Chthonic Matter.

"Last Night ..." © 2015 by Eric J. Guignard. First published in *Mark of the Beast: A Collection of Werewolf Stories*, edited by Scott David Aniolowski: Chaosium, Inc.

AUTHOR'S REQUEST

DEAR READER, FAN, OR SUPPORTER,

It's a dreadful commentary that the worth of indie authors is measured by online 5-star reviews, but such is the state of current commerce.

Should you have enjoyed this debut collection, gratitude is most appreciated by posting a brief and honest online review at Amazon.com, Goodreads.com, and/or a highly-visible blog.

With sincerest thanks,

Eric J. Guignard
Author, *That Which Grows Wild: 16 Tales of Dark Fiction*

THE AUTHOR

ERIC J. GUIGNARD IS A
writer and editor of dark and
speculative fiction, operating
from the shadowy outskirts of
Los Angeles, where he also runs
the small press, Dark Moon
Books. He's won the Bram
Stoker Award, been a finalist for
the International Thriller
Writers Award, and a multi-
nominee of the Pushcart Prize.

As author, Eric has written over 100 stories and non-fiction
works. As editor, he's published six anthologies, including *Dark
Tales of Lost Civilizations*, *After Death...*, and *A World of Horror*, a
showcase of international horror short fiction.

Additionally he's created an ongoing series of primers
exploring modern masters of literary dark short fiction, titled:
Exploring Dark Short Fiction (*Vol. 1: Steve Rasnic Tem*; *Vol. II:
Kaaron Warren*; *Vol. III: Nisi Shawl*; *Vol. IV: Jeffrey Ford*).

Read his novella *Baggage of Eternal Night* (JournalStone) and
watch for forthcoming books, including the novel *Crossbuck 'Bo*.

Outside the glamorous and jet-setting world of indie fiction,
Eric's a technical writer and college professor, and he stumbles
home each day to a wife, children, cats, and a terrarium filled with
mischievous beetles. Visit Eric at: www.ericjguignard.com, his
blog: ericjguignard.blogspot.com, or Twitter: @ericjguignard.